MURDER MASQUE

MURDER MASQUE

A COSMETIC CRIMES MYSTERY

ARLENE KAY

LEVEL
BEST BOOKS

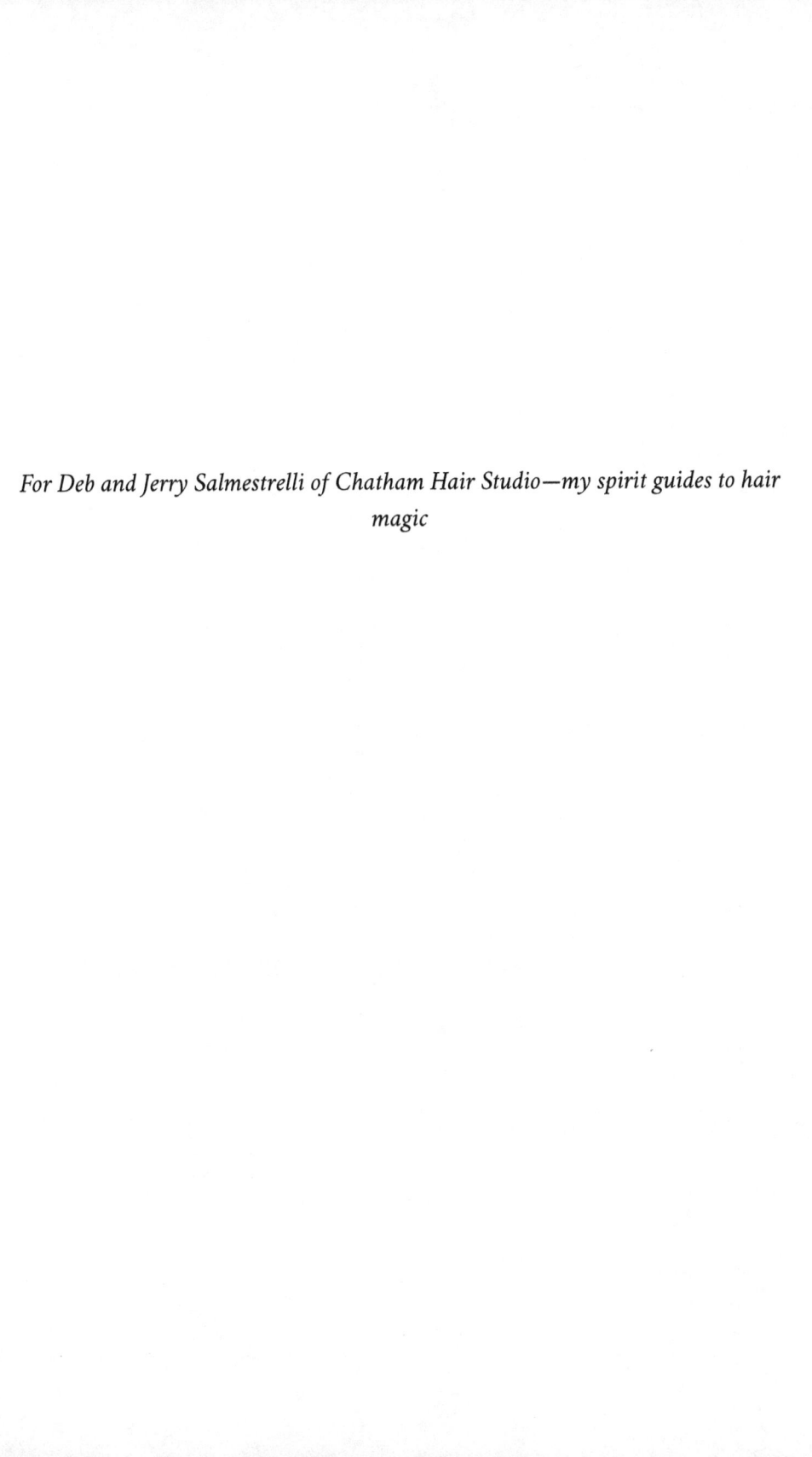

For Deb and Jerry Salmestrelli of Chatham Hair Studio—my spirit guides to hair magic

Praise for Murder Masque

"Written in Arlene Kay's intriguing style of a 'cat and mouse' scenario, *Murder Masque* delivers a suspenseful read. You'll be guessing until the end."—Barbara Eppich Struna, #1 Amazon bestselling author, *The Old Cape House*, The Old Cape Series

"'Splendido! Stupendo!' is how Mario Ricci would describe Arlene Kay's latest offering, *Murder Masque*. And he would be right! Marky and Gemma meet Mario at the launch of his new miracle-promising hair conditioner at the Beauty Expo in Traverse City. Too bad he brought more enemies than Poppet has lipstick shades with him, along with secrets from Aunt Violet's past. Readers of *The Mascara Murders* and *Murder At First Blush* will not be disappointed. The characters and their lives become more endearing with each book."—Lane Stone, author of The Big Picture Trilogy

Chapter One

"Wait 'til you hear the news!" Gemma Watts virtually flew into the stockroom of our store Poppet, the Beauty Spot. Her auburn curls waved wildly as she thrust a circular my way. "I can't believe it! This is our lucky day!"

She was my business partner and best pal, but sometimes, even I was overwhelmed by Gemma's exuberance. I grasped her shoulders and ordered her to calm down while I read the circular. It didn't take long. The event was described in bold capital letters with plenty of exclamation points. **Coming soon! The National Beauty EXPO** to convene at Grand Seneca Resort in Traverse City, Michigan.

"Well," Gemma squealed. "This is our ticket to the big time. Everyone will know the name Poppet before this thing ends." She pointed her talons at the last paragraph, almost stabbing my eyes in the process. When it came to nails, Gemma believed that more was best.

"See. They want us to help. Of course, they gussied it up by calling it sponsorship, but you get the meaning." She twirled about, doing her version of an Irish jig. "Wait 'til Violet hears about this. She'll go nuts!"

Knowing my elegant, sophisticated aunt as I did, that response was highly unlikely. Overreaction was simply not her style. Violet Davis, acclaimed artist and cosmetics genius, had conquered both the art world and the Parisian scene without firing a shot. Her return to Harbor Bay had been a stroke of luck for me, both personally and professionally. I adored my aunt and tried mightily to emulate her. Since my parents relocated to New Zealand, she had become a surrogate mother as well as a trusted advisor.

Once, I also yearned to be a renowned artist until my dreams crashed and burned at the Chicago Institute of Art. Now, I channeled those creative impulses into Poppet, a high-end temple of beauty owned and operated by Gemma and me. I still painted and hadn't totally abandoned the notion of being the next Mary Cassatt. Just call it a dream deferred.

Gemma twirled around the room, brandishing the circular. "Look at the names here. Mario Ricci, Carla Standish, and oh my goodness, Kim Stevens is one of the organizers." Kim, a resident of Harbor Bay, was a glamorous former model and a dear friend. She lived with her sour puss husband Lionel and the cherished memories of their murdered son. I didn't know either Mario Ricci or Carla Standish, but of course, their names were legends to anyone in the beauty biz. He was a showboating purveyor of Italian style, while Carla promoted her all-American line of natural products for the mature woman.

"I hear he's gorgeous," Gemma said, rolling her eyes. "Sexy and suave. You know how Italians are. European men know all the moves."

I faced my partner head on. "I don't know anything about European men or most American men for that matter. Unfortunately, my experience is extremely limited."

Gemma scoffed. "Ah, come on. You're gorgeous. Blonde, beautiful the whole works. And twenty-eight is still young. Don't let a few bad apples spoil the whole crop."

I simply wasn't up for discussing my disastrous love life. Gemma meant no harm, but that subject was strictly off-limits. Besides, my eyes were firmly focused on my career, not the exploits of some playboy.

"What would Benny Soto say about this, Ms. Gemma? Aren't you two engaged or something?" Benny was an officious deputy sheriff in Harbor Bay whose zeal for fame had almost gotten me arrested a time or two. I loathed the smarmy toad and knew he wasn't worthy of my friend. Naturally, I kept my opinion to myself in the interest of business harmony.

Her good nature was one of the things I loved most about Gemma. She brushed off my snarky comments with a toothy grin. "Ah, you know Benny. He's not the jealous type. Besides, I can still look even if we're engaged." She stared at the minuscule diamond on her left hand and sighed. "It's not like we've set the date or anything. His mother still doesn't approve of me."

Benny's formidable parent distrusted any female who came within kissing distance of her boy. I gave her a wide berth whenever possible, and she returned the favor.

The door chimes suddenly announced Aunt Violet's arrival. As usual, her raven hair was perfectly coiffed, her makeup impeccable, and her black Prada sheath tailored to perfection. Otherwise, Violet resembled every matron on the streets of Harbor Bay.

As Gemma launched into a fevered description of the big event, Violet held up her hand. "Stop. I already got the word this morning. Quite a feather in our region's cap, I must say." She scanned the printout and tossed it aside. "Plenty of egos and drama will collide. I can tell by looking at these names."

"What's Mario Ricci like?" Gemma asked. "A real lady's man, I bet."

Violet sighed. "In his own mind, perhaps, but in fairness, Mario is a handsome scamp. Biggest self-promoter I've ever encountered. He's been hawking this new hair conditioner non-stop ever since it was formulated. Calls it revolutionary."

That aroused my curiosity. Any product that generated buzz was worth considering for Poppet. "Is it any good?" I asked. "Or just the typical hype." We featured only high-end brands, but our customers expected an honest appraisal from us.

"Very hush-hush," Violet said. "No samples or promos sent to anyone. Mario swears that *Ricci-Rich* will restore and revitalize tired locks, even help to rescue thinning hair. He uses it himself, and I must admit, the results speak for themselves."

I'd never even heard the name before. *"Ricci-Rich"*?

Violet laughed. "So, like him to use his own name. Modesty has never been a problem with Mario." My aunt seldom discussed her private life, but I detected a distinct hint of intimacy, perhaps even nostalgia, in her voice. Unfortunately, so did Gemma. Nothing deterred my partner when her curiosity was aroused.

"Come on, Violet. Spill. Just how well do you know this guy?"

Her response was evasive. "The European beauty scene is a closed society. Everyone knows everyone else, especially the main players."

I hastily changed the subject to avoid antagonizing my aunt and beloved patron. "I've heard of Carla Standish before. Does a ton of marketing for *Hair Deluxe*. Targets the mature woman who may have thinning hair." I knew from my own customers that with age, many women were confronted by hair loss and were desperate to recapture the look of youthful tresses. Upscale products were a billion-dollar business in the United States alone and women were more than willing to pay for a product that worked.

"She's a good person," Violet said. "No one doubts Carla's integrity or business ethics. I heard that she's going through a rough patch right now. Rival products and ruthless competitors are eating into her market share. Sometimes, the beauty business can get ugly."

Mario Ricci's bombshell launch sounded like a direct challenge to the existing order. No wonder Violet expected fireworks at the Expo. The prospects for intrigue had just ratcheted up, and that intrigued me. Seemed like the Beauty Expo might have some unsavory consequences.

* * *

Kim Stevens convened a meeting the next day to discuss our role in the big show. As always, I found her elegance and style overwhelming and more than a bit intimidating. It wasn't her fault but any woman who was tall, slender as a sylph, with perfect features and doe eyes was bound to arouse my insecurities. Kim was oblivious to her own perfection, probably due to the indifference of her irascible spouse. I'd grown to value her friendship, although my feelings for Lionel were a work in progress. The four of us met at our local patisserie just before the lunch crowd arrived. Gemma dove into the plate of croissants with her typical gusto, but I adopted a more abstemious approach. Kim and Aunt Violet nibbled at the tasty treats, which partially explained the excellence of their figures. I drank plenty of Perrier to mute my appetite but couldn't resist snagging a Pain au chocolat and savoring every delicious morsel.

"I'm so glad you all agreed to participate," Kim said. "Frankly, I'm a bit nervous. This Expo could launch a brand-new career for me if everything goes well." Kim's modeling career had tanked once she reached thirty. Not unusual in that business, but still a painful reminder. I could relate since my dreams of becoming a renowned artist had also been crushed.

Violet patted her hand. "You're a natural for this. How can we help?"

Kim hesitated before answering. "I'm worried about several things. You probably heard that Mario plans a major product launch for *Ricci-Rich.*"

We nodded and waited for Kim to explain.

"Well, that runs right into Carla's pitch for *Hair Deluxe,* and I'm afraid there could be conflict."

I was puzzled. Conventions always drew their share of competitors, and conflict was endemic to the occasion. Gemma immediately jumped to the heart of the issue. "There's something else, I bet. Something personal."

I aimed a stiletto at Gemma's shin, but it was too late. Kim tightened her grip on the table until she was rescued by Violet.

"It's no big secret. Carla and Mario were lovers once upon a time until he discarded her for a younger model. In fact, they were married for several years." Violet shrugged. "Not unusual in any industry but Carla was truly crushed. Mario has a well-deserved reputation as a lothario—and a louse."

Was my aunt speaking from personal experience? I detected a faint flush on her cheeks as she recounted the sad tale.

"Better separate them as much as possible, I suppose. Mario wants to demo his product with him as the model. He'd never miss the chance to take center stage."

Kim swallowed and took a sip of espresso. "Violet. He's asked for you to apply the conditioner to his head. It stays on for twenty minutes before rinsing."

"Me? Why me?" Violet gasped. "Couldn't you do it?"

"He wants someone with gravitas. You don't have a line of hair products, so there's no conflict of interest. And everyone respects you. Plus, according to Mario, you owe him."

Violet's frown resembled a thundercloud but the look of desperation on

Kim's face sealed the deal. Despite her reluctance to become involved, Violet agreed to the plan. "I'll do it, although I can't for the life of me recall owing Mario anything but scorn. It'll be tempting to pull his hair out by the roots, but I promise to control myself."

"Great! That demo is slated for the opening day. I thought about giving Carla a chance to showcase her product, too. You know, sort of a battle for the best."

Violet rolled her eyes. "Sounds fine to me, but Mario will explode. You know how he insists on having center stage."

"Leave him to me," Kim said. "He'll have enough to contend with anyway. Word is that some activist group plans to stage a protest."

Gemma's eyes widened. "I read about that. Just looking at the founder gave me hives. Stringy hair, pockmarked skin—eek! She could use a deep facial and some heavy moisturizer. At the very least. Maybe even some injectables."

An image suddenly popped into my head. Nona Allen, founder of the group Feminists *Against Cosmetic Enhancement (FACE)*, was a fierce opponent of the beauty industry. Gemma's assessment was close to the mark, although Nona was an intelligent, articulate spokeswoman for her cause. She had a first-class education and a law degree as well. Her appearance was another matter entirely. I tried not to judge superficial things, but Nona worked hard to look quite dreadful. I considered myself an ardent feminist, too, one who loved the mystique and artistry of cosmetics. Most of my clients echoed those sentiments, and I believed there was room for both perspectives. Anything that enhanced a person's self-esteem was a good thing, right? That did not comport with the worldview of FACE and its loyalists. Nona herself referred to "tarted-up bimbos" when describing cosmetic junkies like me. Her antics included chaining herself to a plastic surgeon's office door and picketing several prominent Manhattan salons. Based on that, there was no telling what she had planned for the Beauty Expo.

"You'll have to enhance security," Violet said. "Shouldn't be a problem. Badges, vigilance, you know the drill. Maybe we could meet with Nona beforehand and reason with her."

Kim's reaction said it all. She coughed nervously and shook her head. "I tried that.

Even had Lionel threaten legal action but to no avail. Nona matched him word for word. She wears the First Amendment like a banner and isn't above invoking the ACLU and other free speech outfits to aid her cause."

Gemma was never shy and seldom missed a marketing opportunity. "Have you lined up any massage gigs yet? I could partner with one of the herbal crowd and do demos. New techniques for relieving tension. You know the drill. Maybe even a chiropractor or orthopedist could join in."

Kim seemed uncertain, but Aunt Violet nodded approvingly at Gemma. "Great concept. I love it! We could sponsor free foot massages at the end of the day, too. Dangle a drawing for services at Poppet."

"We're having a charity auction to support aesthetic scholarships," Kim said somewhat timidly. "I don't suppose you could donate one of your paintings. I know it's asking a lot."

My aunt was a prominent listed artist whose works appeared in major museums. They went for a minimum of six figures in any gallery. Fortunately, she was also generous and willing to do her share. "Sounds like a plan. There's only one hitch." Violet put her arm around me. "They must feature some of Marky's paintings also. You won't be disappointed."

I blushed to the roots of my hair. Beauty products I could sell with no problem but hawking my own wares was painful for me. I'd graduated from the Chicago Institute of Art and had some minor success. Nothing I'd accomplished approached my aunt's lofty heights despite her frequent pep talks and encouragement. When asked, I described myself as a recovering artist.

"Who's working security for the conference," Gemma asked.

I knew where this was going, but Kim was oblivious. "Oh, I expect the resort will handle everything. They're used to hosting large groups."

"Benny takes on outside jobs, you know," Gemma said coyly. "He's a deputy sheriff."

"Hmm. I'll make a note of that." Benny Soto was the Harbor Bay scold, a perpetual scene-stealer who refused to cut lawbreakers any slack. I applauded Kim's tact under pressure. On the other hand, perhaps a hard case like Benny might be just what we needed to deal with FACE, Nona Allen, and Mario Ricci.

"Any other challenges, Kim?" Violet's voice was warm and reassuring.

"I guess not. We heard that some big-shot lawyer from Chicago could be a problem, though. Does product development for a major cosmetics conglomerate. Name of Killian Blaine."

"So what?" Gemma was fidgeting, ready to stop talking and get back to work.

"His name says it all. They call him Kill for good reason. He's a take-no-prisoners guy determined to acquire the rights to *Ricci Rich* no matter what it costs. Mario has already threatened to clean his clock if he interferes."

Some men! Always settling disputes with fists rather than finesse. I couldn't disguise a grin at the thought of Benny Soto mediating a brawl. His preferred technique consisted of glares, growls, and threats, but nothing physical. This expo might be fun after all!

Chapter Two

It was challenging to focus on mundane matters instead of the Beauty Expo, but as a business owner, I had little choice. There were invoices to send, bills to pay, and customers to entice during what was typically the slow season. Our budget was limited, but at Violet's urging, we managed to splurge by renting a medium-sized booth at the expo. She suggested decorating it with my paintings and designing posters to showcase our services and products. Gemma jumped at the chance to illustrate massage techniques. She hatched a plan to raffle off free treatments and partner with the vendor we used for creams and ointments. I couldn't argue with her motto: everyone loves free stuff! When it came to shameless self-promotion, my partner was a genius.

One afternoon, as we prepared to close for the day, an unexpected visitor arrived. He announced himself by pushing open the door in theatrical fashion with his arms spread wide. A harried Kim Stevens trailed in his wake. I knew without asking that we were in the presence of none other than Mario Ricci, entrepreneur and unrepentant star of his own show. I'd seen his photo numerous times in magazines and on the internet. Despite his small stature, Mario was handsome and a presence to be reckoned with. His full head of curly black hair was a tribute to superior genes, the efficacy of his products, and a fine advertisement for RICCI RICH. His exuberance was contagious as he favored us with a mile-wide grin that seemed to embrace every inch of POPPET. Gemma was gobsmacked when he strode up to her and kissed her hand.

"Aha," said Mario. "You must be the ravishing redhead Kim told me of.

Gemma, I believe. You with the magic hands. The masseuse of my dreams."
He turned my way and spread even more goodwill. "Bellissima! The blonde
angel, niece of my beloved Violet, and a gifted artist as well."

"Mario's visit was unexpected," Kim said. "A pleasure, of course." Her eyes
pleaded for understanding, and she looked close to tears. Meanwhile, Mario
surveyed our shop with the shrewd eyes of a seasoned professional, noting
product placement and range of brands. "Splendido! Stupendo!" He nodded
his approval as he perused the aisles. Mario was a piece of work, but he won
my heart when he spied my rough collie, Fantasia, and bent down to stroke
her beautiful head. She was very much the patrician since her pedigree was
far superior to that of most humans. He respected that and was rewarded
with a handshake, Fantasia's special seal of approval.

"Bella bambina," Mario said. "A fitting goddess for your beautiful shop."

At first, I wondered if the man ever tamped down his enthusiasm, but
I soon learned the answer. He stopped abruptly at a prominent display
in the hair products section that featured *Hair Deluxe, the* brainchild of
his archrival, Carla Standish. Kim lowered her head as if bracing for the
expected fireworks.

"What is this? You stab me through the heart." Mario pounded his chest.
"Are my eyes deceiving me? Kim, how can this be? I see no Ricci products at
all, just this rifiuto—this junk!" With one swift movement, Mario swept the
shelf clean of every trace of *Hair Deluxe*. His temper was such that I feared
he might ravage the entire store. Gemma shrieked, but Kim turned aside
and reached for her phone. When our savior emerged ten minutes later, I
knew whom she had texted. My aunt, Violet Davis, swept into POPPET
like an avenging angel and immediately calmed her tempestuous colleague.
"Mario," she said, "What's wrong? Stop this. You have been a very bad boy
indeed."

Did I mention my aunt's talent for understatement? Mario forgot his fit
of pique and swept her into his arms. "Violetta, my darling. You grow more
lovely each year. How could you abandon me?"

Violet rolled her eyes and patted his cheek. "As I recall, dear boy, you were
occupied with a twenty-one-year-old named Sophia and abandoned me. I'm

surprised you noticed my absence."

His guilty look confirmed what I had suspected. Mario Ricci was a part of my aunt's secret past. "Let us not dwell on that, my darling," he said. "She was a mere child. I prefer a real woman."

Kim had recovered enough to offer a timid suggestion. "Perhaps we could discuss things over dinner? We have an excellent trattoria in Harbor Bay, Mario. The Chef de Cuisine came right from Milan."

"Pasta sounds good to me," Violet said. She herded Mario toward the door, winking at me as she said, "Later, ladies."

* * *

"Whew," Gemma said as she sifted through the debris. "He's quite a handful. What's the story of Mario and Violet? Something juicy, I bet."

"A vast understatement, partner. My aunt can handle whatever their past was, but I suspect there will be fireworks at the Expo with Mario, Carla, and this Chicago lawyer at each other's throats."

"Cool," Gemma said. "I like a good brawl. Better than a wrestling match."

I perused the glossy conference brochure that had arrived that day, noting that snapshots of both Mario and my aunt were prominently featured alongside head shots of cosmetics industry executives. Carla Standish received her share of recognition as well although the *Hair Deluxe* space was less conspicuous.

"Wow! The expo has attracted plenty of firepower. Looks like every major brand is sending someone or sponsoring an event. I can't wait to meet some of them."

Gemma peered over my shoulder and pointed. "Who's that Sophia Laurent? Never heard of her but she sure is hot."

I thumbed through the bios and found her. "Here she is. Represents one of the big international brands. She's French."

"Ooh la la," Gemma said. "Hey. It says she formerly worked for the Ricci company. Could this be the same Sophia your aunt mentioned? You know, Mario's ex-lover?"

I felt uncomfortable prying into Violet's private life, so instead of answering I merely shrugged. Sophia was an exotic blend of brunette locks and enormous cat eyes that was sure to entrance most males. My aunt was a sophisticated woman of the world but there were limits. Being discarded for a vixen half her age who looked like that was must have really stung.

There was no mention of the worrisome attorney Killian Blaine so out of curiosity I googled his name. The firm Blaine and Associates maintained an extensive website that listed areas of expertise and CVs of the staff. It featured the usual retouched glimpses of grinning associates, but oddly enough, It did not contain a photo of Killian Blaine. His impressive pedigree was on full display, but not his face: Stanford, Georgetown, and a Master of Law from Oxford University proved that he was indeed a force to be reckoned with. Perhaps his person was less impressive. I got a mental image of a scholarly nerd with oversized glasses, beady eyes, wispy hair, and a scrawny body. As I soon learned, nothing could have been farther from the truth.

Poppet was listed in the back of the brochure along with the names of other exhibitors. I didn't care. As a relative newbie to the industry, any mention of our name was good business. Violet advised me to be present, observe, and listen to the proceedings with an open mind. I intended to do just that. Gemma, who never shied away from publicity, posted the brochure on our window along with a note urging customers to buy a ticket and join in the fun.

I should have known that our euphoria would be short-lived. The next week, Deputy Benny Soto snarled his way into the shop, determined to rain on our parade.

"They're just using you for free labor," he said. "Anyone can see that." Benny had a talent for curling his lip as he spewed negativity. What Gemma saw in him, I will never know. Even her boundless optimism and sunny disposition seemed to dim in his presence. He wasn't ugly. In fact, Benny Soto was considered attractive by some— mostly those who didn't know him. He had inherited his sainted mother's grim outlook on life, a set of traits that detracted from his generous features and tall fit frame. I wisely refrained from expressing any opinion of the man. Quite inexplicably, he made Gemma happy, and that was all I cared about.

Gemma wound herself around her fiancé like a serpent and tickled his chin. "Did I tell you? Benny will be working security at the big shindig. No need to worry when he's in charge."

Benny puffed up as if he were a king cobra. "You bet your life," he said. "We've already got our eyes on that group of troublemakers. Call themselves *FACE.*" He snickered. "Easy to pick out. What a bunch of uglies they are."

His remarks rankled me, even though they contained more than a grain of truth. Men who judged women solely on their looks were the sworn enemies of any feminist. For Gemma's sake, I swallowed the acidulous comment on the tip of my tongue and remained quiet.

She pinched his cheeks and cooed. "Isn't he the cutest thing? Such a bad boy. I may have to punish him for that remark."

Ugh! That scene was enough to gag a maggot. I reminded myself that as a woman who had temporarily abandoned the dating pool, I had little room to judge. Benny wasn't a prize catch, but pickings were slim in Harbor Bay.

After the lovebirds flew the coop, I settled down at my easel and finished a pen and ink sketch. It had been inspired by a dream I'd recently had about the Expo, but the results were not comforting. To my chagrin the sketch resembled a nightmare straight from the pen of Edgar Allen Poe rather than a fantasy. Did this presage disaster for the event? More likely, I was being fanciful, allowing the events of the day to overwhelm me. Stark lines, corpses, and blood spots were not my usual style. I wondered what Aunt Violet's take on it would be. My mother claimed that second sight ran through the female line of our family. She often said that she, and her mother before her, could predict disasters long before they occurred. My dad and I pooh-poohed her belief in clairvoyance. We were hard-headed pragmatists who attributed things to coincidence. Besides, any snafus in my life thus far had been predictable products of my own bad decisions.

* * *

Kim Stevens called me the next morning, full of apologies for ambushing me with Mario.

"He's some piece of work, isn't he? You'll have your hands full with him, Kim."

She sighed. "Frankly, he's only one of several prima donnas at the show. I called to enlist your help." Kim explained that she planned to survey the convention space and wanted a second opinion. Violet was unavailable and suggested me as her substitute. Since business was slow and Gemma was there to staff *Poppet*, I jumped at her offer. Perhaps seeing the actual locale would allay my misgivings and sweep away the bad dreams.

Traverse City was close enough to Harbor Bay to make an easy day trip, provided that the weather cooperated. Spring was a lovely season full of blossoming flora and fauna, with only the occasional vestige of snow remaining. The conference center was collocated with an academic and culinary institute on the shore of Lake Michigan and the edge of Grand Traverse Bay.

"We're limited to three hundred participants," Kim said as she pulled her Cadillac to the curb. Her voice quivered, and I could tell that she was anxious to succeed in this new venture. "I hope that protest group won't cause too much trouble. This Nona Allen has a bad reputation. Kind of an in-your-face person. I tried calling her, but she never returned my texts, emails, or phone calls. Probably thinks all models are bimbos."

"Nonsense," I said. "Your appearance probably intimidates her. It would most women, you know. Just ignore her and the entire FACE crowd. No one's forcing them to use beauty products."

"Lionel said I should let Violet handle things. I wish I had her self-confidence."

I chuckled. "Don't we all! By the way, who is Sophia Laurent? We saw her name in the brochure."

Kim explained that Sophia was a former actress, brand representative, and close friend of Mario. I didn't probe any further in case I strayed into my aunt's private life. Based on the way Kim shifted in her seat, I saw that the topic made her very uncomfortable.

As soon as we arrived, the event coordinator, Lin Baugh greeted us and invited us to lunch at their culinary institute. He was a trim, middle-aged man with closely cropped hair, copper skin and a wide grin. Small wonder that he was their go to person for public relations. His easy manners instantly made friends out of total strangers.

"Let's see. Marky Davis. I know that name. You're a painter, right? I've seen your works at a gallery in Detroit. Very impressive."

I was flabbergasted, gobsmacked and totally euphoric. Painting was my passion. Parting from that dream had been an extremely painful thing for me to confront. I was pathetically grateful for even a crumb of recognition. "Maybe you mean my Aunt Violet Davis. She's a listed artist and world renown."

Lin shook his head. "Nope. I'm kind of an art groupie, so of course I'm familiar with your aunt's work. But yours is quite unique as well." He ducked his head and grinned. "I own one of your paintings. The impressionist one of a collie and a young ballerina. Beautiful!"

"No kidding! That one was special to me because my dog Fantasia was a model."

Kim put her arm around me and hugged. "She's so talented, Lin, but a successful business owner and a detective as well. I own several works by both Davis women that I cherish."

"Detective? What's that all about?" His reaction surprised me. Lin Baugh's genial manner became more impersonal and less effusive, as if he were threatened by Kim's comment.

"She's exaggerating," I said. "I got involved in several crimes, strictly by accident."

He nodded and immediately switched back to professional mode. "I think you'll be pleased with our arrangements," he told Kim. "We've hosted many groups with a minimum of fuss and received great feedback." He frowned. "I see that you've augmented security. Not expecting any problems, are you?"

Kim explained about the protestors and her wish to avoid confrontation.

"I get it," Lin said. "Better safe than sorry. Because we're not near any of the big cities, we've been able to avoid most of that stuff except for a few environmental protests. But I know the world we live in."

Lin Baugh was an attractive man, a fact that was not lost on either me or Kim. Her husband Lionel was a cantankerous coot who seldom paid her any attention or compliments, so it was good to see the sparkle in her eyes.

"We're selling tickets to the general public," I said. "And we'll have a raffle after the dinner dance."

Lin shared the menu with us and explained that a local disc jockey would play a variety of music. "Nothing like dancing to liven up a group," he said. "No karaoke, though. There are limits." He paused as he scanned the brochure. "I see that Mario Ricci is guest of honor."

"Do you know him?" I asked. "His products are very popular."

Lin shook his head, but I sensed that he wasn't being totally candid. "My sister knew him. She interned for his company in Italy during college and got to work with his staff. She loved cosmetics and everything in that world."

Manners dictated that I refrain from asking anything more, although he had aroused my curiosity. Lin had used the past tense when referring to his sister so perhaps some tragedy had occurred. Probing further would have been unseemly.

"It sounds like a lovely event," Kim said, "and you've been very helpful. I think we've got everything covered."

There was an added spring in her step as we walked toward her car. "Just wait 'til I tell Lionel. He'll be astonished. My husband, prophet of doom. He underestimated me, and for once, he was wrong." On the way home we reviewed our day and agreed that things were well in hand. Unfortunately, optimism triumphed over reality and brought us closer to disaster.

Chapter Three

"What did you think of Mario?" my aunt asked. "Getting used to him takes a bit of practice. He has what they used to call a big personality."

"That's one term for it." I mentioned our trip to the expo site and meeting Lin Baugh. Violet paused when I said his name.

"Baugh. An unusual name but one I think I recall. Let me think." She snapped her fingers. "I've got it. About ten years ago, Mario had an intern named Baugh. Linette. Beautiful girl. Very into Mario and all his nonsense, unfortunately."

"How so?" I asked. "Her brother was vague, but I sensed there was some problem."

Violet scoffed. "Problem? More like a tragedy. The girl was young, innocent. Totally in love with Mario. She lived in kind of a fantasy world. You know, love, poetry, passion. I tried to warn her, but she wouldn't listen. When he discarded her as he inevitably does with all his lovers, she fell apart."

"Oh no!" I had to learn the ending of this sad tale.

"The girl just pined away. Stopped eating and became anorexic. Her brother came over and took her home. I lost track of Linette after that."

No wonder Lin Baugh had spoken of his sister in the past tense. I did a quick Google search and found her obituary.

Linette Annabel Baugh, 1990- 2012, beloved daughter of Dorothy Baugh and cherished sister of brother Lin. Brilliant literary scholar known for her beauty, style, and gentle heart. 'She walks in beauty like the night' Always loved, never forgotten.

It was a lovely tribute, with an homage by Lord Byron, if I recall correctly. She was a child, only twenty-two, when she left the earth. Small wonder that her brother bristled when he saw Mario Ricci's name.

"He's a monster," Gemma said when she heard the story. "What about this Sophia Laurent? Did he destroy her, too?"

"Hardly." Violet closed her eyes and smiled. "Quite the reverse. Mario was obsessed with Sophia. Called himself her slave. Typical hyperbole, but not that far from the mark. He showered her with gifts, even proposed to her, but she wouldn't have it."

"Serves him right," Gemma said. "Bad karma. What goes around comes around or something like that."

Violet explained what had happened. Mario imploded when Sophia discarded him. Became a virtual recluse until the next pretty girl caught his eye. That made me wonder. How would Mario react when he came face to face with Sophia at the beauty expo? Based on what I'd observed, sparks would fly. We might need Benny Soto's services after all.

* * *

I found Gemma unpacking a large shipment of *Hair Deluxe* products. Our customers were loyal fans of the entire line, particularly the hair rejuvenator, *Love Locks*. I found that very few men understood the link between self-esteem and female hair. After all, some prominent male celebrities made shaved heads a fashion trend. Not so for women. An intimate bond was forged with any substance that worked or appeared to. Carla Standish understood this and had made a fortune mining that vein of gold. She also understood the personal touch. Each shipment included a photo and a personal note penned by Carla herself. I looked forward to meeting her and sharing those sentiments. I knew plenty of people who would provide testimonials for her. Fingers crossed, she and Mario could coexist in a reasonably professional manner during the Expo.

We'd already sold tickets for the big event to several patrons, including Benny Soto's mom, the redoubtable Josephine Soto. That puzzled me since

Jo-So, my secret name for her, eschewed using most beauty products. Once again, Gemma enlightened me.

"Mrs. S. is a stealth consumer," she said. "Didn't you know she joined FACE? Yep! Benny spilled the beans. His mom thinks this Nona Allen is the bee's knees. Calls her the Susan B. Anthony of the anti-beauty movement."

Come to think of it, Jo-So, an ample woman with a pronounced mustache, resembled some of those fierce feminist pioneers herself. I tried to avoid her because, quite frankly, she terrified me. The woman was twice my size and age, with a frown that would stop a pit bull. On the few occasions when she visited POPPET, disapproval radiated from her every pour. If Nona Allen were even half as fierce, we were in for a very rough patch indeed.

* * *

"You never asked about me and Mario," Aunt Violet said with a smile. "Aren't you curious?"

We were counting our receipts after a particularly profitable day of sales. "I wondered, but didn't want to intrude," I said. It was cowardly, but truthfully, I was a teeny bit afraid of my aunt. Any rebuke from her would have wounded me.

Leave it to Gemma to break the ice. "Well, I wanted the story, but Marky told me to back off." Her eyes gleamed as she awaited the news. "I could tell there was something there. Mario obviously adores you."

My aunt laughed. "We shared a moment many years ago, but the romance didn't last long. In some ways, we were too much alike, ambitious, driven to succeed, and self-involved. He needs a more pliant woman. One who defers to his genius."

Gemma's instincts went on high alert. "So, who dumped who? Was that Sophia part of the deal?"

I was embarrassed by her brashness but eager to learn more. Violet apparently found the entire subject amusing. "To be honest, Mario let me down gently. Just a slow slide into oblivion. Oh, I kept my dignity, and we remained friends, but it was obvious that he was obsessed with Sophia and had no time for any other woman, including me."

If Mario Ricci followed the same pattern with every woman, he might also have zeroed in on Carla Standish too. When I asked Violet about it, she shrugged. "Who knows? I haven't kept up with that man's peccadillos. It wouldn't surprise me, though. You'll like Carla. She's very sensitive, kind, and a bit naïve. Just his type until she became a competitor."

I mentioned my research on attorney Killian Blaine. "Impressive CV but no photo. Strange, don't you think?"

"Probably some little nerd with a big ego and lots of degrees." Gemma tended to be overly sensitive about formal education or the lack of it. Violet had never met Blaine but his tenacity and success at acquiring companies were legendary. His firm specialized in Mergers and Acquisitions, and by all accounts, Blaine had his eyes set on Ricci Enterprises.

The Expo was only two weeks away. I spent time evaluating my paintings to select three that best showcased my work. Lin Baugh's praise still rang in my ears, and I vowed to rise to the occasion. Meanwhile, Gemma arranged posters and brochures proclaiming the glories of POPPET. She planned to plaster the walls of the expo with them if she could. Her motto was never waste an opportunity for shameless self-promotion, and I readily admitted that her sales skills were far superior to mine.

We hadn't seen much of Kim Stevens of late. When she swept into POPPET one morning, her frayed nerves and anxiety were on full display. "Some of the participants are driving me crazy," said Kim. "Simple things like the dinner menu become major roadblocks. Vegan, vegetarian, Keto—my Lord, these people obsess about trivia. Lionel says to ignore them, but I'm desperate to get things right. It's my debut as an event planner."

I patted her arm and prescribed herbal tea. Gemma slid a luscious lemon croissant on a plate, saying, "Here. Eat this. Nothing like pure sugar to calm the nerves. Screw those entitled fools. You're doing a great job."

"How can we help," I asked.

"You mean it? I'm going nuts trying to collect all the auction items." Kim handed me a list. "Could you possibly gather them and drop them off at the Expo? I'll be forever in your debt."

I agreed, and Gemma seconded the motion. Most of the items had been shipped directly to the Expo from cities all over Europe and the States, but more than a few were local. The star of the show with a six-figure estimate was an oil painting by Violet Davis, listed artist. My humble offering ranked far below that, but I was honored to be included at all. I had chosen an abstract impressionist work of a young girl seated at a tea table with an older woman, probably her grandmother, and labeled it "Tea with Grand -Mere". I feared that it would sound pretentious, but Violet assured me that buyers appreciated a title. "It helps frame things for them," she said. "Some people can visualize things better if you set the stage for them."

Gemma had assembled a few things from Poppet for the silent auction. She'd devised a package featuring a day of beauty with massage, manicure, and makeup application at a bargain price. We'd had quite a bit of success with that during the holiday season. It helped draw new customers into our store and was particularly popular with desperate husbands and boyfriends. Kim donated her services as an image consultant and the local doggie day spa offered a special for pampered pets looking for beauty. High-end pet products had become a significant part of the beauty business as indulgent pet parents vied for ways to show love for their pooches.

After we'd scoured the market for donations, Gemma and I carefully packed the spoils into my Jeep, added Fantasia, and headed toward Traverse City. Lin Baugh met us at the loading dock with several laborers who carefully removed our treasures and stacked them in a storage facility. Gemma was entranced by Lin, and despite being an engaged woman, she flirted shamelessly with him. I dismissed her antics since I knew full well that they were harmless, just part of her normal routine. Lin won my heart by fussing over Fantasia, stroking her soft fur, and admiring her beauty. Anyone who ignores my dog earns my lasting enmity.

"I'm a bit concerned about your aunt's painting," Lin said. "I'll store that and your lovely work in my office. They'll be secure there. And there's a place for Fantasia, too. I'll have the chef bring her water and some chicken treats."

I was flattered, of course, but also comforted by his prudence. We'd given my painting a range of $1000-1500, but the sales price of Violet's work was estimated at $80-100,000. Lin explained that he received that figure from DuMouchelle's, a respected Detroit auction house. "Tell your aunt that they considered that a bargain price for her work," Lin said. "She has plenty of fans in the art world." Lin hesitated. "Violet's work is a tad rich for my blood and pocketbook, but I plan to bid on your painting, Marky. It's lovely."

I'm certain that I blushed when Gemma barged into the conversation. "I keep telling her that. After all the Art Institute doesn't have the final word. Marky is so talented."

We spent some time chatting over an excellent lunch of broiled white fish with morel mushrooms. The dining room was filled with customers, eager to sample the offerings of the culinary institute. According to Lin, that was not unusual. Prices were reasonable, and many of the student chefs showed extraordinary promise. Suddenly, the conversational buzz stopped as a newcomer entered the room. A man with incredible presence stood silently in the doorway and surveyed the crowd. Something about him inspired other men to suck in their stomachs and square their shoulders. The distaff part of the audience tended to gape, open-mouthed. He must be a celebrity, I decided, for outside of the cinema, I'd never seen a more handsome creature. My powers of description failed me, even though, as an artist, I was accustomed to noting physical traits. He was tall, with lush brown hair styled in a ponytail, perfectly molded features, and a museum-quality body. That summed up my assessment of this elegant stranger, but as usual, Gemma voiced it better. She rubbed her eyes and exclaimed, "Good Lord! Who in the world is that dreamboat?"

Lin Baugh quickly rose, hurried to the door, and greeted the newcomer. There was a decided air of arrogance to the man, although he accepted the stares of my fellow diners with a type of noblesse oblige that suggested he was accustomed to such a reaction. I lowered my eyes, trying to salvage a modicum of dignity and unwilling to feed what was probably a gigantic ego. Aunt Violet would have handled things with aplomb, but she modeled the behavior of a Parisian. I was merely little Marky Davis from Harbor Bay, Michigan, trying her best to be cool.

"Oh no," Gemma whispered sotto voce. "He's coming over here." She fluffed her hair and managed a seductive smile.

"Ladies, let me introduce one of our Expo sponsors," Lin said. "I'd like you to meet Mr. Killian Blaine."

Killian Blaine! Was this the elusive nerd with the exalted academic pedigree who terrorized his competitors? The one whose nickname was Kill. No wonder he concealed his appearance. Otherwise, female clients would flood his offices begging for his services.

I glanced up furtively and did a quick appraisal. His eyes. I was mesmerized by them, but not in a good way. Windows to the soul, I've heard them called. His were glacial blue—probably tinted contacts—without even a hint of warmth. Shark eyes—cold and lifeless as a relentless predator. Probably earned the title Kill many times over. I resolved to remain strong and appear indifferent. Gemma took no such vow.

"We wondered who you were," she said. "You caused quite a stir, but I guess you're used to that."

His reaction wasn't friendly. It wasn't even civil. Killian Blaine ignored Gemma's comment and turned to Lin. "May I have a word in private," he asked. After nodding curtly to us, he motioned Lin toward a corner table for two and strode away. Lin excused himself and followed. I envisioned the possible confrontation between hot-blooded Mario Ricci and this iceman. Hard to predict who would emerge victorious, but I gave Mario a slight edge. Fire melts ice, after all. Meanwhile Gemma did her best to eavesdrop on the conversation. She was adept at lip reading, and her hearing was as acute as any bat's. Killian Blaine's massive frown told me he was one unhappy camper. In contrast, Lin Baugh's impassive countenance gave nothing away.

"I couldn't make much sense of it," Gemma whispered, "but I distinctly heard the name Ricci several times. Didn't Kim say that the dreamboat was trying to muscle in on Ricci Enterprises?"

Before I could respond, Lin returned to our table. "Sorry, ladies," he said. "Just a slight kerfuffle. Nothing serious. Conflict management is part of my job."

"He's not very friendly," Gemma said. "Kind of rude, but I guess a guy who looks like that is used to getting his way. What ruffled his feathers anyhow?"

I decided to pile on, even though it was none of our business. "Kim told us that man's firm does mergers and acquisitions. I suppose he's looking for victims at the show."

Lin laughed. "That about sums it up, although I would say partners, not victims. Apparently corporate America thinks the beauty biz is a good investment. High finance is beyond me, thank goodness. I just concentrate on giving customers their money's worth and a good time."

His act was good, but it didn't deceive me. Lin Baugh was one smooth operator who was aware of anything that might sabotage his operation. After exchanging business cards, we concluded our meeting, collected Fantasia and headed for the parking lot. Gemma was bursting with excitement, but I managed to contain her comments until we reached the car. As I unlocked my Jeep, I saw that it was blocked by one of the most elegant vehicles I had ever seen—a sleek, ebony Mercedes Maybach sedan that matched its driver, the redoubtable Killian Blaine. Like most Michigan natives, I have a deeply ingrained automotive DNA. I'm not car-obsessed, but I can identify and appreciate a thing of beauty, particularly one that costs about two hundred grand. There was an aura of exclusivity about it that suited Killian Blaine, but I was not intimidated. When he rolled down the window and poked his head out, I remained aloof.

"You're Marketta Davis. Violet's niece, I presume. Sorry if I was rude back there. Sometimes I forget my manners."

Gemma jabbed me in the ribs with a sharp elbow and whispered. "Say something."

I lowered my sunglasses and said, "You know my aunt?"

Killian elected to be charming, or his version of it. "Not personally, but I'm a great admirer of her talent. I own several of her oils."

That didn't surprise me, and he could certainly afford it. I try to be courteous to everyone, but something about this man raised my hackles. Perfect looks, perfect car—just a bit too much perfection for my taste. I would love to paint him, but that's where my interest ended. Besides, I resented his treatment of Gemma. He excluded her as if she was unworthy of his notice. I would not tolerate that, even if he was the most gorgeous male specimen I had ever encountered outside of a museum. Inner beauty counted, too.

"I'll be sure to mention it to my aunt," I said while closing the car window.

"Hold on." Killian Blaine jumped from his mega-car and tapped my window. "Please take my card. I'll be down your way next week. Maybe we can have dinner."

I toyed with snubbing him outright but that would make me as rude as he was. Meanwhile, Gemma was bug-eyed as she watched our encounter. She acted quickly, thrusting one of our business cards into my hands and leaving me little choice but to exchange it with his. Killian smiled, gave us a half-wave, and retreated into the lap of luxury. I waited a full two minutes before pressing the Jeep's accelerator. No doubt his interest had more to do with my aunt than me. Still, I had to admit that even a smidgeon of attention from such a man was flattering. Overwhelming. Gemma was temporarily speechless, a condition that seldom afflicted her. She fanned herself as she pulled down the passenger mirror and checked her lipstick. "Can you believe it?" she asked. "Wait 'til I tell my mom. She loves stuff like this. Love at first sight."

"Hardly. Just because you're engaged, don't throw me in the mix. That man isn't even my type. He probably uses and discards women like tissues. Maybe you should dump Benny and pursue him yourself if you think he's so hot. Leave me out of it."

Gemma has a talent for ignoring what she disagrees with. She continued to weave her romantic fantasy despite my objections. "He wasn't wearing a wedding ring," she said. "First thing I noticed. Did you get a load of that car he drives? Pure class all the way."

Money didn't impress me, even though I enjoyed having nice things and strove for success. Maybe I'm just an artist at heart. So many of the world's greatest never achieved financial riches during their lifetime but created enduring treasures. Aunt Violet achieved the perfect balance: financial security, artistic acclaim, and business success. Those were my goals, and they didn't require pandering to any man, no matter how gorgeous he was.

"Mario Ricci's name came up in his conversation," Gemma said once she had revived. "Wonder what that was about? Lin certainly played it cool."

Not surprising. Lin Baugh was one cool customer whose livelihood depended on placating clients of every stripe. I decided to call Kim as soon as we got home and ask for advice. She knew the players and probably had insights on all of them. The Expo was only one week away. Information was power and I intended to muster every particle of intelligence available before the big event.

Chapter Four

"Sounds like you had quite an exciting trip." Aunt Violet looked amused, not surprised, but Kim was distraught. She dug her nails into her palms, a gesture that had to hurt. They listened to Gemma's highly colored account of our adventures without interrupting.

"He didn't say anything, I hope. Killian won't cause any trouble at the Expo, will he?"

"I suspect that he's far too civilized to do that. Besides, Killian Blaine is an art lover and a lawyer to boot. They always calculate the cost of lawsuits before acting." My aunt chuckled, sharing a private joke that no one else was privy to. "Mario is the one to watch. That man is a magnet for trouble, and he enjoys making a scene. So volatile."

We reviewed the agenda and checked the timetables and the guest list. Despite Kim's urging, Mario insisted that Violet must be the one to apply his Ricci Rich conditioner. His big moment came on day two. Lin Baugh had arranged a mini salon for the occasion, complete with a rinse station and blow-dry stand. Kim allotted 45 minutes for the demo, far more time than any other promoters received. Since Mario had paid extra for the privilege, there was nothing she could do. Major cosmetic companies had gobbled up time slots to showcase their products, and the schedule was packed. The reception, banquet, and auction were featured on the first evening, with one of the premier French makeup tzars serving as master of ceremonies. I loved his products and stocked Poppet with them. Gemma and I also agreed to act as ticket takers and timekeepers during the event. I didn't mind. Kim needed the help, and any task, however menial, that enhanced our visibility was worth it. As a newcomer to the beauty scene, my goal was to watch and listen. Aunt Violet was an established star, but I was merely a functionary. Gemma and I were only twenty-eight, so our time would come. Patience and persistence would ultimately pay off. At least, that's what I told myself.

* * *

I paid special attention to my appearance that next week in case Killian Blaine came to town. He did not. Gemma contrived several excuses for his absence, but I was above all a pragmatist. Men like him were always on the prowl for arm candy. I'd seen enough of that during art school. To some, I was decorative enough to qualify, but it meant nothing in the overall scheme of things. I was not surprised. Perhaps a tad disappointed but not surprised.

Gemma and I spent an inordinate amount of time agonizing over wardrobe choices. In the after-hours, we each modeled several options and, with the advice of my aunt, Kim, and Gemma's mom, made our final selections. I opted for bright colors but nothing too daring. Gemma toned down her usual look since the beady eyes of Benny Soto would be following her every move. He bragged that he was privy to the event's secret security plans, although I suspected that Lin Baugh would tamp down his excess zeal by confining Benny to guard duty.

When the big day finally arrived, we packed Fantasia and our supplies into my trusty Jeep and started our trek. Aunt Violet opted instead for the comfort and luxury of Kim's Mercedes. I didn't blame her. A luxury vehicle was far more her style than a muscular off-road one like mine. Gemma was beside herself with excitement, but I maintained a steady course. This was my chance to mingle, observe, and learn from beauty's best practitioners. Any gaffes would immediately brand us as parvenus unfit to join the elect. My mantra was "fake it til you make it."

The moment we arrived, Mario Ricci charged toward us, waving his arms in what was either excitement or a medical emergency.

"Where is she?" he said. "You must tell me immediately. This is a disaster."

I assumed that the "she" in question was either Kim or Violet and that

Mario's emergency was nothing critical. Fortunately, before his anxiety reached critical mass, Kim and my aunt came to the rescue. The garbled mixture of Italian, English, and French was impossible to decipher save for the names Carla Standish and Killian Blaine. Kim did plenty of nodding while Violet absently patted Mario's shoulder. As we unpacked, they slowly walked toward the registration desk where Lin Baugh stood, ready to take command. Mario's arms were still flailing, but at least his diatribe had lessened. Our time was limited, and both Gemma and I were anxious to unpack and dress for the reception. Fantasia, who was already groomed and gorgeous, kept us company as we primped.

"Wonder what that was all about," Gemma said.

I shrugged. "Who knows or cares? Violet says it's a crisis a minute with that man. No big deal."

Gemma always fancied herself a clairvoyant or something very much like that. I had to admit that her heightened senses had come in handy a time or two, but I did my best to discourage her flights of fancy. This time, there was no deterring her.

"I've got a funny feeling about this," Gemma said, frowning. "Something bad is brewing, mark my words."

I zipped up her dress and focused on the positive. "You, my girl, look ravishing. Benny will be overcome with jealousy."

"Look who's talking," she said. "I'll bet a certain dreamboat lawyer will lose his mind when he sees you. Ravishing red. It's really your color."

I glanced at the mirror and was pleased with my reflection. There would be plenty of glam and bling at the night's festivities, but Gemma and I could hold our own. Others boasted diamonds and jewels, but we had youth on our side. I was especially eager to meet two of the guests: Carla Standish and Sophia Laurent. If any fireworks emerged, they would probably be right in the thick of things.

As low persons on the volunteer totem pole, we staffed the registration table. Lin Baugh chose discrete lanyards rather than those obnoxious sticky tags that cling to fine fabrics. Kudos to him for that and his ability to maintain a bland expression in the face of conflict. His sister's tragic end would cause most men to strike out at Mario Ricci, but not Lin. I doubted that Mario even realized the connection between the suave event coordinator and the young woman he had ruined. Self-involved people seldom saw beyond their own needs and according to Violet, the list of Mario's conquests was extensive.

My first customer was a female with a soft Southern twang. "Name please," I said, keeping my head down while searching the roster.

"Carla. Carla Standish."

I raised my head and stared at the woman I had heard so much about. Carla was tall and slim, clad in an all-beige ensemble that looked like either cashmere or silk. Her blonde hair was skillfully highlighted and precision cut by a master stylist. I knew her age. Kim mentioned that Carla was on the sunny side of fifty, although she could easily pass for a decade younger. The ravages of time had been tamed by the judicious use of fillers and a masterful makeup application.

"Oh, Ms. Standish, I'm so pleased to meet you." I tried not to gush, but it was hard to restrain myself. I quickly introduced Gemma and mentioned Poppet. "We love your products, and our customers rave about them, especially the *Hair Deluxe* regimen."

Gemma overheard our conversation and chimed in. "You bet they do! You have a solid fan base in Harbor Bay."

Carla flushed with pleasure. "Hearing that warms my heart. This business can be difficult, as I'm sure you know." She scrutinized me. "Hold on. I bet you're Violet Davis's niece. There's quite a family resemblance."

Carla noticed that a line of impatient registrants had formed behind her. "Maybe we can talk later," she said as she fastened her lanyard and moved away. It was difficult to imagine such a refined, courteous lady mixing it up with the likes of Mario Ricci. On the other hand, who could envision my lovely aunt having a moment with him?

We were so busy for the next hour that I barely noticed the sultry brunette who sidled up to me sporting a large Chanel tote. Her curvaceous body was on display in a skintight dress that left nothing to the imagination and fulfilled the fantasies of every male in the place. Next to her, I felt like a hopeless ingenue. The woman had to be at least forty. Skillful use of cosmetics and a flawless complexion conspired to mask the effects of age, but beauty was my business. She reared back as the eye-popping diamond studs in her ears flashed defiantly at my humble gold hoops. Even Gemma gasped as she surveyed the new arrival.

"I am Sophia Laurent," she said with a heavy accent that was both imperious and seductive. "Why is my suite not ready?"

Somehow, I managed to salvage my dignity in the face of her onslaught. "I'm sorry," I said. "Accommodations are handled at the front desk." I pointed to the line on the other side of the room. "They can help you there." I handed her a lanyard, which she promptly tossed back at me. "I do not wear that trash. Everyone knows Sophia anyway."

Sophia's sharp intake of breath suggested that she was working her way into a major snit. Only the timely intervention of Lin Baugh averted a crisis.

"Ms. Laurent," he said. "How lovely you look. It will be my pleasure to assist you with your suite." He guided her toward the elevator, but not before turning our way and winking. As they passed, I heard them converse in a steady stream of flawless French. Lin was a true marvel, someone to measure my own customer service skills against.

"Talk about a spoiled brat," Gemma hissed. "Mario had to be nuts to drop your aunt for that creature."

I wondered about that but kept the speculation to myself. Violet deserved her zone of privacy if she so chose. Still, Mario Ricci dropped several notches, in my estimation. There was no comparison between my elegant aunt and the vulgar tart Sophia Laurent. Only a fool would be beguiled by such a creature.

I checked my watch. The registration period had officially ended, and that freed Gemma and me to join the festive crowd. Most were milling about the bar or cadging snacks from the waiters' trays. No sign anywhere of that sizzling legal eagle, not that I cared at all. A string quartet set the right mood by playing a selection of Mozart and Beethoven tunes. I was captivated by the subtle scent of high-end fragrances blending seamlessly with the alluring notes of oriental lilies. Tuxedo-clad attendants armed with gift baskets ringed the auditorium. Famous faces with equally famous names mingled with beauty purveyors, engaging them in muted sales pitches for their products. An understated carnival air prevailed as participants mixed business with pleasure.

Gemma spied Benny Soto and sped across the room to join him. Benny, like several other security officers, wore a navy blazer, grey slacks, and an earpiece. Any weapons they carried were inconspicuous. True to type, Benny preened in front of the gilded rococo mirror and soon sent Gemma packing. "Back so soon?" I asked. "What's up with Benny?"

Gemma leapt to his defense. "You know how serious he is when he's working. I should have known better." She sighed. "Doesn't he look handsome?"

I gave her a perfunctory nod and continued to scan the crowd. Mario was easy to spot. He was surrounded by a cluster of admirers, mostly female, and appeared to be emoting at some length. Over to the side, like the proverbial wallflower, stood Carla Standish. Despite the smile she wore like armor, I sensed that this was an essentially shy woman who was uncomfortable in unfamiliar surroundings. Fortunately, Kim joined her and soon had Carla engaged in an animated discussion. With a dollop of luck, I managed to overhear most of what they said.

"Don't let him get to you," Kim told Carla. "You've earned your place here without Mario's help. Very few women could have done that. People admire you. Besides, you look devastating. You're a great advertisement for Hair Deluxe."

Carla closed her eyes. "I'm sorry. It's just that seeing Mario revives all the sad scenes in our marriage. I honestly loved him, and it wasn't enough. I wasn't enough."

"Horse feathers," Kim said. "You developed some of Ricci's best formulas. If anything, Mario should fear facing you. That man acted like a cad. Ignore him."

They linked arms and laughed. It seemed as if Kim's pep talk had restored Carla's fighting spirit.

That didn't last long. Mario Ricci left this throng of admirers and marched toward the two women with an ominous frown on his face.

Kim tried to placate him, but the volatile Italian seemed determined to cause a scene. To her credit, Carla remained poised and unflappable. She turned aside, shook Kim's hand, and glided toward the bar. Who knows what would have followed had not Aunt Violet suddenly appeared? Without descending to hyperbole, I can truthfully say that she was a vision in lavender. Mario thought so, too. He abandoned his pursuit of Carla and focused on my aunt, who handled things with her usual flair. Peace and tranquility returned until another player entered the mix. Sophia Laurent's arrival caused a temporary lull in the conversation. Men leered, and women faltered as the French woman made her mark.

Gemma jabbed my ribs with those sharp elbows of hers. "Look who's with her," she whispered. "They make a stunning pair."

Sometimes, when Gemma states the obvious, I'm tempted to pummel her. Not often. This was one of those times. Killian Blaine, the other part of the duo, placed a propriety arm around Sophia and guided her toward the drinks table. I got it. Whatever their shortcomings all men look better in a tuxedo, but Killian Blaine set a standard for perfection unequaled by any other male in the room. I'd seen images of his glorious handmade suit in upscale magazines. It wasn't even a tuxedo. Brioni called the royal blue bespoke item a *Brunico*, and it retailed for well over $10,000. Once again, Shakespeare nailed it. Polonius, that sage advisor, opined that apparel oft proclaims the man. Who was I to dispute the Bard? That Brioni suit proclaimed that Killian Blaine was a certified hottie with taste, money, and a killer body. From my limited perspective, he was also a cad who enjoyed toying with women.

"Go on over and greet him," urged Gemma. "Give that Frenchie something to think about."

"No, thank you. I don't intend to lower myself to that. Besides, the opening ceremony is about to start."

Kim, joined by Lin Baugh, greeted the guests and welcomed everyone to Beauty Expo. She then invited us to be seated for dinner or, as Lin phrased it, 'a moveable feast.' Gemma and I found a seat in the peanut gallery, a table populated mostly by staff and the personal assistants of the mighty. I still had a bird's-eye view of Sophia and her devoted swain although I tried to appear disinterested. Gemma showed no such restraint. She openly gawked at them, reporting their every move.

"Oh, Oh. Incoming." Gemma pointed toward Mario Ricci, who charged toward his former love like a guided missile. Emotion made Mario lose his bearings and he collided with a waiter bearing a tray of shrimp cocktails. The resulting commotion might have been disastrous had Lin Baugh not inserted himself between Mario and his prey. In record time, a squad of waiters armed with dust bins arrived and quickly tidied up the scene. I looked for Sophia and Killian, but they had magically disappeared. Most of the diners, especially one, appeared to enjoy that bit of theater. Carla Standish's face was wreathed in smiles as she watched Mario pluck shrimp from his tuxedo. I understood her reaction. A vanquished adversary was an awesome sight for anyone to behold.

The rest of the evening passed uneventfully. The menu was superb, from appetizer to dessert. I shamelessly cleaned my plate, but Gemma went even further by scrounging a second dessert. When the dancing started, I slipped away to repair my makeup. On the way back, I ran into the very person I had hoped to avoid.

"Marketta Davis. I've been looking for you." Like most lawyers, Killian Blaine had perfected the art of dissembling. Fortunately, I am equally skilled in deception.

"I saw that you were occupied and didn't want to intrude."

That momentarily floored him, but Killian quickly recovered. "Oh yes. Sophia is an old and valued client. Business before pleasure, unfortunately." He patted my cheek. "Sorry, I couldn't make it to Harbor Bay last week. Things got chaotic at the firm."

I beamed my most beatific smile his way. "No problem. I know how that is. We were swamped preparing for this anyhow."

When the orchestra played a lively tune, Killian grinned. "Care to dance?" he asked. "That song's one of my favorites." I had absolutely no doubt that the man danced divinely. It was a tempting offer, especially since I adored dancing. Self-restraint was one of my superpowers, however, and I exercised it in full.

"I'd love to, but I promised my aunt I'd help out with the auction and tomorrow's arrangements."

His puzzled look told me that Mr. Blaine was not accustomed to rejection. "Yes, of course. Mario does his big show and tell tomorrow. Perhaps we'll have some time together after that. I would like to get to know you."

We parted then, and I rejoined Gemma. She immediately noticed the flush on my face and the spring in my step. No detail eluded my partner.

"Okay, spill. I bet you ran into the dreamboat, didn't you? You have that look."

"Don't be silly." I turned away to avoid a telltale blush. "We're here to help with the auction in case you forgot. Come on. It starts in twenty minutes."

Lots for the live auction were stacked on the stage behind a thick red curtain. The lesser items, including my painting for the silent auction, were arranged around the ballroom on tables. Notepads listed the proposed range and allowed the prospective buyer to make a bid. I was tempted to peek at my painting, but once again, willpower came to my rescue. Besides with Gemma around I didn't need to worry. She circled the room and gave me constant updates.

"Someone already bid on your painting," she said, smirking. "More than the asking price, too. I'll bet we know who that was."

I shrugged, affecting nonchalance. If someone appreciated my work that was enough. Nothing would wound me more than my painting sitting lonely and ignored, like the last muffin on the plate. "It's a charity event, Gemma. I won't get a dime from it. I feel grateful to be included." I've known Gemma all my life, and she reads me like a well-worn book. She scoffed at that falsehood and turned away.

As I scanned the crowd, an interesting scene caught my eye. Carla Standish and Sophia Laurent were engaged in what appeared to be a heated discussion. Nothing violent, although from Carla's rigid posture, I suspected that she was prepared for anything. They were a study in contrasts: Carla, an aristocratic Brit, versus the sensuous Sophia oozing French glamour. On the surface, they would seem to have little in common, but the beauty business encouraged several odd alliances. I edged closer to the duo, hoping to overhear something.

"Sophia will own Ricci products," she hissed. "Very soon."

Carla folded her arms. "Unlikely. Mario lives for that brand. He'd never sell, especially to a vile strumpet like you."

Her words ignited a firestorm in Sophia's eyes. "He will change his mind." She curled her lip. "French women know how to convince a man. You have ice water in your English veins. Mario told me so!"

Carla flushed and pointed a finger at her tormenter. "Leave me alone. You and Mario deserve one another."

Their squabble was halted by the start of the live auction as the crowd returned to their seats. Kim and Lin served as auctioneers, a task that required focus, tenacity, and more than a bit of charm. The first lots sold quickly with brisk bidding and competition from the floor. They included several vacations for two at luxury ski resorts, sunny spots, and a tempting trip along the French Riviera with Viking cruise lines. All of them reached heights that far exceeded my meager budget, but I applauded the successful bidders. I did hunger for the custom jewelry that had been donated by several of the large cosmetic firms. Emeralds captured every one of my fantasies, but they usually commanded a dizzying price. True to form, when the hammer came down, the successful bidders ponied up a big chunk of green to match the jewelry. There was a momentary hush followed by murmurs from the crowd when my aunt's painting came up for bid. I held my breath and crossed my fingers, hoping that someone in the audience appreciated such fine work. My misgivings were unfounded. Bidding was spirited, and the final hammer price far exceeded the initial estimate. Violet Davis's painting was the star of the show! I couldn't see who had won the day, although I suspected that it might be a certain attorney from Chicago. There was little time to wonder since Gemma and I were busy tagging and bagging the silent auction items and presenting them to the lucky winners. At evening's end, Kim was flushed with pride. Lin whisked away after congratulating her on raising such a sum for the beauty foundation's scholarship fund.

"Wow!" Gemma said, pointing to the final totals. "What a haul!"

I summoned my courage and asked the question that had been plaguing me. "Okay. Who was the lucky bidder? Who snagged my aunt's painting?" I braced myself, expecting to hear Killian Blaine's name. To my surprise, a totally different name surfaced.

"Sophia Laurent won it," Kim said. "That woman must have some deep pockets to outbid Mario and that lawyer from Chicago. Mario was fuming. Oh well. All proceeds go to charity, and Violet's work was a bargain even at that steep price."

Lin had offered to house the more expensive items in his office, and we carefully transported the emeralds and Violet's painting to safety.

Gemma urged me to join her at the bar for one last nightcap, but I declined. Her look of innocence didn't deceive me for a minute. I knew she was hoping to eavesdrop on some of the more prominent folks in the group and glean salacious tidbits of gossip. That didn't interest me. Besides, I was so weary that the only thing I yearned for was the big, comfy bed in my room.

She shrugged when I mentioned that. "Okay, party pooper, act like your own grandma. See if I care. Benny's shift just ended, so maybe I'll hook up with him." Her eyes sparkled at the thought. "He may need some help getting out of that uniform. Don't wait up for me."

The thought of Benny Soto, dressed or undressed, was enough to send me fleeing for the elevator. Carla Standish was also waiting there, and I introduced myself to her once again. Her manner was gracious, and she seemed a tad shy.

"I admired your painting," Carla said. "Put in a bid, but someone topped it in a hurry."

Despite my best efforts, I couldn't hide my pleasure. My painting sold for a considerable sum to an unnamed bidder. I hoped it was Lin Baugh because he would give it a good home.

"Your demo is scheduled for tomorrow," I said. "Lots of people are interested in it."

Carla pointed to my hair and asked which products I used. That led us to an animated discussion of the pros and cons of extensions, blow-drying, and the current penchant for going grey. "I don't understand it," she said.

"For centuries, cosmetics have been every woman's secret weapon. Think of Cleopatra, or Madame Pompadour. All the great beauties throughout history have known that. Why even men used some enhancement."

I mentioned that a growing number of Poppet's customers were men. Skin care products were popular with an upscale male clientele, and massage was always a big item.

Carla laughed. "Thank goodness guys have learned that good hair is very attractive to us women. I was talking with Sophia Laurent about that, and we agreed that male hair enhancement was the next big growth sector in our business. She's already an investor in a French company that specializes in that. Trichology is very popular in France." She grinned. "It was one of the few things we agreed upon. Sophia is such a spiteful creature, but she's shrewd about business. Wants to acquire Ricci Beauty to augment her portfolio. That's why she brought her attorney with her. He's quite a pirate, or so I hear."

I contemplated the lush locks of Killian Blaine and admitted to myself that I'd love to run my fingers through that manly mane. The mere thought shocked me back to reality. The elevator had come and gone but I'd enjoyed my discussion with Carla. Now it was time to walk Fantasia, complete my beauty ritual, and fall into the arms of Morpheus. I dared not hope for any dreams.

* * *

Gemma didn't return that night. When my cell phone buzzed, it took Fantasia's frantic barking to rouse me. Through bleary eyes, I noted that it was only six a.m. That's practically the middle of the night!

What kind of a monster awakens someone that early?

I growled a greeting and prepared to do battle. Only the dulcet tones of Violet Davis saved me from unleashing a stream of very naughty words.

"Get dressed and come over to Lin's office," she said in that same calm tone she always used. If the hotel was smoldering, my dear Aunt would still speak soothing words. "We've had an incident."

Thoughts of mayhem and murder ran through my muddled brain. "What happened?"

"Lin's office was robbed. I'll fill you in when you get here."

When the occasion demands it, I can pull myself together at warp speed. This was one of those times. I slipped into my running clothes, applied a minimum of makeup, and grabbed Fantasia's leash. The hotel corridors were, to use that old cliché, silent as a tomb. No right-thinking convention goer would darken the doorways at this hour. At least, that was my fervent hope. As Fantasia satisfied her potty needs, I considered the possibilities. Between the emeralds and my aunt's painting, a considerable amount of loot had been stored in Lin's office. I computed the figure and realized that it was well north of $200,000 dollars. That was a pretty prize for any enterprising thief, and it represented a potential disaster for Lin Baugh.

Flashing lights from two police vehicles announced that the authorities were already present and accounted for. My path to Lin's office was barred by the mighty figure of Benny Soto in full uniform with his weapon openly displayed. Come to think of it, Benny and resort security were responsible for safeguarding the valuables and preventing just this type of crime from happening.

"Stand clear," Benny thundered. "No civilians allowed and absolutely no dogs." He pointed to my beautiful Fantasia as if she was a potential terrorist.

I shouldered him aside without a second thought. "I was summoned by my aunt. Maybe you should be hunting for clues unless this is a case of locking the barn door after the horse has bolted."

Rage mottled Benny's face. "You're quite a comedian, Ms. Davis. Maybe we should search your room first. You brought some of that stuff in here, didn't you?"

I ignored him and studied the door. Nothing looked amiss, in fact, the thief had been remarkably tidy. That didn't bode well for Lin or the hotel management itself. I texted my aunt, and within a few seconds, the door swung open to admit me. Much to Benny's consternation, Lin Baugh waved me into the scene of the crime. Although he said very little, the enormity of the crime had taken its toll. Lin's face was ashen, and his usually impeccable suit was the worse for wear.

Lin quickly summarized the details in a monotone. Sometime between midnight and three AM, his office had been burglarized. The security system malfunctioned and failed to alert the local police or Lin. By the time the theft was discovered, the culprits were long gone.

"Wait a minute," I said. "I thought a guard was posted outside 24-7."

Lin looked away, and Aunt Violet cleared her throat. "Actually, a guard was assigned to watch the office, but he stepped away for a brief time."

Suddenly the truth dawned on me. Benny Soto! That big lug had probably been canoodling with Gemma instead of guarding his post. No wonder she hadn't returned to our room. Kim and Lin were up the proverbial creek without a paddle.

"Now what?" I asked.

Lin assured me that the valuables were insured, so ultimately, everyone would recover their losses. Nevertheless, the breach had sullied the reputation of both the resort and its management. When Kim joined us, it was obvious that she, too, was distraught. Beneath the impeccable makeup and perfect coif, lines of strain that no amount of cosmetics could eradicate now appeared.

"I explained the situation to the couple who purchased the emeralds," Kim said. "They were most understanding. I wish I could say the same about Sophia. She launched into a tirade, a virtual fit of hysterics even though I told her that Violet would provide a substitute painting."

My aunt gently squeezed Kim's shoulder. "This too shall pass. Sophia loves a bit of theater, but ultimately, she's a realist. Meanwhile, we should consider altering today's program to accommodate the police. They'll want to question everyone."

"It's worse than that. I'm afraid they plan to search everyone's room," Lin said. "High-profile patrons will be offended, but there's no avoiding it. In fact, they've already started."

Kim covered her face with her hands. "More disruption. Mario will be livid if his big unveiling is ruined. I don't think I can face another tongue-lashing at this point."

Violet grinned. "You can and you will. Besides, I have an idea. Privileged people adore free bees. Why not serve mimosas and have a raffle with the breakfast buffet? I can offer to sketch the lucky winner, and Gemma can redeem herself by offering free massages."

For a moment, I thought Kim would bawl, but she quickly composed herself. Making lemonade from lemons was Violet's specialty. Feeling more optimistic, we agreed to reconnoiter in the ballroom after freshening up. I chose to jog around the complex with Fantasia before returning to my room. No one was around, and both of us would profit from some rigorous exercise. Besides, I needed time and solitude to think. Had someone deliberately sabotaged the conference, or was the theft a well-planned crime for profit? We had publicized the auction items, particularly the emeralds and Violet's painting. Any enterprising thief could have seized the opportunity to profit. Benny Soto's dereliction of duty would not go unnoticed either. He might lose his job or worse. And what about Gemma? Her daring side had surfaced at the most inopportune time. With any luck, Poppet wouldn't be associated with the unsavory incident, although gossip and speculation were still the main events at the Beauty Expo. Sophia was certain to spread the word as quickly as possible.

"Hey. Wait up."

I pretended not to hear that rich baritone, but he quickened his pace and called me by name. There was no denying it—Killian Blaine in form-fitting sweats was a sight to behold. He blocked my path, reaching down to pat Fantasia's silky coat. "I heard there was a big dustup at the hotel," he said. "A robbery."

Those icy eyes looked warmer now, although it might well have been my sleep-deprived imagination. My hair was tangled, and I was certain that mascara had seeped down under my eyes. He'd now seen me at my worst, so I had nothing to lose by confronting him.

"You seem to know what's going on. What have you heard?" Hands on hips, I challenged the arrogant attorney.

Instead of answering, he laughed in my face. "Touchy, touchy. Don't kill the messenger. My client woke me from a sound sleep screeching like a banshee about her stolen painting."

That sounded plausible enough, especially since Sophia had already heard the bad news from Kim. No harm in answering his question. "Yeah. There was a break-in. The emeralds and my aunt's painting were stolen."

Killian didn't feign shock or sorrow. He chuckled as if the entire incident had been staged just to entertain him. His glee was almost insulting, and I wanted to strike back.

"The cops are all over this. They're probably searching your room as we speak. No one, even an attorney, is exempt. Of course, if you have nothing to hide, it shouldn't be a problem."

The thought of police rummaging through his things made him react. "I have confidential files in that room. Attorney client matters." Killian abruptly turned around and sped back toward the resort.

Score one for me.

* * *

Gemma slunk back to our room soon after I returned. Her face was a study in misery-guilt mixed with a healthy dose of shame. She bowed her head at first, refusing to meet my eyes. There was no trace of the ebullient Gemma who enlivened my daily life. I took pity on her.

"Fess up. What in the world happened last night?"

Her hands balled up into fists as she carefully chose her words. "There's not much to tell. I met Benny thinking he'd finished his shift, but the big goof promised his buddy he'd cover for him."

"And...?"

Gemma bit her lip. "It wasn't his fault. Not really. We stayed an extra thirty minutes. That's all he promised his pal. Then we left, and one thing led to another. You know how it is."

Unfortunately, it had been a while since passion had robbed me of my senses. "You mean you just left the office unguarded?"

"We thought the other guy would be there right away. Who knew some criminal was casing the joint?" Gemma whined with the best of them, but her excuses cut no ice with me.

"What did they tell Benny?"

Deputy Soto was told to guard the door and await a decision by his superiors. Possible penalties ranged from verbal reprimand to termination depending on the outcome of the case. Things looked grim for the amorous policeman who deserved every bit of the blame. I sympathized with Gemma though. After this, her big romance might fizzle and even more frightening was the thought of confronting that mad matriarch, Josephine Soto.

"Cheer up," I said. "Maybe we can help them find the culprit or, better still, recover the loot. Did you see anyone lurking around the office last night?"

Gemma shook her head. "We weren't looking for that."

I got a sudden brainstorm. Lin's office was large and included a sizable walk-in closet. No one was concerned with security until after the loot was left in the room. Suppose the thief was already in position, hid inside that area, stole the goods, and escaped while the door was left unguarded? That would explain the pristine condition of the office. It wouldn't identify the culprit of course but it was a start.

"Dry your tears and get ready for the public. Violet wants you to give free massages as your penance."

We took turns in the bathroom sprucing up. I gave my hair a thorough scrubbing and applied plenty of product to tame any errant strands. Gemma's style was strictly wash and wear, so she finished well before I did. After realizing how ravenous I was, I scampered down to the ballroom, hoping that the buffet was still open. It was. Lin had outdone himself by plying his clients with piles of smoked salmon, made-to-order omelets, and freshly baked croissants. The mimosa station was also doing a thriving business. None of the crowd appeared surly except for Sophia Laurent, who flounced around the room, regaling everyone with the tale of her lost painting. Killian Blaine was nowhere to be found. Perhaps he had lost his appetite after watching peons rifling his belongings.

As we savored our breakfast, Lin Baugh addressed the group. He explained about the unfortunate incident (his words), apologized for the disruption, and shared the proposed changes to the schedule. At the conclusion of his remarks, he provided an update. The emeralds, along with the frame for Violet's painting, had been found unharmed in a service closet. Sadly, the painting itself had not been recovered. To augment the private security, the resort had contacted Gideon Hall, Harbor Bay's former police chief, to lead the investigation. I wasn't certain if that was good or bad for Benny Soto. Gideon had recently been promoted to head Traverse City's police force. He was Benny's former boss, but he was also a no-nonsense lawman who would pursue all avenues no matter where they led. I'd tangled with Gideon a time or two when he accused me of interfering in police business, but something about the man inspired confidence and security. His large frame was reminiscent of a sequoia, sturdy and reassuring. It helped that he was also intelligent and measured when trouble arose.

"That's weird," Gemma said. "Why would someone dump the emeralds but steal the painting? Jewels would be easier to fence than artwork." She grimaced. "And why bring Gideon Hall into this mess? Poor Benny. He'll be chewing his nails off."

That was one visual I could do without. As far as I was concerned Benny Soto had deserted his post and should pay the price. A hot romance was no excuse for dereliction of duty, even if it involved my best pal.

Gemma clutched my arm. "We've got to help him. If Benny loses his job, it'll kill him. Plus, there's no telling what that mother of his will do. She'll blame me!"

Envisioning that scene made me shudder. The formidable Josephine Soto would pulverize poor Gemma if she got the chance. Like many mothers she thought that her son could do no wrong and only a temptress like Gemma could lead him astray. Like many mothers, Josephine had no idea what her boy was capable of.

Most of the main players were already seated. Mario commanded a place at the head table next to my aunt and alternated between guzzling mimosas and whispering into Violet's ear. All things considered, he seemed less agitated by the change to his schedule than I'd expected. Every time he glanced at Sophia Laurent, he smirked. No doubt his glee had to do with her missing painting, although with Mario, one never knew. Carla Standish nibbled at her omelet while keeping her eyes downcast. *What was her problem?* I'd grown fond of the woman and sympathized with her business woes, but instead of fighting for her livelihood, she appeared to be succumbing. *Hair Deluxe* was a successful product that compared favorably with anything Mario might produce. His braggadocio was all that stood between the two items.

Violet stopped by our table to commiserate with us about her painting. When I pointed to Carla, my aunt gave me a look of pity. "I thought you knew. Carla was Mario's first wife. It was her genius that developed the Ricci line. Mario stole all her intellectual property and dumped her like a hot potato when Sophia sashayed in. Carla almost didn't survive."

"You mean…?"

Violet nodded. "At least one suicide attempt that I know of." She closed her eyes. "Luckily, I found her before she overdosed. No man is worth sacrificing your life for. Trust me on that. When Sophia returned the favor by discarding him, Mario went through his usual histrionics, but he never even considered harming himself."

I'd dealt with double-dealing men before, so I understood. My courage failed me however and I didn't ask my aunt about her own romantic adventures with the volatile Italian. Sometimes, silence was indeed golden.

"Hey, look who just walked in." Gemma gestured toward a figure at the buffet line. "You got to admit he's a dreamboat," she said. "Now there's a man who doesn't need to use *Ricci Rich*."

I opted for a subtle approach to avoid gawking at Killian Blaine. He was perfectly groomed and attired in Italian sportswear straight from the pages of *GQ*. I shook myself to return to reality. Perfection was boring, especially when the specimen in question knew just how perfect he was. Kindness, courtesy, and humility counted, too, and from what I'd witnessed so far, Mr. Blaine came up short in those areas. I yawned just to show Gemma that I wasn't interested.

"He's coming this way," she squealed, elbowing me. "Act natural."

Violet had vacated her seat, and she offered it to Killian. He commiserated with her about the theft of her painting, proving that he was at least capable of empathy when the occasion demanded it.

"I bid on it myself," he said. "Another devoted admirer of your prodigious talent, ma'am."

My aunt was no stranger to praise. She acknowledged it with poise and dignity because she knew it was true. My suspicious mind was working overtime. Suppose Mr. Blaine took a five-finger discount and absconded with Violet's painting. He had no need for emeralds and could easily have discarded them. Would he risk his reputation and career on a whim? Unlikely.

"I suppose they searched your room?" Gemma said. "Join the club. If I'd known, I would have tidied up my things."

Killian gave her a bland smile and devoted himself to savoring the eggs heaped on his plate. A long table at the back of the room was filled with law enforcement types from all over who were also wolfing down the delicious chow. I nodded at Chief Gideon Hall and one of his deputies, noting the conspicuous absence of yet another. Benny Soto had chosen to skulk around the ballroom rather than join his fellow officers. Humility was a welcome change from his usual pose of macho bravado, although Gemma might not agree. She had always favored bad boys or bullies for reasons known only to her. No amount of counseling or lectures from me would ever change that, especially since my own track record with men was mixed.

"I understand you're giving a massage clinic this afternoon," Killian said. "Sign me up. I overdid it on the Peloton yesterday, and my back aches."

"That's Gemma's bailiwick. She's the massage maven," I said. "Her clients call her a miracle worker."

Gemma ducked her head to avoid blushing. Ironically, she bristled at any insults, real or perceived, but was embarrassed by praise.

Killian ignored that comment and focused those icy blues directly on me. "Perhaps you might join me for a walk after breakfast."

Talk about being between the proverbial rock and a hard place. I'd already planned to take Fantasia for some much-needed exercise, but three was a crowd. Still, it would look churlish to refuse his suggestion. A walk was not a date.

"Want to join us?" I asked Gemma.

"Nope. I need to set up for the massage clinic. Besides, time is short. You promised to join Carla at her skin-care session. Moral support. Girl-power. You know the drill."

I agreed to join Killian outside after collecting my patient partner, Fantasia. No one could ask for a better friend and protector, and like many women, I cared more for my dog than for any man I'd ever dated. Upon reflection, that was either a sad commentary on my love life or a sensible response to reality.

He was waiting patiently for me outside the lobby. Since time was limited, we immediately headed down the trail at a brisk pace. I pride myself on being in fine form, but keeping up with Killian's stride was taxing. Fantasia had no such problem, but to be fair, she also had four legs.

"Need a breather?" he asked. I detected a faintly patronizing tinge to his remarks, so naturally, I lied. "Not at all. I was just thinking about the theft. Lin Baugh must have been worried even though they recovered the emeralds. He's a nice guy, and I'd hate to see him get in trouble."

"Hmm. I'm sure everything's insured, although that painting is irreplaceable."

Praising my aunt's genius was a winning strategy, even though I recognized that he was probably exaggerating things for my benefit.

Killian finally slowed down giving me the chance for a much-needed breather. Why did so many men treat a casual stroll as a competitive event? That question always confounded me. When I spied a bench, I surrendered my pride and plopped down on it.

"I plan to leave tomorrow after Mario's big presentation," Killian said. "I suppose you know that I've tried to acquire the Ricci line."

"How's that working out for you?" I asked. My response was cheeky, but something about this man activated my baser instincts.

"Not so well. Mario drives a hard bargain, and he's stubborn. If we can't come to an agreement, I'll simply look elsewhere. *Hair Deluxe* is another option, and Carla is far easier to negotiate with."

That floored me. Carla never breathed a word about selling to Killian or anyone else.

"Why would she even consider giving up her independence?"

He gestured with his hands. "Money. The oldest motive in the world. She needs capital, and my client can provide it. Besides, some of the independents like Kiehls and Bobby Brown did that with great success. L'Oréal bought Kiehls and Bobby Brown went to Estee Lauder. The formula worked like a charm, and the corporate honchos used sense. They left the brand and boutique factors that customers crave alone. Expanded market and advertising sales are just two advantages the companies gained. Prestige products sell in high-end retail markets, not drug stores. Carla understands that she'd still be the face of the *Deluxe* line. Mario's more ego-driven. If *Ricci Rich* is even half as good as he says, it's an attractive product. I'd advise my client to focus on marketing it for men's hair."

Something suddenly clicked in my mind. "Wait a minute," I said. "Doesn't Sophia Laurent represent one of those giant conglomerates? No wonder Mario freaked when you approached him. I've heard that their parting was anything but amicable."

Killian shrugged. "All that's confidential. Suffice it to say that I originally planned to announce a merger during the Expo. Who knows how things will work out? Mario's the stumbling block, but that situation can turn on a dime."

I checked my watch and jumped up. "Oops! I've got to get going. Carla's session starts in ten minutes."

He reached out and touched my hand. "Enough business talk. I'd like to see you again. Socially."

I paused, uncertain of how to respond. From what I'd heard, Killian Blaine was a major player who enjoyed toying with women. Besides, he lived in Chicago. Granted, that was only a six-hour drive to Harbor Bay, but it was still a trek. I took the coward's way out and punted. "Next time you're in Harbor Bay, I'd like that." That put the ball squarely in his court. He acted pleased, although I doubted that a man like him got turned down very often. Since time was of the essence, I whistled to Fantasia and headed back to the resort at a brisk trot with Killian at my side. Carla's presentation had barely begun, and I was able to slip into a rear seat without disrupting the show. The room was full, and the audience was attentive. I joined them in taking notes and asking questions. Skincare was a big concern for my customers, and *Deluxe brands* featured several new products that would appeal to them. Carla stressed simplicity, speed, and results in a daily routine. Busy women demanded it. As the session ended, someone from the audience raised his hand. I heard a collective gasp as Mario Ricci leapt up.

"Your competitors say your line is old-fashioned, Carla. They call it the grandma's go-to favorite. What's your response?"

Carla's face was drained of emotion, and for a moment, I feared that she might faint or, worse still, weep. To my delight, she quickly recovered and wagged her finger at her former spouse. "Women over forty form a tremendous market share, Mario. I'm proud if they support my products. They encourage their daughters and granddaughters to sample *Deluxe Cosmetics* too. Quite a formula for success, wouldn't you agree?"

Her plucky response earned Carla a round of applause from the audience. Mario didn't share that sentiment. His face darkened like an approaching thundercloud as he stormed out of the room. The seminar concluded on a high note when gift baskets heaped with samples were distributed. Everyone loves a freebie, even beauty experts!

Afterwards, Violet gave her friend a vigorous hug. "Congratulations! You handled that perfectly. Couldn't have done better myself."

Carla was a bit wobbly, but she maintained her poise. "I just couldn't let him win. Not again. Especially with Sophia in the audience."

"Maybe I'll tug his hair tomorrow during the demo," Violet said. "Bad boys deserve some punishment." They wandered off arm and arm in search of some liquid refreshment while I sought out Gemma's massage session. In her typical fashion, my partner had the crowd chuckling as she explained techniques for advanced massage and the products that worked best. Somehow, Gemma had corralled Chief Gideon Hall to serve as a model. He was middle-aged, practically ancient by my standards, but I had to admit that the lawman still had an impressive build. Perhaps his native American heritage had something to do with that. Either way, I noted that he drew admiring looks from the female contingent, particularly the New York crowd. When I glanced at the clock on the back wall, a tall figure lurking in the shadows drew my attention. It was Benny Soto who was blatantly sulking at his fiancée's performance with another man. *Good! Let the pompous little jerk suffer. Gemma can do so much better.*

Lin Baugh stopped me as I exited the room. He looked harried but otherwise untouched by the constant drama and recent crime wave.

"Got a minute?" he asked. "Help me check out the setup for Mario's big event tomorrow." As he led me to the main ballroom, he asked about Carla's dustup with Mario.

"No big deal," I said. "Mario was being Mario—a big bully. He probably thought that Carla would fold under pressure, but she showed him. How in the world do you manage so many big egos at these things? I felt like knocking a few heads together, and I was just a spectator."

Lin smiled. "Comes from being the oldest of five with a widowed Mom. I played enforcer all my life it seems."

"Wow!" You had a big family."

"Yep! Three younger brothers and my little sis. She was no trouble at all, though. A little angel. That was my dear Linette."

I kept silent at that point, wondering what words of consolation a stranger could offer. Lin suddenly got a text that put him on alert. "Oh, oh," he said. "Trouble. Nona Allen and her crew have arrived." Lin pointed out the window. "You can just hear them chanting. I rather hoped Nona's plans might have changed, but no such luck. If you're up for adventure, you can join me."

"Sure. Why not?"

He led the way to the area where a group of about twenty-five women had assembled. "Into the Valley of Death. Tennyson, here we come!" Lin winked as he approached them. "Ladies. I'm the event manager. May I be of assistance?"

I immediately recognized their leader. Nona Allen was unmistakable in her drab pantsuit with FACE emblazoned on the pocket. She made no attempt to conceal the ravages of a severe case of acne with makeup. Instead, she seemed proud of her scars and the wisps of blonde hair that framed her face.

"Ladies? My members are women. And who is this?" she asked, staring me down. "Your personal assistant?" Nona snarled the question in such an offensive manner that I yearned to throttle her on the spot. Unfortunately, she looked extremely fit and could probably have given me a run for my money. I tried a charm offensive instead. If it worked for Violet, maybe I could do the same. I extended my hand. "I'm Marketta Davis, Ms. Allen, an artist and business owner." Nona brushed me off as if I were lint. That told me it was time to ramp up my people-pleasing skills if I hoped to survive this crowd.

"We're hoping to avoid any trouble," Lin said mildly. "This is a private event."

"Huh!" she snorted. "Every one of us bought tickets to your so-called private shindig. You don't have a legal leg to stand on, and you know it. The First Amendment still means something in this country."

Instead of grimacing, Lin grinned. "You are so right. All I ask is that you show our other guests courtesy. I promise you they'll return the favor. If you like, I can arrange a booth for your group to display your material."

Nona started to snarl a retort but then thought better of it. FACE was equipped to counter opposition, not accommodation. She quickly regrouped, however. "We may take you up on that after we circulate around the exhibits."

At that moment, a savior arrived in the person of Violet Davis. She advanced on the gaggle, wearing the smile that had charmed European audiences around the continent. After introducing herself, my aunt addressed the group. "I couldn't help overhearing your conversation. FACE has quite a following, doesn't it?"

Heads nodded, and Nona Allen asserted herself by explaining her group's credo. "We're feminists, and we oppose cosmetic enhancement. It enslaves women and reinforces the patriarchy.

"I understand. My home base is Paris, and many French women focus on skincare rather than cosmetics. Check out the firms represented here.

You'll be surprised at the variety." Violet herded them toward the front desk, where tickets were collected, information packets distributed, and lanyards provided. She stayed at Nona's side until the group disbursed.

Lin heaved a sigh of relief. "Thank heaven for Violet." When Kim joined us, he explained the situation and asked her to circulate throughout the convention floor and pour oil on troubled water.

"Glad to," Kim said. "I've spent my morning trying to placate Mario. Those FACE ladies may be easier to handle." She ran her fingers through her beautifully coiffed hair. "I suppose they'll hate me on sight, won't they?"

Lin assured her that it was impossible for anyone to dislike her. Meanwhile, I sauntered off to check out the setup for Mario's *Ricci Rich* presentation. Everything appeared to be in order. Promotional materials and jars of the cream were stacked neatly against the curtain. Signs extolling the product's virtues were everywhere. I couldn't help thinking that Nona Allen's sad locks could benefit from a healthy dose of this miracle conditioner. That was one thought I vowed to keep to myself.

"So that's the big star of this show. How pathetic." Nona had crept up behind me so noiselessly that I jumped a foot. "I suppose you use that junk."

I counted way past ten before responding. Since when did the loudest voice in the room always win out over respect? I neither feared nor opposed her views, but they were opinions, not holy writ. I whirled around and stood toe to toe with her. "As a matter of fact, I do. It's my choice and still a legal option I believe. The people here aren't monsters. They have businesses, employees, and families. Don't demonize them or pretend to know their motives."

Nona puffed up like a cobra, but before she struck, Gemma entered the room with Fantasia. "Here's your little sweetheart, Marky. She thought you had deserted her."

Nona's face softened, and her scowl disappeared. She bent down and stroked Fantasia's beautiful head. Immediately she cooed with that mixture of joy and soothing baby babble so familiar to animal lovers. I succumb whenever I see a dog or cat. Can't help it. No excuses.

"I love animals, especially dogs," Nona said with the ghost of a smile showing. "Cosmetic companies do horrible experiments on animals, you know, just to satisfy women's vanity."

Gemma leapt into the conversation. "Awful, isn't it? Most products are now cruelty-free. I know that we refuse to carry anything that tests on animals."

I introduced my partner to Nona and suggested that she show her some brands that protect animals. Peace was partially restored, and a rapprochement based on shared animal love was close. All would have been fine had a wind machine named Mario Ricci not appeared. He snorted several vile comments, waved his arms wildly about, and confronted Nona Allen.

"You! You are the troublemaker! Telling lies about Ricci products!" I saw that Mario was working himself up to a major snit, spewing a mixture of English and Italian. "You never use them. I can see that for myself. You disgrace the female sex. Such an ugly woman!" His disdain was obvious, and it banished our goodwill mission in a hurry. Nona's fighting spirit rose to the fore as she struck back with a vengeance.

"You're a pig! We know all about you and your miracle cure. Wait 'til you see the surprise you'll get tomorrow, little man. Oink. Oink." She stormed out of the room, leaving us dumbstruck and in a quandary. Should we notify Lin or the security people?

"She's crazy. Pazza!" Mario screeched. "That ugly woman."

I tried to calm him, but the effort was futile. Mario paced and fussed until Lin Baugh appeared. Lin uttered some magic words that soothed him and quelled Mario's outburst. Together, the two men strolled toward the bar for some liquid consolation.

"Whew!" Gemma said. "What a mess. Should I find Benny and tell him?"

I bit my tongue. The last thing we needed was the clumsy efforts of Benny Soto.

"No. They'll both calm down sooner or later. No need to worry."

Whether from naivete or unfounded optimism, my words would soon come back to haunt me.

Chapter Five

That evening, Kim hosted a reception for exhibitors. Since attendance was limited, I prayed that Nona and her crowd would find some other cause to champion and leave us in peace. We'd already had more than our share of drama. Thank you very much!

Gemma and I were deputized to circulate among our guests and keep everyone happy. The event was black-tie, and I confess that both of us spent extra time primping. Gemma chose a steamy black silk gown with a slit up the side, but I opted for a less showy ensemble in muted colors of gold and cream. If Killian happened to glance my way, I certainly wouldn't object.

Kim assured me that security was extra tight to avoid any repetition of the previous night's disaster. With Gideon Hall on deck, I felt an enormous sense of relief. Unlike his distracted deputy, Gideon would stay focused on his task. Gemma agreed and pledged not to beguile any other lawmen with her charms. Benny's fate still hung in the balance, so he was being extra cautious. I suspected that if anyone made even one false move, Benny would swoop down and arrest the offender.

From the first moment that we arrived, it was evident that Kim had outdone herself. Tuxedoed student waiters bearing trays of champagne circulated around the ballroom while others staffed long tables of delectable finger food. I stole a glance at the offerings and couldn't resist. Lobster mac and cheese bites competed with mini–Beef Wellington snacks and shrimp scampi. No partygoers in this fashion-forward crowd dared to gorge themselves. Counting calories was an Olympic sport with them, so they nibbled on the tidbits and daintily sipped champagne. My rumbling tummy sent me an urgent message, and I suddenly realized that I was hungry. Ravenous. After glancing around, I edged toward the buffet table and filled my plate. There was no time for delicacy when I was fainting from starvation. Naturally fate in the person of Killian Blaine intervened. I ran straight into him and nearly upended my plate.

He glanced at me and my plate and laughed. Not a refined sound but a big hearty guffaw. "Oops. Looks like you're a woman with a mission."

I knew better than to make any excuses. Sometimes, I stuff myself like a stevedore even though I seldom gain a pound. This was one of those instances.

"My fault entirely. Let me get out of your way."

"Hold on," he said eyeing me head to toe. "I admire a woman with a hearty appetite, particularly when it doesn't show. You look particularly lovely tonight."

I should have lobbed a glib response his way, but I drew a blank. Instead, I said the first thing that came to mind. "Thank you."

The glow I felt evaporated quickly when Sophia Laurent arrived on the scene. Clad in a red draped Grecian gown with her flowing brunette hair she looked stunning. There was no other description that would do her justice. Her eyes flicked momentarily at my plate before she turned to Killian. "Mon cheri, come and sit with me. We have much to discuss."

He nodded at me and followed Sophia like an obedient lap dog.

She's a client I told myself. Its business. If that were true, why did I feel like an errant ingenue being dismissed by her older brother?

I spun around and slid into a seat next to Gemma, Carla, and Kim. Aunt Violet had yet to appear. As usual, Gemma had joined the full plate club, and her portions put mine to shame.

"Absolutely fantastic," she said, savoring a bit of lobster. You scored a ten with this, Kim."

Kim twisted her napkin as she scanned the room. "Everyone seems content, but I have this feeling of impending doom. At least that awful woman and her posse haven't shown their faces, and even Mario's behaving."

When she heard that name, Carla blanched. I vividly recalled Violet's comments about the marital split between Mario and Carla, and they obviously rang true. Time to change the subject. I complimented Carla on that afternoon's presentation, especially on the defense of her customer base. "It's so easy to ignore the obvious and forget which segment has the time and money to buy our products," I said. "Teens and twenty-somethings have very separate needs from mature women."

Kim laughed. "You know my great-grandmother was a huge fan of Dorothy Gray, a brand that was very popular in her day. She was proud of her complexion and took good care of it. Although many were scandalized by what they considered her frivolous ways, everyone admitted that her skin was perfect right up until she passed in her late eighties."

We all chuckled and provided our own anecdotes about friends and relatives. Carla shared the three things she urged customers to consider: avoid suntans, never smoke, and be disciplined about using high quality products. Gemma added a tip about daily exfoliation to sweep away dead skin cells. "I swear by that," she said, "and weekly moisturizing masks too. Some clients say they're too busy, but they pay the price."

Despite the lively chatter, I was distracted by worries about my aunt. Where in the world was Violet, and why was she missing? That question was answered when she appeared in the doorway escorted by Chief Gideon Hall. She was a vision in lilac, a silky couture creation that probably packed a stratospheric price tag. Chief Hall held up his end of the bargain, too. He stood tall, trim, and handsome in his dress uniform. I'd always pictured him and my aunt as a couple, but she brushed away my hints without commenting. Considering my romantic track record, I could hardly blame her.

"How does she do it?" Gemma whispered. "No matter who is there, Violet steals the show without even trying."

Kim laughed. "Maybe that's the secret. Effortless elegance. Violet's time in Paris was well spent."

We focused on reviewing the conference schedule and speculating on Mario's big reveal. Carla joined in despite the tender feelings she must still harbor for her ex-spouse. "*Ricci Rich* sounds fantastic," Kim said. "He's kept it hush hush, so I have no idea what it looks like or which ingredients it contains."

Carla grimaced. "Why not ask me?"

Gemma clutched her hand. "You know something. Come on. Spill the beans."

Carla hung her head while she collected her thoughts. "Unless I'm mistaken, Mario's using the formula I developed when we were together. He may have made some changes, of course, but I suspect it's basically the same."

That left us speechless. If *Ricci Rich* was successful, it would be worth millions, money that Carla, who was struggling to survive, would never see. No wonder Mario had enlisted Violet to be by his side. Her presence would add credibility to his performance.

"That's outrageous," Gemma said. "Can't you do anything? Sue him or something."

"I tried that. Consulted a lawyer, but the laws in Italy are very different than here. Besides, I can't prove anything. We worked together on developing all our products."

I glanced across the room at Killian Blaine. If Carla became his client, Mario's crooked ways could be challenged by that man with a reputation as a ruthless predator.

"Besides," Carla said. "When Mario left me, it destroyed every ounce of business sense that I had. I...acted unwisely. Signed a whole bunch of things I shouldn't have. Whatever his lawyers put in front of me. I just wanted it to end, and I didn't care how."

Kim reached over and hugged her friend. "I understand that. When we lost our son, I felt the same way."

"You probably heard this," Carla said, "But I was so desperate I tried to take my own life." She shrugged. "I should have killed Mario instead. It would have saved some unsuspecting women a lot of heartache."

That reminded me of Lin's sister and her sad end. It was easy to dismiss Mario as a loveable eccentric but, when it came to women, he was a monster, as ruthless and determined to get his way as any sociopath.

"Sophia Laurent knew how to handle him," Carla said. "She tied Mario in knots and left him twisting. I understand that when she left, she took several valuable formulas with her."

I had to applaud the sultry brunette for beating Mario at his own game. She was one adversary I wouldn't care to tangle with, although Killian seemed eager to do so. When the disc jockey cranked up a lively tune, the dance floor quickly filled up. Violet and Chief Hall made a fetching pair as they moved to the beat of *Another One Bites and Dust*. Killian chose Sophia as his partner and proved that he was as deft at dancing as he was in every other facet of life. That gave me a momentary pause as I considered his expertise in more private arenas. Soon, Kim, Carla, and even Gemma found partners from among the gathering. I tried not to sulk, but playing the role of wallflower was simply not my style. When Lin Baugh approached, my anxiety lessened. Even a pity partner was preferable to social ostracism.

"You look lovely tonight," he said. "I hope that doesn't offend you."

"Are you kidding? Compliments are always accepted, especially from the evening's host." We shared a laugh and quickly got down to serious dancing. Afterwards, I asked him how the conference was going.

"I'm always an optimist," Lin said, "But in this business, one must be. Nona and her crowd aren't here, so that's a plus, but they're probably saving their thunder for tomorrow. I've got extra security on alert, particularly for Mario's big show. That guy is a magnet for trouble, but he's met his match in Nona."

I recalled the veiled threat Nona made to Mario and wondered just what she had planned. "No trace of my aunt's painting I presume."

"Nope. The police haven't searched the vehicles, but they can't without the owners' permission. I gave them the okay to search the hotel rooms, but that's where it ends. Your aunt is being a real champ about the whole mess. Too bad Sophia didn't follow her example."

I'd seen the sultry vixen stamp her feet and pout. It was an amazing performance, but not one I could ever emulate. Admirers had called me pretty, wholesome, even beautiful, but never once had I been described as sensuous. Call me your typical girl next door.

When the music ended, Lin disappeared. I was astonished when Killian

Blaine glided in and took his place. "May I have the next dance, or is your dance card filled?"

He was teasing, of course, trying to replicate a scene from one of Jane Austen's classics.

"I'd be delighted unless you need to rest first." My smile was saccharine sweet, but he felt its sting.

"Yow! That hurt. I'm not that much older than you."

I shrugged. "what's a decade or two among friends."

"You know how to hurl those zingers, Ms. Davis. Well done." He led me to the dance floor where a Lionel Richie ballad, *Three Times a Lady*, was playing. I had to admit that his arms felt good around me. So good that I quickly reverted to business. "Sophia managed to snag some of Mario's formulas, I hear. Must have caused quite a dustup."

"Really?" His expression was impassive, devoid of any reaction. Killian's version of a tabula rasa belonged etched on Mount Rushmore. I'd never perfected that art, and friends laughed when they described my nonexistent poker face.

"Thought any more about what we discussed?" he asked. "You know. Our long-delayed dinner date."

"Hmm. Call me when you're within striking distance of Harbor Bay. Then we can make plans."

The song ended, and so did our tete-a-tete. Killian bowed, thanked me for the dance, and whisked away to enchant some other worthy female. There were plenty of them in this comely crowd, and I told myself they were welcome to him.

When Mario appeared at my side, I did a double take. His perfectly tailored tuxedo and heavily moussed hair were both standouts, but he seemed agitated and out of sorts. Perhaps he was nervous about his big reveal. I wondered if being in the presence of so many foes might have put him off his game as well.

"Where is she?" he asked. His body tensed as he looked around the room. "Who?"

"Your aunt. My beautiful Violet." He clutched my arm in a near panic and squeezed it hard. "I must see her."

"Ouch! Calm down, Mario. She's somewhere around, but she's busy."

That didn't satisfy him. His eyes glowed with an intensity that alarmed me, and his fingers twitched. "Don't you see? Tomorrow is my big day. All the world that counts will see the miracle of Ricci *Rich* and the glory that is Mario."

I'm normally patient. It's a critical skill in any sales job. But everything has limits. Mario's preening and pouting had robbed me of any shred of self-restraint. It took every bit of my willpower to keep from thrashing him.

"Maybe I can help you."

"No, no." He savaged his perfect waves by running his fingers through them. "Here. Look. Someone dares to disrespect Mario." He thrust a crumpled sheet of paper into my hands. I read it and gasped. The perfectly typed message was brief and explicit. *"Send not to know for whom the bell tolls. It tolls for thee."*

"It's a threat," Mario screeched. "Someone plans to kill me."

Despite his many talents, Mario's genius didn't extend to poetry. *"For Whom the Bell Tolls by John Donne* is a sonnet. Part of a very famous poem, Mario."

He looked at me as if I was possessed. "Who is this man? Why does he hate Mario? I will fight him, and we will see what kind of man he is."

I tried for womanly compassion but could only find derision for this emotional wreck. "He's been dead for almost 400 years, so it wouldn't be much of a contest. Where'd you find this?"

He patted his side. "In my pocket. An assassin is stalking Mario, waiting to spring at him." He took a beautiful linen handkerchief and mopped his brow.

"Relax. It's just a prank. Don't let one little thing rattle you." His reaction gave me pause. "You haven't gotten anything else, I hope."

Mario produced a fine leather wallet, Bottega Veneta, if my eyes were accurate. He removed yet another slip of paper from it and handed it to me. "Here. See. Someone is torturing Mario."

Although the wording differed, the author was the same John Donne.

"...and Death shall be no more. Death thou shalt die."

"You see! I must say my prayers, make my final confession before he strikes."

It was unkind, but I told myself that Mario's litany of sins might take a while to recite. "When did you get this?"

He shook his head. "How should I know? I found it yesterday after that awful woman assaulted Mario. She must be guilty. She hates me for making the world beautiful."

I thought of Nona and her confrontation with Mario. She got close enough to slip something into his pocket, but it was a stretch to say that she assaulted him. On the other hand, Nona was probably conversant with literary greats and poets such as Donne. That last quote was from his most famous work, *"Death Be Not Proud."* It wasn't a threat. Not really but it was disquieting.

"Never mind, Mario. Someone is probably teasing you. Maybe you should show these to Chief Hall or my aunt. They'll know what to do."

I pointed Mario toward the exit sign where the chief's stolid figure could be seen. As it happened, Violet was also with him. Mario made a beeline for them, clutching the evidence as he did so.

"What was that all about?" Gemma asked. "He looked frantic."

I explained the snippets of poetry, although Gemma was as clueless about the departed John Donne as Mario had been. She had little patience for what she termed nonsense.

"So, what's the bottom line," she asked.

Some clever person knew how to rattle Mario's cage. Was it anything serious, or merely an attempt to throw him off his game? Hard to tell. Either way, the sender was someone with a firm grasp of the classics and an equally piquant sense of humor. There were plenty of suspects in this literate, sophisticated crowd, although John Donne was certainly an unconventional choice. Most would be tempted to quote Shakespeare. His works contained enough ghoulish scenes to frighten even a self-absorbed rascal like Mario. Nona's name immediately leapt to mind; however, Mario had made so many enemies that she was certainly not alone. Cara, Sophia, and Killian, that scourge of the unprotected everywhere, were also in the running. Kim,

Violet, and Lin were more remote possibilities, although each had reason to terrorize the feisty Italian. Come to think of it, I wasn't too fond of him myself. Short men with big egos didn't interest me.

Whatever Gideon said seemed to calm Mario, and when Violet brought Lin over to join them, peace was temporarily restored. Lin signaled to a waiter who scurried to the bar and supplied a large snifter of brandy for Mario. I'm not much of a drinker, but at times, brandy does have a salutary effect. Under other circumstances, I would have enjoyed Mario's discomfort. Tonight, my concern for Kim and Lin robbed me of that pleasure. The Beauty Expo was a major coup for Traverse City, and anything that threatened its success would impact them, too. I trusted Violet to sort things out. She always restored calm and had a balanced perspective that could tame even the fractious Mario Ricci.

"Aren't you the least bit curious?" Gemma asked. "It serves him right, of course. He's trampled on enough women. Someone wants to take him down a peg."

I threw up my hands. "Oh no. You're not going to involve me in this mess. My detective days are over. Finished!"

Gemma knew how to hit me where it hurt. "Okay. If Kim or Lin get stiffed, it won't be your fault. I'm not asking you to go all Sherlock Holmes. Just use that big brain of yours to help Gideon before it's too late."

She had a point, but I stubbornly refused to concede it. I loved an intellectual challenge, and this one was a doozy. Doozy. That was my grandma's expression, but it fit perfectly. Perhaps I could drop a few hints to the main suspects, grill them about poetry in general and greats like John Donne. It couldn't hurt, and it might help Gideon. Not that he wanted or appreciated my help. He'd told me on more than one occasion to butt out of police business. I elbowed Gemma to get her attention.

"Hey. Find Benny and see if they're taking Mario's situation seriously. Maybe they're just blowing it off."

Her eyes glowed at the mention of her fiancé. "I suppose I could do that. Gideon never makes a move without asking Benny, even now. He trusts him."

I bit my lip to avoid laughing hysterically. Gideon Hall knew what a dolt Benny was. How could he not? Meanwhile, Gemma sped away in search of her sweetie. That old saw about love being blind must be true, but you couldn't prove it by me.

Chapter Six

I slipped out of the party early. Fantasia needed her exercise, and I needed a sound night's sleep. Between Mario's antics and the unexpected attention from a certain suave attorney, I was out of my element. The resort featured an inviting walking trail that was well-traveled and secure. Besides, with Fantasia by my side, I felt insulated from harm. She kept a weather eye on anything or anyone in our path that might pose a problem. That gave me time to consider the poetry puzzle and its impact on Mario. According to Kim, he was very superstitious and more than a bit paranoid. It didn't take much to rock his world, and the anonymous sender probably knew that. I suspected that he—or she—was probably watching from afar and snickering. There wasn't much the authorities could do except be on the alert during the *Ricci-Rich* demo. As word spread through this gossip-loving crowd, attendance at the demo would soar. I was confident of that.

Fantasia suddenly stopped, ears on high alert. I'd been woolgathering and hadn't noticed that anything was amiss. My faithful companion was far more focused on her job, and I was thankful for that.

"Thought you'd be at your party." The voice was raspy, the tone snarky. I whirled around, prepared to confront Nona Adams. She bent down, captivated once again by my beautiful dog. That gave me time to collect my wits and turn to poetry.

"Why weren't you there?" I asked. "All ticket holders were invited."

Nona scoffed. "Black tie? Do you think I packed formal attire? Do you think I'd even consider appearing in that?" She pointed to my dress. "I don't own girly things. Symbols of the patriarchy. Wouldn't be caught dead in them."

There were several tart replies on the tip of my tongue, but I chose forbearance. "I enjoy the occasional dress-up party. Makes a nice change. It's fun. Most women enjoy having a choice or is that against your group's rules too?"

Nona continued to stroke Fantasia's silky coat. The act calmed her although it didn't improve her disposition one jot. "Why would I even consider mixing with a bunch of phonies like them? I loathe everything they stand for. Men don't tart themselves up with makeup, and they seem to do just fine. Rule the world." She leaned toward me and sneered. "Men like your boyfriend. That attorney."

That woman knew how to get under my skin. "Boyfriend! I beg your pardon."

"I know Killian Blaine. All too well. Mr. Perfect. Gets all the women in a tizzy. Huh!"

Her eyes telegraphed a different message than her words and I suspected that Nona had a personal connection to Killian. Had she been one of his many conquests? Hard to envision but anything was possible.

Nona grunted. "Killian Blaine lives to destroy others. Everything's a conquest to him. Mergers, hostile takeovers, the works. Out with a different woman every night and never happy unless he's ruining someone's livelihood."

I saw my chance and took it. "You prefer a more literary crowd, I bet. How do you feel about poetry? Famous names like Byron or John Donne."

Nona tilted her head as if I were slightly addled. "Poetry? You're delusional. Why dwell on old white men when female poets like Elizabeth Barrett Browning, Sylvia Plath, and Gwendolyn Brooks surpass them? Sounds like even at your age, you've been drinking the Kool-Aid." She snorted an unprintable insult and stalked toward the hotel, muttering epithets like "pathetic" and several less flattering terms.

Based on her reaction, I doubted that Nona was the secret sender. Subtlety simply wasn't part of FACE's playbook, and she was far more likely to favor direct, in-your-face action. Mario's tormentor wanted him to suffer and twist in the wind. Nona preferred to publicly draw and quarter him. FACE would confront those they considered to be gender-phobic when they could garner the maximum attention. Lin mentioned that several national news outlets would be present at the expo for Mario's big show. I expected Nona to capitalize on the press presence.

I whistled to Fantasia and skipped back to the hotel having crossed one potential suspect off my list. A niggling doubt still troubled me. Nona was wily enough to deliberately mislead me and anyone who would disrupt her plans. For the foreseeable future, she must remain on my suspect list.

Violet was waiting in the lobby for me, and for once, my laid-back aunt was anything but.

"There you are," she said. "Gemma said you were sleuthing, and I got worried." She embraced me. "I guess I lost my head. All this hysteria surrounding Mario must be contagious."

I hugged her and described my encounter with Nona. "Admittedly, she's unhinged, but I doubt if she's homicidal. Besides, if she were the culprit, she'd use quotes from female poets. The woman is obsessed with sexism or her version of it and sees enemies behind every corner." I shrugged. "She's probably harmless. Most attorneys are all talk anyway."

Violet smirked. "Not all of them. I bet there's one here who believes in taking charge. His eyes never left you all evening, dear niece. Even Sophia's charms didn't sway him."

I'm much too old to blush, especially when my favorite relative teases me. Nevertheless, my cheeks felt warmer than I liked, and I found myself unable to respond. I'm no ingenue. Men had pursued me before, so why did this feel so different? Had Gemma's romantic obsession begun to rub off on me? Ultimately, my aunt took pity and changed the subject. She handed me a detailed agenda for the morning's *Ricci Rich* program. The specificity impressed me, and it was apparent that Kim had left nothing to chance. Each step was listed in order. Kim would explain the process and Ricci brand's use of their special detoxifying shampoo prior to treatment. I'd tried that product myself, and it was a marvel at scrubbing residue left by sprays, mousse, and the like. When the curtain rose, Mario would appear on the stage, freshly shampooed and ready for the transformation. Violet would then apply the conditioner, place a plastic cap on his head to increase absorption, and close the curtain. After thirty minutes, when the curtain parted, Mario, freshly shampooed and blown dry, would be shown to the crowd. After extolling the virtues of his miracle and its impact on hair care, testimonials from prominent male entertainers would circulate. I had to admit that Mario had corralled some rather big names to lend their support. At the conclusion of the program, amidst popping champagne corks, each member of the audience would receive a goody bag filled with *Ricci* products, including the conditioner.

"Well," Violet asked. "What do you think? Kim worked hard on that pamphlet."

I hated being a naysayer, but the entire event reminded me of a third-rate magic show rather than a serious product launch. "Isn't it a bit cheesy?" I asked timidly. Violet's reputation for elegance was at variance with this extravaganza.

She didn't take offense. In fact, Violet threw back her head and laughed. "You are so right and so very Midwestern. The entire spectacle is ludicrous, but that's the point. Everyone here tends to be a stuffed shirt. So serious and professional. Mario wanted to upend things by injecting a bit of fun into the proceedings. You know how theatrical he is anyway. And as for me, I don't mind shedding my staid persona for a change. Think of the *Folies Bergère*. You've seen the sketches and comic revues in that show. The French know that a bit of levity keeps things lively." She patted my cheek. "Does that make sense?"

I still didn't approve, but in an odd way, it made sense. Even if Mario played the buffoon, no one would forget the launch of *Ricci Rich*. According to Violet, the police dismissed the poetic snippets as pranks by some overwrought fan or a business rival. Modern minds weren't attuned to metaphysical poets, especially ones like Donne, who had been dead for almost four centuries. Where I saw a threat, they saw only garbled words from a world that was quite foreign to them. Mario finally accepted that, although he maintained that his foes lurked everywhere, waiting to strike. They assigned Benny Soto as his bodyguard until after the big show."

Benny Soto, the Inspector Clouseau of Harbor Bay? By the time he stumbled and bumbled about, Mario's adversary would be long gone. "Any ideas about the identity of the mystery poet?" I asked Violet.

Her response surprised me. "Carla studied English literature at Oxford, you know. Did quite well, as I recall. And don't be too quick to judge Sophia. She may look like a bimbo, but her family is one of the most cultured names in France. In fact, either her father or uncle was quite an accomplished poet."

"What did Lin say about all this? The poor man must be at his wit's end by now."

"These big events always have their share of drama. Lin can handle things without overreacting." Violet put her arm around me. "Now, forget about the intrigue and get a good night's rest."

As usual, her advice was sound. Just before I dozed off, I recalled something that made me jump up in bed. Killian Blaine had also studied at Oxford University. He'd likely be quite familiar with the works of the poet and might relish the chance to get under Mario's very thin skin. To top it off, like the perfidious Mr. Blaine, John Donne was also a lawyer.

* * *

"You overthink things," Gemma said. "Always have. That's why I beat you on those multiple-choice tests in school. You read too much into every little question, but I just picked something at random. All this poetry junk—let it go. Besides, Benny says it's just PR stuff. Mario probably made it up himself."

She had a point, but I refused to concede. "Benny's the designated bodyguard, I hear. Someone's taking it seriously."

Gemma yawned. "Not really. It's all cosmetic." She made a face. "Hey. I made a joke."

I ignored her and continued my grooming routine. Today, I planned to pull out all the stops. I told myself it was to properly represent POPPET, but that was a pathetic excuse. If Violet was right, if Killian truly was interested in me, I refused to disappoint.

The *Ricci Rich* presentation was scheduled for 10 am to be followed by a buffet luncheon. Would anyone have an appetite after suffering through Mario's routine? I wondered. Kim had deputized Gemma and me to distribute the goody bags and solicit orders for the products. I planned to add brochures touting POPPET while we were at it. Mario had paid a hefty premium for this time slot and the response had been gratifying. Male improvement products were a hot topic that many other companies were interested in. If they followed Mario's lead, the Ricci company would net a handsome profit. Perhaps the theatrical approach was worth considering after all.

Carla was the first person I saw after entering the ballroom. She was seated front row center with a group of like-minded pals from other beauty outlets and wore a fixed expression devoid of either pleasure or pain. From the chatter I overheard, most of the group were expecting an over-the-top spectacle ala Mario but were also intrigued by the new product. After age thirty, very few men sported the thick, glorious locks of their youth. Mario's exuberant ringlets were indeed the exception, although they were probably attributable to sound genetics and luck rather than any conditioner. Still, hope springs eternal in both genders and consumers were beguiled by dreams. My female customers were often frantic when their hair thinned. Despite the rhetoric from FACE and its supporters, hair was inextricably linked to self-esteem, beauty, and youth. Both genders would benefit from *Ricci Rich* if its claims were proven. The company touted vague clinical studies validating Mario's claims, but those might easily be manufactured. In this instance, the proof was in luxuriant locks, not the pudding.

I scanned the room for any missing audience members. One could hardly miss the officious Benny Soto, who patrolled the ballroom with a ferocity that inspired wonder and a niggling sense of impending doom. Perhaps they were taking Mario's fears seriously after all.

"Isn't he handsome in that uniform," Gemma gushed. I expected my lovelorn pal to drool when her sweetie swept past us. Benny wasn't armed although that baton he clutched could do some damage to an unlucky skull.

"I don't see Nona and her posse," I said. "Maybe she thought better of making a scene."

"Huh!" Gemma could scoff with the best of them. "That nut case wouldn't miss an opportunity like this." She pointed to the rear of the room. "Look. The local press is already on the hunt, and the Chicago and Detroit crew should arrive shortly. Ghouls! Always hoping for some disaster."

I convinced myself that all would be well. Unfortunately, optimism was often an expendable commodity when passions were ignited. Our hosts tried to do their part. Lin Baugh and Kim circulated among the tables, spreading good cheer and looking spiffy. Sadly, it wasn't enough. Just as the lights dimmed, my worst fears materialized. Nona's henchwomen had positioned themselves at each table. Before the curtain rose, they leapt to their feet, produced placards, and started chanting the theme of FACE.

"Feminists against cosmetic enhancements. Feel like a natural woman. Fight the patriarchy."

The newshounds lapped up the controversy like cream. They snapped photos of the protestors and the outraged audience. No one resorted to fisticuffs, but it was a near thing.

Lin Baugh grabbed the microphone and asked for quiet. "Thank you, ladies, for your energy and commitment. Please respect the rights of the audience and be seated."

"Would our foremothers back down?" Nona bellowed. "No, indeed. In the name of Susan B. Anthony, I protest this sexist session."

The photos I'd seen of Susan B. Anthony suggested that worthy as she was, some cosmetic enhancement would have been a big improvement.

Lin's face looked pained, and Kim appeared to be close to tears. Benny Soto's expression was impossible to gauge. Suddenly, the curtain rose, and the stars of the show appeared. That sparked a rousing round of applause as the audience drowned out the chanting FACE protestors. Nona grimaced but motioned her troops to take their seats.

Mario, garbed in a flowing purple robe, sat on a gilt chair that resembled a throne. A towel-wrapped turban-style concealed his wet curls, adding to the special effects. Aunt Violet, wearing purple gloves, stood at his side adjacent to a pyramid of *Ricci Rich* products. The histrionics didn't faze her one bit. In fact, my famous aunt appeared to be enjoying herself. I wasn't certain, but it occurred to me that, being an excellent businessperson, Violet might have demanded financial incentives for her role in the production.

An overhead projector listed the main points of the conditioner, but it was Mario's presentation that impressed. After Violet applied the thick white cream to Mario's scalp, she placed a plastic processing cap on his head to maximize absorption and rewound his turban. All the while, Mario kept up a constant stream of chatter extolling the virtues of his product. After the curtain closed around him, Violet conducted a thirty-minute tutorial on the causes and cures for hair loss. No claims were made for regenerating lost locks. She was far too wily to fall into that trap. The pitch was focused on preventative care for both men and women and the use of topical enhancements. A timer dinged at the thirty-minute mark, and Violet disappeared behind the curtain to shampoo Mario's hair. When she reappeared five minutes later, I knew by the look on her face that something was wrong. Very wrong. Her famously creamy skin was ashen, and she staggered up to the microphone.

"Is a physician present? We have a medical emergency."

Gasps from the crowd alternated with an alarming silence. When I joined her behind the curtain, I was greeted by a chaotic scene. Mario Ricci was vomiting, muttering incoherently, and sweating profusely.

My usually unflappable aunt was shaking, mopping Mario's brow, and speaking softly to him in Italian. By then, a tall, slim woman appeared and announced that she was a dermatologist. She whipped out a blood pressure cuff from her medical bag and fired questions at Violet.

"Is he subject to seizures or allergies? Did he eat or drink anything unusual?"

Violet shook her head. "I don't think so, but I simply don't know. He started getting sick right after I shampooed his hair."

Mario lifted his head. He tried to speak but was too weak to utter anything but gibberish. At that moment, Lin Baugh, accompanied by an EMS crew, arrived on the scene.

"Stand back, everyone," said the paramedic. We all complied except for the doctor. She barked orders to the crew and agreed to accompany them in the ambulance. By listening carefully, I heard the words poison and police. I wrapped my arms around Violet and led her to a nearby chair. Lin Baugh joined us and squeezed her hand.

"Are you okay? Here, take this." A tumbler of brandy had magically appeared in his palm.

We waited until Violet sipped it before peppering her with questions. Gemma's words exploded into the void. "Is he dead? What happened?"

Violet gulped and shook her head. "I can't say. He complained of feeling queasy, and then when I rinsed off the product, Mario started vomiting and moaning."

We were then joined by Chief Gideon Hall and a wild-eyed Benny Soto.

"How's Mario doing?" I asked. "He's going to be okay, right?"

Gideon's response was non-committal. "Hard to tell. Meanwhile I need to confiscate those jars of goop. If he was poisoned, they should tell us something." He looked at Violet's hands. "Good thing you wore gloves, Violet. They'd protect you from poison if that's what got to Mario."

I knew what he was inferring, and it wasn't pretty. He liked and respected my aunt, but Gideon was still a cop. Best to clarify things right away, especially in a high-profile case with the press swarming about. "We always wear gloves when doing color or even conditioner, Chief. Standard procedure." I stared straight into his eyes as I said that. Gemma nodded vigorously, acting as backup.

Violet blinked as if she couldn't believe what was happening. I found it hard to accept myself. Benny scooped up the containers of *Ricci Rich* and placed them in a plastic evidence bag. He also collected Violet's plastic gloves while he was at it.

Everything moved at breakneck speed as Gideon and his troops did their duty. The entire episode felt surreal to me. Mario was annoying but scarcely worthy of a lethal response. Pests like him were swatted away, not smashed.

I got a sudden jolt recalling the samples we distributed in the goody bags. Suppose they, too, were contaminated? Lin acted swiftly when I explained my concern. He stepped out to the microphone, greeting the guests, and requested that they relinquish the samples to one of the uniformed officers. When Gideon Hall appeared, the audience erupted with questions. Crisis management wasn't part of everyone's skill set but Gideon had mastered it. He addressed the looming question first: Mario was at the hospital receiving treatment. No one knew the source of his ailment, but as more information was received, his associates would be kept informed.

"Suppose it's food poisoning," Nona Allen yelped. "We could all be in danger."

Sophia clutched her chest and even Carla looked green around the gills. Once again, Lin Baugh saved the day.

"I understand your concern, but Ms. Davis informed me that Mario ate nothing before his performance. His nerves didn't permit it."

That calmed the group and even restored the appetite of most participants. They were invited to enjoy the buffet while waiting for the police to interview them, and most dug in with a hearty appetite. The beauty business tended to be collegial, but I noted little concern for Mario among his peers. A few even whispered that this might be yet another stunt by the drama-loving Italian. That seemed like a stretch to me. Vomiting was extreme and unsightly. Mario might have fainted or even feigned a heart attack, but I very much doubted that he would soil himself.

The police fanned out in the auditorium and started interviewing those seated by table. It was an effective and efficient way of handling such a large gathering and once again I saluted Gideon Hall for his perspicacity. Kim regrouped and announced that the conference would resume at two p.m. In the meantime, guests were invited to circulate amongst the many booths and sample the products on display.

Gemma shivered. "Benny says things aren't looking good for Mario."

I grimaced. "Oh. So now Benny's a doctor? Wait for the official word. Violet will know the real story. Let's find out what the cops are asking. Stand near one of the tables. Lurk and try not to be conspicuous. And watch the reaction, particularly from his competitors."

My partner was very task-oriented. She immediately brightened and pulled up a chair at one of the farthest tables. I followed suit, choosing the table where Carla, Sophia, and Nona Allen were seated. Unfortunately for me, Gideon Hall was acting as chief inquisitor at my table. His stern glance was more of a glare when he noticed me leaning in. From prior experience, I knew that despite my wiles, this man was not easy to fool. In this instance, however, I was genuinely disturbed and worried about my aunt. Mario, too, of course, but mostly about Violet. Would anyone believe that she was avenging a failed romance with Mario? That story ended long ago. By all accounts, their relationship seemed friendly enough, and he had begged her to assist him. As I precaution, I texted Violet, asking for an update. She responded immediately. "No change."

Gideon started off with softball questions, a sound tactic in my book. "How well did any of you know Mario?"

Nona Allen leapt to answer. "I didn't know him at all. Well, hardly."

"Hmm. I understand you had a dustup with him only yesterday," Gideon said.

Nona was a lawyer and knew the value of caution. "A disagreement, Chief. A clash of values. Nothing more." She turned to me. "Ask her. Ask anyone. I never touched the man. Didn't threaten him either."

I recalled the conversation quite differently. Better to say nothing at this point. Someone had already provided Gideon with enough ammunition to focus on Nona. "What was the surprise you promised Mario, Ms. Allen? I believe you called him a pig as well."

Nona scoffed. "Hyperbole. A war of words, Chief. Our group certainly didn't poison Mario Ricci if that's what you're suggesting."

"Did I say he was poisoned? Maybe you'd better explain this surprise you planned. Somehow, that conversation didn't sound friendly." Gideon's tone was affable. Firm but affable.

"Maybe you'd better read me my Miranda rights," Nona said, folding her arms. "Until then, I'm electing to remain silent."

"It's your right, Ma'am. But we'll resume this conversation later." He turned to Carla. "You were once married to Mr. Ricci, I understand. Was yours a friendly parting?"

Carla bit her lip until she almost drew blood. Her complexion looked as waxy as anything Madame Tussaud could produce. She clasped her water glass and took a sip before answering. "In my experience, few divorces are friendly. Ours certainly was not, but it was years ago. Both of us have moved on from it."

I didn't believe her, and I doubted that Gideon did either. Carla was spared further questioning when Gideon received a text. He hesitated as he read the message and acted immediately. "Pardon me, ladies, I must go. One of my deputies will continue."

He sped away only to be replaced by the one person I most abhorred. Benny Soto pulled up a chair and sat with his legs spread wide. He consulted his iPad and unleashed a spate of questions directed at no one in particular. Nona Allen made short work of him. She narrowed her eyes, pulled out her iPhone, and placed it on record. "You realize I'll have a copy of any of the foolish things you say, Deputy. I advise everyone here to refuse to answer anything without having an attorney present." She stabbed a finger his way. "Besides, we don't even know what type of incident we're dealing with. That Ricci man may have a stomach virus for all we know."

Benny Soto met the challenge head-on. Judgment had never been one of his attributes, and he proved it anew. "Do whatever you want, lady, but we're dealing with a murder now. Mario Ricci died ten minutes ago."

* * *

I heard a collective gasp as the news sunk in. Carla was the most affected. She slumped down in her seat and fainted. Sophia shrieked and immediately became hysterical. Nona remained stoic but watchful. I admired her Sphinx-like pose in the face of tragedy, although it did appear rather unfeeling. My own reaction was different. I felt numb, as if a sudden frost had enveloped me. Once again, I feared for my aunt and checked to see if she had returned my message. No response. Benny must have realized just how big a blunder he had made. Instead of helping Carla, however, he sat stupefied like the lox that he was.

I pulled myself together and attended to Carla. After chafing her wrists and applying a moist napkin to her forehead, she finally revived.

"Dead? Did he say that Mario died?" The sound was hoarse, a croak, unlike her normal speaking voice. "Oh no. It can't be true."

Sophia's sharp cries caused Killian Blaine to rush to her side. For once, I welcomed the intrusion since Benny Soto was hardly a match for that legal eagle. First, Killian whispered something into Sophia's ear. That calmed her and reduced the noise level considerably. He then turned his baby blues on Benny. I'd seen ice shards that looked warmer than those eyes, and apparently, so had Benny. He didn't cower, but he dialed down his level of aggression.

"What's the problem, officer? I trust you're not harassing my client." A slight sneer was evident on Killian's face. Sophia leaned against him, sobbing softly into her handkerchief. Her cosmetic firm featured a waterproof mascara that must have served her well during her frequent fits of emotion. In this instance, however, it didn't matter. Her eyes were bone dry with no telltale marks underneath them. I assumed that sorrow for Mario was feigned and intended to evoke sympathy from Killian or any available male. Sophia hardly seemed like the sentimental type to me, although prejudice and a smidge of jealousy may have blinded me to her finer points.

"I'm told you were once involved with Mario Ricci," Benny said. He did his best to intimidate Sophia, but with the strong arm of Attorney Blaine supporting her, she became defiant. "True, Mario and I were once lovers," Sophia said, "but that was long ago when I was very young. Besides, I discarded him. He was devastated and begged me to return. So many men act that way, but it means nothing." She pointed at Carla. "Ask her. She was married to Mario, and everyone knows he stole her formulas and destroyed her life. Why not pester Violet Davis? She was the one with him today." Sophia's eyes narrowed with malice. "Violet was once his lover until he set his eyes on me. I was younger and more beautiful, you see. Maybe she got her revenge."

I refused to let such slander go unchallenged. "Hold it. My aunt isn't here to defend herself, and furthermore, Mario asked her to help. Practically begged her. Obviously, they were still close friends, unlike his relationship with you."

Sophia spat a retort like a scalded cat. "Huh! So that is your story, little niece. How sweet." She swiveled toward me, eyes blazing. Had Killian not restrained her, I believe she would have struck me or clawed my eyes out.

Benny frantically waved his arms about trying to restore peace. "Calm down, ladies, or you'll spend the night in a jail cell. Both of you." It was an idle threat that no one dignified with a comment.

Nona Allen suddenly leapt into the fray. "I certainly wasn't involved with that horrid man, although he deserved whatever he got, believe me. I'll bet half the women in here hated him. The half that knew him."

I was curious about the surprise that Nona had promised Mario. Had she or one of her confederates introduced some substance into his drink without realizing its toxicity? More likely, she planned some innocuous protest to publicize FACE to the press corps.

Benny's interrogation techniques left much to be desired. He was tenacious, however, much like a terrier with a bone, and he was better prepared than I expected. That convinced me that Gemma had plied her sweetie with tidbits about the principal suspects and their relationship with Mario. It was his chance to redeem himself after the unfortunate theft of my aunt's painting.

"You threatened Mr. Ricci," Benny said, pointing an accusing finger at Nona. "That makes you a prime suspect."

"Prove it!" Nona brushed him off with a show of panache that I admired. She was either innocent or extremely clever. Maybe both. "Unless you intend to arrest me, I'm going up to my room. I suffer from migraines."

That bit of insolence inspired Carla and Sophia to also abandon ship. Benny responded by sputtering and uttering useless threats that were ignored. I am by nature a compassionate soul, but I felt nothing but contempt for this pathetic authority figure. To me, he would always be Benny Soto from high school, a pimply kid with mother issues. Our table was now almost empty. Only Killian Blaine and I held our ground and awaited further developments. That should have fostered a type of kinship, but

I still didn't trust him. Killian was a slick lawyer determined to protect his client's interests. I was equally focused on safeguarding my aunt.

A murmur swept through the group as word spread of Mario's demise. Kim breezed by like a wraith, wringing her hands, pale and close to her breaking point. Even Lin was subdued. He maintained his poise, but I could tell what an effort it was for him to do so. When Chief Hall reappeared, he approached the microphone and asked for everyone's attention. Immediately, the room became tomblike—an unfortunate metaphor in view of the situation but an accurate description.

"Ladies and gentlemen, I'm sorry to inform you that your colleague Mario Ricci expired at the hospital. As standard procedure, the medical examiner will conduct an autopsy, and forensic tests will be made. For now, pending further results, we are treating this as a suspicious death. I must advise all of you to remain on the premises until told otherwise. If anyone has information to share with me on this matter, please contact my office immediately. Thank you."

A cacophony of protest erupted as participants absorbed the awful news. No one appeared to be grief-stricken or gleeful, but despite his faults, Mario had been a larger-than-life presence in their profession. His sudden absence left a void that would be hard to fill. I did sense one strong emotion born more of self-interest than love—fear. Suppose some madman was roaming about, ready to strike? Were they helpless pawns condemned to await a similar fate? Predictably, when the dust settled, out came the iPhones. Frantic calls to New York, Chicago, and the West Coast competed with pleas to European and Asian locales. Reporters seized the day by skulking about the room, interviewing anyone who volunteered a morsel of information, an opinion, or an anecdote about the deceased. Mario's colorful past would provide plenty of fodder for the gossip columns. I just hoped that Violet's role in his life would fade away.

When Lin reappeared, it was to pour oil on the troubled waters. His demeanor, calm and professional was a tonic to the befuddled group hoping for answers.

"Ladies and Gentlemen," he intoned, "condolences on the loss of your friend. Mario Ricci was the consummate professional, and despite the tragedy, he would have urged us to continue this expo. I propose we do so in his honor."

Lin didn't really know Mario. That much was obvious. The volatile Italian would have favored two days of mourning for him rather than business as usual. Under the circumstances, however, it served the needs of the conference and participants to pretend otherwise. The afternoon sessions resumed at two pm—right on schedule. One popular feature was a heated debate between a dermatologist and a plastic surgeon on the use of injectables. I was captivated by the topic until I recalled my duties as a pet parent.

I raced back to my room to redeem Fantasia and give that good girl her lunch and a long-delayed walk. She was a patient soul; however, I noted a distinct look of reproach in her lovely eyes. I begged for indulgence, gave her a treat, and added yet another failure to my list of offenses.

As we exited the front door, Violet returned looking more disheveled and shaken than I had ever seen her. Her eyes were red, and it was obvious that she had been weeping. I folded her into my arms and gave her a full-body hug. "How about a walk? Looks like you could use some fresh air."

Fantasia sealed the deal by licking Violet's hand. No one could resist that, and my aunt was no exception. "Okay. Just keep those reporters away from me. They're like a plague of locusts."

We set off at a brisk trot, with Fantasia taking the lead. When we reached a bench, Violet held up her hand. "Let's rest for a moment. I must catch my breath."

That wasn't like her, and it alarmed me. Exercise was almost an obsession with Violet, who valued maintaining her figure. On the other hand, clutching a dying man in her arms wasn't exactly routine either. I curbed the urge to question her and eke out every detail of the tragedy. That would have been rude, and I pride myself on having good manners. Mario and Violet had once been close. I wasn't certain about the depth or duration of their romance, but it must have meant something at one time. When she finally spoke, Violet was wistful. If she harbored any animosity towards the late

Mr. Ricci, it wasn't evident.

"Mario was one of a kind," she said. "Essentially a child with enormous talent and the ego to match. I knew that when we first began dating." She laughed. "Dating? Seems like an archaic word to describe our relationship. What started out as passion ultimately became friendship. Quite an enduring friendship as it happens."

"Did he hurt you when it ended?" I hated to pry but felt I had no choice.

Violet smiled and shook her head. "No. By then, I understood that Mario was so self-involved that he never considered anyone else's feelings. What he liked, he grabbed. Food, fashion, or flesh, it made no difference to him."

I became indignant on her behalf and that of every woman Mario had touched and damaged. His treatment of Carla and Linette Baugh for example was inexcusable. Who knew how many other women he caused to suffer?

Violet dabbed at her eyes. "Now, that really doesn't matter. Mario's legend will live on, and Ricci Products will endure. They're really that good, you know."

From what I'd heard, the excellence of the brand was attributable to Carla, not her greedy ex-spouse. I kept my own counsel about that. I had no right to dispute Violet's tender memories, even if they clashed wildly with reality.

"So, what happened? We've heard all sorts of speculation and rumors."

Violet took a deep breath while collecting her thoughts. "I really can't say. I've been wracking my brain, trying to piece everything together, but it's all a blur."

"What do the cops say?"

"They're taking things slowly. Very methodical." I saw a ghost of a smile flit over her face as Violet said that. "Thank goodness Gideon is in charge. Otherwise, I'd probably be in manacles by now."

"You? How is that possible?" I felt outraged. No sentient being could believe my aunt was a killer. On the other hand, this was a high-profile case, and the authorities were under pressure. The Benny Sotos of this world would act first and think later.

"Try to retrace your steps," I said. "It might be important."

She closed her eyes. "Everything was routine. At least, at first. We'd rehearsed everything so many times. I applied RICCI RICH, the treatment cap, and that turban thing. Then, while I was on stage, Mario sat behind the curtain."

"Did he say anything? Complain about feeling ill?"

Violet thought about that. "The only glitch was with the cream. Something minor. Mario thought the mixture was too thin, so I stirred it up." She smiled. "A bit of it dripped down his chin, and he yelped like a schoolgirl. You saw how vain Mario was."

"Did he eat or drink anything unusual?" I envisioned someone spiking an exotic brew and enticing Mario to try it.

"Nope. He was too nervous to eat. He sipped some Perrier, but that was from a bottle they got him from the bar. He wouldn't touch anything in plastic, you know. Mario was a water snob."

I shared thar prejudice myself, so I understood Mario's preference. Pellegrino, Perrier—imported European water was my lifeline but never anything encased in plastic.

"Everything went according to plan. Mario was wary about that FACE group, worried that Nona Allen might try some kind of stunt to upstage him. You see he'd invested most of his profits into Ricci Rich. He hinted that he'd borrowed from some rather unsavory characters to finance the big launch."

"Loan sharks? Mafioso?" I envisioned an enforcer infiltrating this crowd of beauty enthusiasts. It was easy enough to do at a public event. On the other hand, why kill the golden goose? Like it or not, Mario was indistinguishable from Ricci Rich. His smiling face was even featured on the label.

Violet shook her head. "Nothing so dramatic. Modern businesspeople use lawyers to do their dirty work."

That startled me. I could think of one brash attorney who was determined to acquire Mario's business. At any cost? That remained to be seen. Killian Blaine had quarreled with Mario. I'd witnessed that myself at the opening reception. I didn't want it to be true for selfish reasons, but I had to consider the possibility.

"Gideon knows you were once involved with Mario," I said. "Benny blurted it out. That spells motive to some people."

Violet laughed. It was refreshing to hear that sound, a light, lilting laugh with a musical quality. My joy was tempered by fear and caution. This was hardly the occasion for levity.

"What's so funny? They might try to pin his death on you. After all, you were right there on the scene." If I sounded testy, it was only out of concern for my aunt.

"Oh, I very much doubt that," Violet said. "Besides, plenty of other people, mostly women, had grievances with Mario. He was a bit of a rogue, you know."

Nona Allen's description sprang to mind. Mario was more of a porker than a loveable scoundrel. That made me wonder.

"Who inherits his estate? Money is always worth considering as a motive."

"I guess his attorney in Rome would know the particulars," Violet said. "Ricci Enterprises was privately held. I know that much. He had a staff, of course, but the power stayed at the top. Mario resisted all efforts to go public even though he would have made an enormous profit."

"I suppose he didn't have any children or obvious heirs." A womanizer might have sired some offspring on the wrong side of the blanket. It was not unheard of, even in modern times.

Violet looked pensive. "No. Mario couldn't have children. It was a big blow to his ego. That European machismo, you know. He had no siblings, and his doting mama passed some time ago." She hooted. "Now there was a femme formidable. Signora Ricci would put Josephine Soto to shame. She hated me and didn't try to hide it. That was one of the reasons that our affair ended."

I considered the basic motives for murder. Money, love, and revenge were a powerful triumvirate that inspired evil acts. Mario's shady dealings in love, life, and business certainly rang each of those bells. His murder had been carefully planned for maximum exposure. It was no spontaneous act, and the killer wisely capitalized on a gathering filled with suspects who held grievances against him.

"What about those poems he got? You know, the John Donne ones."

Violet frowned as if she had forgotten all about them. "Oh yes. I'm not sure he took those seriously. Whoever sent them didn't understand Mario that well. He was no scholar, as you know, and analyzing poems simply didn't interest him. Matter of fact, he found one in his pocket only this morning and shrugged it off. Gideon has it somewhere."

Fantasia raised her head and growled softly. I recognized several of the conference goers as they somberly ambled along the path. My aunt bowed her head seemingly oblivious to their presence. Out of respect I restrained my urge to shake her out of her torpor.

"What did this latest poem say? The one you got a chance to read." I felt certain that there was a connection between the sonnets and Mario's murder if only I could find it.

"I can't recall the entire thing, but one line was familiar. 'The paths of glory lead but to the grave.' Rather prophetic when you think of it."

Poetry has always been my thing, and I recognized those lines immediately. "*Thomas Gray. Elegy in a Country Churchyard.*" I felt a sudden sensation of triumph. "Don't you see? The killer was warning Mario of impending death. Playing on his vanity and need for glory."

Violet shrugged. "Maybe. But I don't see where that helps us find the culprit. Anyone can copy a poem. Most policemen focus on practical things. They zeroed in on me, asking why I agreed to help him and making me repeat every step I took."

I checked my watch. The next session started in ten minutes, and I'd promised Kim I'd help. It was a panel discussion, with a breezy title like "What's new in the beauty biz". At one time it had sounded like fun, a lighthearted touch to entertain and inform. Now, in view of Mario's death, that approach bordered on obscene. Violet wanted to rest, so I led her back to the hotel. Everyone we passed gave her a second look, but in this sophisticated crowd, they were too well-bred to intrude. Unfortunately, the strictures of Emily Post didn't inhibit the Fourth Estate or deter them from their mission. As we waited for the elevator, a toothy matron joined us, firing a barrage of rude questions at Violet.

"Harriet Scott, *Detroit News.* What killed Mario, Violet? Any ideas?" "Did you have a lovers' quarrel? What were his last words?"

I'd seen this pushy woman before lurking around Nona and her group, pen and pad at the ready. Her overuse of cosmetics and badly colored hair suggested that she desperately needed the services of a competent stylist. Her bad manners needed some work as well.

"No comment," I said rather forcefully. "My aunt just lost a close friend. Show some respect." A sudden glimmer of inspiration came to me. "Why not ask Nona Allen what she knows? She bragged about some sort of ambush she planned for Mario. Her group opposed everything he stood for. Who knows how far they were willing to go?"

That stopped the newshound in her tracks. She stared, mouth agape as if she had been stupefied. "Gee, thanks for the tip," said she. With astounding speed, she swiveled around and loped toward the conference center, presumably in search of Nona.

Violet grinned as she watched her disappear. "Quick thinking, Marky. Nona knows how to handle the press. She'll send that woman packing so fast her head will spin. We might even learn something in the process." She entered the elevator and urged me to leave for the seminar. "Nose around while you're at it. Information is power, you know. Have Gemma grill her fiancé. They're probably doing the autopsy as we speak." Violet shivered as she said those words. I pictured Mario's corpse, naked on that cold metal table, no longer adorned in designer duds. For someone like him who so valued appearances, it was indeed a sad end.

Chapter Seven

I left my aunt and joined the panel discussion just in time. The other participants included a perfumier, the CEO of a pricey boutique brand, and Sophia Lauren, spokesperson for the large international conglomerate she represented. There was also one more addition to our group. At the very end of the table sat that handsome hunk with insights into the acquisition process and the role of the legal community. Killian caught my eye and bowed. Kim had recovered sufficiently to serve as panel master, and she had also done her homework. The list of talking points she devised explored the less glamorous aspects of cosmetics—the financial bottom line and research and development. I felt certain that Kim's husband, Lionel, had advised her on the questions. He was a crusty, crabby attorney but sharp as the proverbial tack when it came to business matters. Her first question fired up the group. "Can small brands or privately held entities survive in today's competitive climate?"

I thought immediately of Ricci Enterprises, a ferociously guarded, privately held company. Killian Blaine and several competitors had been circling around like vultures waiting to pick its bones. What would happen to the business now with its founder and protector gone? Killian was far too tactful to mention it by name, but he did allude to the difficulties such entities encountered when their namesake left or refused to modify their practices. Many floundered, and more than a few lost the battle entirely.

Sophia Lauren surprised me. Her argument touting the advantages of alliances with well-funded corporate sponsors was both lucid and logical. Had I been blinded by my own prejudices against this woman? Sophia's switch from spoiled bimbo to savvy businesswoman made me reconsider my attitude.

Kim posed an interesting question to me as a small business owner. Did I plan to expand the reach of *Poppet* or remain as a sole proprietor? We debated the perils of rapid expansion versus the dangers of stagnation. It was an intelligent, vigorous discussion that left me with plenty to consider. Afterwards, Killian sidled up to me and proposed that we share a coffee. We found a server and ordered two steaming cups of espresso with biscotti. Killian motioned toward an alcove that boasted a secluded seating area and two comfy chairs.

"You made a sound case for yourself just then," he said. "Good to see that you're not just another pretty face."

That bit of blatant sexism made my blood boil. "I was going to offer you the same compliment," I said. "Even handsome lawyers can have gravitas. Who knew?"

"Touché," he said, laughing. "I guess I deserved that. Here's something for your aunt to consider when she deals with the police." He held up his hands. "Speaking as a lawyer now and a friend. No charge. They're searching everywhere for motives, and number one on any cop's hit parade is money. Love is a close second."

An uneasy feeling gripped me, gnawing at my innards. Did he know something that threatened my aunt? He couldn't possibly be serious. Violet Davis was a renowned artist and entrepreneur. Everybody knew that. She was certainly no killer.

"So what? How does that affect Violet? She was just doing a favor for an old friend. No strings attached. Plus, their romantic involvement ended decades ago. No hard feelings, no bitterness on either part."

Killian grimaced. "Look. Keep this confidential. I spoke to one of my contacts in Italy an hour ago. Someone who knows what he's talking about."

"And...?" I resisted the urge to shake the words out of him. "What's this have to do with my aunt?"

Killian hesitated as if he was groping for the right words. "My buddy knows Mario's lawyer. The guy who prepared his will."

When I'm nervous, I sometimes resort to sarcasm. "I thought you guys couldn't discuss that sort of thing. Don't you take an oath of omerta or something?"

He sighed. "You're not making this any easier. Yes, we're committed to client confidentiality, but we're also human." Killian's lips twitched. He was clearly exasperated with my constant interruptions. I vowed to button my lip and let the man speak. "Sorry," I said. "Go on. I'm listening."

"As you can imagine, Mario left a sizable estate. He designated two people as his heirs. One of them was your Aunt Violet."

My mouth felt dry, and I took a long swallow of espresso before speaking. Crumbs from the biscotti tickled my throat. "Who else?" I croaked. "Anyone I know?"

"His former wife. Carla Standish."

My head was reeling, and for one of the few times in my life, I felt faint. "That can't be right. My aunt would have told me. It's got to be a mistake."

The look in Killian's eyes dashed my hopes of a misunderstanding. I clutched the edge of the table to steady my nerves. My next move was done on autopilot. I reached into my purse, found my iPhone, and dialed Violet's number. She sounded groggy when she answered but this was no time for slumber. At any minute, Gideon Hall might learn about Mario's will, and when he did, Violet and Carla Standish would be in grave peril.

"Get dressed," I said. "I'm coming up and bringing Killian with me."

Violet heard the urgency in my voice and responded accordingly. "What's wrong? Are you okay? Has something happened?"

"No time to talk. I'm on my way." Out of the corner of my eye, I spied Benny Soto patrolling the aisles. Fortunately, I also saw Gemma. She took one look at my face and sped over.

"Hey, you two. What's going on?"

I clasped my partner's hand and squeezed it. "Trouble. Find Benny and distract him. You know how to do that. Find out what's going on with the investigation."

"Ouch! That hurt! Tell me what's wrong. You're scaring me."

I was playing for time. Time enough to brief my aunt and perhaps save her from disaster. "Just trust me. I'll tell you everything after I speak with Violet. And while you're at it, find Carla Standish and tell her not to discuss anything with the police."

Gemma wasn't happy, but her loyalty was unquestioned. She gave Killian a hard stare and sped off to fulfill her mission.

"I should have asked you for your help right away. Will you come with me? I know you're not a criminal attorney, but my aunt needs advice."

Killian took a deep breath before answering. He obviously was wrestling with an ethical dilemma and trying to avoid any conflict of interest. Unless, of course, he was the killer. "True. I specialize in corporate law, but I still recall a few things from the criminal side of the house. I'll act as Violet's temporary advisor if she asks me to. Then we'll see where things go. You realize that your aunt is in a very vulnerable position. Former lover, heir, and the last person to touch Mario."

I tried to maintain my composure, but he was frightening me. *Relax,* I told myself. Until we knew Mario's cause of death, it was no use agonizing. He probably had a seizure or even a heart attack. After all, the man was no youngster, and he lived life to its fullest—plenty of wine, rich food, and women—especially women. Violet said he abhorred drug usage in any form, so that was probably off the table as a cause of death. He didn't smoke except for the occasional cigar. Cubans, of course.

The elevator was jammed with convention goers chattering about topic number one—Mario Ricci. Speculation ranged from epilepsy to suicide, with several people who obviously didn't know him hinting that Mario was deeply depressed. Quite the contrary. Mario was the eternal optimist convinced that *RICCI RICH* would dominate the market and add to his fame. I would bet my meager savings that suicide was the farthest thing from his mind. Killian and I kept our ears open and maintained a studied silence. I closed my eyes, and he looked up at the ceiling. Never had an elevator ride felt so endless.

Violet was waiting for us when we reached her room. The nap must have refreshed her because she was her composed, coiffed, and cosmetically perfect self once more.

"Come on in," she said. "I can't wait to hear your news. Gideon hasn't told me anything."

I exchanged glances with Kilian and plunged into the icy waters. "Did Mario ever talk about his will?"

"I told you before he was very secretive about money matters. Almost paranoid. Besides Mario was superstitious. He had that old Italian aversion to ever speaking about death. Thought it brought bad luck." Violet gave me a hard stare. "Why? Don't keep me guessing."

Killian was used to broaching sensitive topics with clients, so I deferred to him. He spoke candidly, almost bluntly. No beating about the bush for this boy. I think Perry Mason would have handled things more tactfully, but Della Street would have chimed in, too.

"I learned today that you are one of Mario's two heirs, Violet. Except for a few modest bequests to servants, you split everything he owned with Carla Standish. I'm told it amounts to quite a legacy."

My aunt was seldom at a loss for words, but she seemed stunned by this revelation. "You're kidding, right? Why would Mario do that? I understand wanting to rectify things with Carla. He owed her that. But why me?"

"He never mentioned it to you?" Killian asked. "That's the first thing the police will want to know."

"Police? You don't seriously consider me a suspect, do you? Mario must have had a medical emergency. They don't even know how he died yet." She looked directly at him. "Or do they?"

Killian's demeanor could only be described as grim. The sparkling, flirtatious lawyer of yesterday had morphed into a prophet of doom. "I can't answer that question," he said, "because I don't know, but I'll offer you some free advice. If they find anything irregular about his death, don't speak to the police without an attorney present. This was just a heads-up. You and Ms. Standish will automatically jump to the head of the suspect list."

Violet looked incredulous, as if she hadn't fully processed the situation. "Gideon knows me. I trust him to do the right thing."

I approached my aunt and hugged her. "He's a good guy, but he's still a cop. Listen to what Killian said. Be cautious just until we get this thing settled.

Please." I turned to Killian. "Can't you help her at least until we figure out where we stand? On television, the lawyer always asks for a retainer. You know, to establish the attorney-client relationship."

Apparently, my pseudo-legalese amused him. Killian bowed his head to conceal what I suspected was a grin. "You spend too much time on social media. That's obvious. If Violet agrees, I'll do what I can. But first, I need to speak with Chief Hall to figure out where things stand."

A ferocious banging on the door caused all three of us to jump. I envisioned a swat team bearing weapons and manacles breaking down the door. Then I heard Gemma's voice.

"Let me in, you guys. I have news."

When Gemma gets excited, her untamed curls bounce wildly, and she nearly levitates. I was relieved to see that she had ditched her shadow, Benny Soto, and convinced Carla to join us. Knowing Gemma, she hadn't given Carla much choice.

Carla's naturally pale complexion looked ghostly, and her eyes consumed her entire face. Without Gemma to support her, I doubted that she could remain upright. Violet waved her into the chaise and poured Carla some Perrier.

After taking a healthy swallow, Carla reached out. "I don't understand. Gemma said not to speak with the police. Why? I've got nothing to hide. I still resented Mario, but not enough to kill him. Besides, I thought he had some medical emergency."

"What did Benny tell you?" I asked Gemma.

"Nothing important. Just that they airlifted the test samples from the autopsy to Chicago for analysis. Top priority; you know the drill. They should know something tomorrow or the next day." She shivered. "He really got off watching the autopsy. Ugh. Not sure I want to marry a ghoul. Poor Mario. Now he's just a pile of bones and body fluids." Gemma added an impish grin. "And, of course, incredibly lush hair."

That was more candor than Carla could take. She gasped and leaned back in the chaise.

Violet took charge and comforted her friend. "Did you know Mario's financial arrangements? Ever speak with him about his will?"

Carla's eyes widened. "His will! You must be joking. Mario was as tight as a clam about money matters. After our divorce, we spoke only through our attorneys. Trust me, he probably had a pile of money stashed somewhere the Italian tax authorities couldn't find it. He was cagey that way."

We were all tiptoeing around the main issue. If Carla knew that she benefited from Mario's death she didn't admit it. Time to face the beast. "There's something you should know, Carla. You and Violet are Mario's heirs. At least, we think you are." It went without saying that if either Violet or Carla had dispatched lover boy, she couldn't inherit anything.

She couldn't believe what she heard. Carla tilted her head, looking quizzically at me as if I were speaking in tongues. "Heirs? I don't believe it." She turned toward Violet for validation.

"Apparently, it's true. Either way, that gives us a powerful motive for murder. Say nothing until we learn more. I'm certain there's some reasonable explanation for this."

If she had plotted Mario's demise, Carla was an Oscar-caliber actress. She leaned back, wilting right before our eyes like a desiccated orchid.

"Benny didn't mention any of that," Gemma said. "Probably didn't know. That boy cannot keep anything secret from me. He was too busy shadowing Nona and her group. She still won't tell them what big surprise she planned for Mario."

A rather ominous silence descended upon our group as if we were awaiting the executioner's noose. I couldn't help calculating just how much money my aunt was now privy to. Lots if *Ricci Rich* and the other products were involved. By all accounts, the stuff was amazing.

Finally, Killian spoke up. "Here's my advice. Say nothing, acknowledge nothing. Wait for the authorities to bring up the subject and insist on having an attorney present."

That was sound advice but an essentially passive approach. I'm a woman of action. I refused to leave my dear aunt in limbo while the prospect of disaster loomed over her. Gemma and I had some aptitude for detection. We'd proven that several times before.

"I suggest we join the group and circulate. Find out what we can even if it's pure speculation. Act innocent." I turned to Killian. "Think you can access the autopsy report and the blood work?"

His smirk said it all. "I have a few contacts. Until we know the cause of death, let's not panic." Carla slumped even further on the chaise. The latest news, coupled with Mario's death, had totally unnerved her. When Killian put his arm around her and spoke softly, she agreed to leave with him. As soon as the door closed, Gemma sprang up.

"Okay, you two. We need to regroup. Enough of this nicey-nicey stuff."

I couldn't disagree. We needed a plan of action that would allow us to anticipate what came next. Violet, who had made a quick recovery from her shock, responded first.

"Maybe this is tied to the theft of my painting. I could nose around and get Lin's help. Remember I promised to replace it. That gives me an excuse to approach Sophia."

"Great!" I turned to Gemma. "Your task is harder. Ingratiate yourself with the FACE crowd. Play on their sympathies. You know, sisterhood forever. That kind of stuff."

Gemma looked uncertain, although duplicity was her strong suit. "I guess so. Undercover work has always appealed to me. Suppose I'll have to scrub off my makeup and find something dowdy to wear. Trust me. I'll find out what little surprise they planned for Mario no matter what lies I must tell."

Violet crossed her arms and faced me. "Okay, dear niece. Tell us what your role will be. Nothing dangerous, I trust."

There was unintentional irony in her statement. Who would have suspected that modeling a new hair conditioner would leave someone dead? On the face of it, that seemed like a supremely safe task, although it proved fatal for Mario.

"I'm still stuck on the literary angle. You know, those poems. They meant something to someone, and I think it was the killer. Someone wanted Mario to suffer before his death. Whoever it was gave him too much credit, though. Mario had a creative mind, but his intellect didn't stretch to include poetry." I paused. "If only we knew what that final note said. I'll bet it's the key to the entire puzzle."

"I could ask Gideon," Violet said. "He might let something slip. For old times' sake."

That was an inspired idea. As long as I'd known him, Gideon had admired my aunt. Oh, he was subtle. The guy had too much class to make overtures. He merely stayed in the background and pined for her in the great old tradition of courtly love. It was easy to picture Gideon that way, although I recognized that he would still do his duty if he believed that Violet was guilty.

Gemma's brusque comment interrupted my thoughts. "Hey! Wake up and stop dreaming. This is serious stuff we're talking about."

She was right. Violet and Carla were in serious peril if the forensic results spelled murder. Violet had hit the trifecta—motive, means, and opportunity. We probably had forty-eight hours at most before the hammer dropped. I am an inveterate mystery reader, and in my favorite novels, the sleuth always focuses on the character of the victim. Mario's public persona was on display for anyone to judge, but I wondered about the private man. Which of his habits, traits, or flaws would drive someone to murder?

Violet was uniquely positioned to provide those insights. She'd known him on a most intimate level, a bit too intimate for my taste. Still, she'd watched his behavior over the years as a lover and businessman. That had to be useful.

"Come on," I said. "Let's take Fantasia for a walk and have a little chat."

"Little chat? That sounds rather ominous," Violet said, "although a walk would be most welcome. Okay. I'm game."

Gemma skipped off to don her undercover outfit while I rescued my canine companion from total boredom. Fantasia's plumy tail wagged, and she jumped up to give me a kiss. Wouldn't the world's problems vanish if everyone shared that kind of love?

* * *

The brisk air alongside Grand Traverse Bay provided the perfect antidote to the doldrums. Fantasia's ears pricked as she trotted ahead, sniffing the area for imaginary foes and fending off the occasional shards of gravel.

"Ah," Violet said, lifting her head. "I needed this. Natural beauty puts everything in perspective, doesn't it?"

I agreed. Our situation was perilous but not hopeless. Not if we kept calm and used our deductive skills.

"Tell me more about Mario," I said. "Anything, even if it seems inconsequential. I don't believe his death was accidental. Natural maybe. His lifestyle was high risk."

Violet gave it some thought before responding. "I told you before, Mario was capricious, selfish but curiously innocent. A child inside a very complex character. Brilliant business instincts, insatiable appetite for success, ruthless competitor."

"And women?" I asked. "Seems like he always made time for them."

She laughed. "Count on that. He genuinely loved women that's why he developed so many great products. Didn't keep him from breaking their hearts when he finished with them, of course."

"Carla and Linette seemed to take it especially hard," I said. "Anyone else you can think of?"

Violet hesitated once more. Dredging up old scandals was obviously painful for her.

"What made Sophia so special? Granted, she's quite lovely, but I assume all his lovers were. Bet he never even looked at an average or homely woman."

"True," Violet said. "I think Sophia's greatest asset was her indifference. Mario wasn't used to that, and it made him crazy. She used him and left when he no longer served her needs. He was devastated, I can assure you."

I gave a silent cheer for the French femme fatale. Men like Mario were all too common. Scheming women less so.

"One other thing," Violet said. "Sophia did what none of us ever even thought of. She conned Mario out of money. Lots of it. Maybe she was angling for more to finance her business ventures."

That was a revelation. Love and money were often a deadly duo. The only problem was that Mario lost his life instead of Sophia. That put paid to a revenge motive.

A sickening thought suddenly assailed me. "You didn't…he never took your money, did he?" If that were true, Violet graduated to suspect number one.

She hugged me. "No, my dear. Haven't I always told you that love and money are very separate things? Besides, we had our romance when I was just starting out. Starving artist, you know the drill. Mario helped me out by introducing me to contacts, gallery showings, the works. I had no regrets when we parted. At least no broken heart and certainly no empty wallet."

"What about Carla? You said she was devastated."

"Ah. Carla was a different matter entirely. Remember, she was Mario's wife. Her family left her well off, but most of it went to Mario. He siphoned off almost every penny, then fleeced her in the divorce settlement. I never forgave him for abusing her that way."

"I agree, but don't mention that to Gideon. It makes you sound vengeful." My aunt merely smiled as if I was exaggerating the danger. If Carla was one of Mario's heirs, she certainly deserved every penny. "Suppose you do inherit. What would you do with RICCI enterprises?"

Violet didn't hesitate. Her savvy business instincts immediately asserted themselves. "Oh, I wouldn't think twice. I'd urge Carla to sell to one of the big cosmetic giants. That way, we could merely sit back and reap the profits." Violet winked at me. "Someone like your Killian Blaine could handle it perfectly. He's quite a smooth operator."

Killian was smooth, but he was not mine! We'd never even had a date or shared a kiss. I felt myself blush just thinking of it. Some men enjoyed romancing a host of women like the sailor with a girl in every port. For all I knew, Killian was inclined that way.

"Look, Marky, I'm an artist with a profitable side business in cosmetics. Running an empire has never appealed to me. Forget about that, and let's try to extricate me from this mess." Violet's eyes twinkled. "Besides. Unlike a prominent lifestyle guru I could name, prison would simply not suit me. I'd look dreadful in those dreary orange jumpsuits."

We exchanged fist bumps, and I went about my assigned task with a much lighter heart.

* * *

I returned to my computer and with an assist from the conference brochure, researched the academic pedigrees of the registrants. The absence of a liberal arts background didn't preclude having a love for poetry. I recognized that. Still, with an additional assist from Google, it was one place to start. The results were both interesting and informative, although there were no red flags. Carla earned a BA in English from Barnard. That fit the profile and put me on high alert. Lin Baugh graduated from the Cornell School of Hotel Management and held a graduate degree in the field from that same institution. Not surprising. It explained his exquisite devotion to detail and superlative skills. What it didn't explain was why someone with those sterling credentials would land in Traverse City, Michigan, instead of the major markets. Perhaps he enjoyed winter sports or had family connections in the area. A point to verify, although not a very salient one. Nona Adams required more scrutiny. She was not a panelist or listed attendee, but the internet exploded with tales of her exploits. Bryn Mawr College was her undergraduate home, and to my surprise, her major was fine arts. I tried and failed to envision Nona's gangly form of

dancing, weaving, or painting. It seemed far more likely that her field of concentration was civil disobedience. Nona's legal studies made more sense. The woman was a born rabble-rouser who was ready and all too willing to file lawsuits in the name of gender equality. I never doubted her intellect, just her sanity. Nona nursed grievances against most men and women like me who enjoyed conventional feminine pursuits. That made her difficult but not homicidal. She could kill someone's spirit but leave their corpse intact.

Perhaps my biggest surprise came from researching Sophia. Frankly, I expected a finishing school background at best. Imagine my chagrin when I learned that she was an engineer! That revelation ended my cyber snooping for the day. It had been a timewaster that yielded nothing of value.

I devoted myself to my toilette and emerged, ready to do battle. Marky Davis was no Mata Hari, but on occasion, with enough effort, I could pass for sultry, even slinky. This was one of those occasions. I painted my face, donned a flame-red slip dress, and made the ultimate sacrifice by pairing it with stilettos. My appearance wouldn't please the FACE crowd, but they were not my target audience. That was Gemma's assignment.

As luck would have it, my first encounter was with Lin Baugh. He glided among his convention guests, chatting amiably and looking dapper in a tuxedo. When he saw me, he stopped in his tracks.

"Marky! You look fabulous. A breath of fresh air in this sober crowd." He kept his voice low so as not to offend anyone else.

"Not too festive, I trust. I didn't want to seem disrespectful to Mario."

Lin assured me that I hadn't violated any social taboos. "In fact, you lifted my spirits. The expo lasts another five days and we simply can't sustain a funereal atmosphere. Besides, we took a vote, and the group overwhelmingly opted to continue with the program." Lin's lips twitched in a wry smile. "I'm sure Mario would have wanted it this way. For the good of the conference." For the first time, Lin traded his mask of civility for sarcasm. A welcome change in my book.

I elected to confront the topic head-on. "What's the latest on the police investigation? I'm worried that Violet might be implicated."

"Violet? That's nonsense. Mario adored her. Besides," Lin said, "I'm sure it was a medical emergency. Some underlying condition we weren't aware of." He was being evasive, and I called him out on it. Despite his claims, Lin had to stay attuned to anything that might damage the hotel's reputation. His livelihood depended on that.

"You must have excellent contacts at the hospital. What's the word?"

I hate to make a grown man squirm, but my aunt's safety overcame my scruples. Lin guided me toward a secluded alcove before speaking. "This isn't official. It's pure supposition since the lab tests haven't concluded." He cleared his throat. "My sources think Mario was poisoned."

"Poisoned! How can that be? He hadn't eaten anything and was only sipping Perrier. What could poison him?"

"I'm no doctor," Lin said. He sounded rather testy the more I quizzed him. "But I understand that some poisons are slow-acting and might be administered hours before. As I recall, Mario had quite the lusty appetite. For food and other things."

"Hmm. I suppose the cops searched his suite." Knowing Gideon Hall, I had no doubt that he had covered all the usual bases. Lin's reaction told me I had struck gold.

"They cleared out everything and blocked off the suite. Apparently, Mario entertained someone after the reception. A woman. They found lipstick on one of the flutes and an empty bottle of champagne. *Krug,* one of our most exclusive brands."

At least his final evening was a celebratory one. I adored *Krug*, but it was way out of my price range. I felt a pang of anxiety. Violet loved the stuff. Had she joined Mario for a toast? If only I knew the shade of lipstick found on the flute. In this cosmetic-loving crowd, that would narrow down the suspect pool. Without being too indelicate, I wondered if Mario's bed sheets showed any signs of carnal activity. My courage failed me, and I couldn't ask. Gemma would have forged ahead without batting an eye, but she was far more intrepid and twice as worldly as yours truly. I was confident that she could inveigle Benny into spilling the beans. He relished discussing sordid details. Probably considered it a type of foreplay.

Lin escaped my clutches with a graceful maneuver and sped away. Before I evaluated what I'd learned, Kim sashayed up to me. She looked elegant as befitted a former fashion model, but faint shadows under her eyes suggested a troubled sleep.

"Marky, let me look at you." She spun me around and nodded approvingly. "Lovely. Nothing surpasses the sweet bloom of youth."

"Very poetic, Kim. Are you a fan?"

She flushed. "It sounds pretentious, but I've always read and written poetry. Lionel scoffs at it, of course."

"What about the scraps of poetry that Mario received? Any thoughts?"

She furrowed her brow. "Curious, wasn't it? How many people quote John Donne or Gray or even know who they were? Shakespeare is far more common. There's obviously a message in that, but I can't figure it out."

We agreed that the final message might hold the key. Gideon hadn't mentioned it to anyone, but my aunt might coax him into revealing it.

"What about that dreadful Adams woman?" Kim asked. "She would enjoy that type of cat-and-mouse game. Someone told me that Mario insulted her to her face. Called her ugly."

Nona came here on a mission, but was it murder? Most protestors, even zealots, stopped short of that. I mentioned Mario's late-night amour and the lipstick on the champagne flute.

"Let me check with the room service manager," Kim said. "Not many people spring for a bottle of *Krug*. They must have been celebrating quite an occasion."

All that skullduggery had made me thirsty. I sidled up to the bar, ready to order something strong and smooth. That's where I found Killian Blaine. The look in his eyes told me that my makeover had the desired effect. His gaze was anything but brotherly. It was tinged with lust and a pinch of longing. Quite a satisfying result!

"May I buy you a drink?" he asked. I was thrilled by the husky tone in his voice. A true sophisticate would have ordered a martini, but I loathed the vile taste. I opted for a Bellini instead.

"Nice choice," he said. Killian's drink of choice was scotch. Johnny Walker blue label, to be precise. As he sipped it, his icy blue eyes never left me. "Red is your color, Marky. You should wear it more often. Mesmerizing."

Seduction was a foreign concept to me although I tried to match his moves by flashing a sultry smile. I failed miserably. My fear for Violet consumed me, making any games playing impossible. Mother always said that honesty was the best policy. Why not put that cliché to the test.

"I need your help or at least your advice."

"Okay." He raised an eyebrow and sipped his scotch. Killian must be one heck of a poker player because he never moved a muscle. His face betrayed absolutely nothing.

"If *Ricci Enterprises* was gobbled up by one of the cosmetic conglomerates, would the owners make a killing?" *Bite my tongue!* Could I have chosen a less incriminating expression?

He saw the humor of the remark. "Better not let Gideon Hall hear you talking like that.

But to answer your question, the owners would profit enormously from the sale." He flashed an evil grin. "Assuming Mario's death wasn't associated with his products, of course. Any sharp lawyer would use that as a cudgel to get more favorable terms."

My nerves were stretched to their breaking point, but visions of Aunt Violet made me persevere. "What did your contacts tell you? Was Mario murdered?"

He shrugged. "Search me. Hall is keeping a very tight lid on things. But fear not. I'll find out. Sooner or later, I always get what I want."

Was that a double entendre or merely an innocent statement? Either way, I chose to ignore it. "Come on. Promise me you'll tell me as soon as you find out."

He reluctantly agreed.

I had information to trade, and now was the time to do so. "By the way, did you know that Mario had a visitor the night before he died? A female visitor."

That surprised him and gave me a faint taste of victory. "No kidding?"

"Who has a taste for *Krug*? Anyone you know?"

Killian hooted. "Honey, anyone with a refined palate loves the stuff, including your dear aunt. That means about half of the three hundred or so gathered here. I exclude the FACE contingent on moral grounds."

"His visitor wore lipstick, so you're probably right. How did Sophia take Mario's death? I understand that they were once a couple, and you seem rather close to her."

"I'm attentive to all my clients, Ms. Davis. Part of the service offered by my firm. Sophia was distraught, as you might expect. She has a tender heart."

Tender heart, my foot! I managed to choke down the response I yearned to give and substitute a wan smile. "Of course."

I finished my Bellini and excused myself, citing pressing business. He didn't believe me, but I really didn't care. Killian Blaine had risen to the very top of my enemies list.

* * *

Glamour exacts a heavy toll, and by seven o'clock, my feet were killing me. Maybe Nona Adams and the FACE group had the right idea after all. Sneakers would have felt so comforting. I gingerly eased into a wing chair and heaved a sigh of relief. That's where Gemma found me. I barely recognized her. She had taken her role as a FACE supporter very seriously and looked every inch the part. Her face was scrubbed clean of makeup, and she substituted drab clothing for her usual festive garb. I squinted as I looked up at her. "Freckles! I never knew you had freckles! How cute!"

"Stuff it, glamor girl," she said, "Maybe I should bunk elsewhere tonight. Looking like that, you might have company."

"Go soak your head. I am not in the mood, Gemma." Blisters had formed on my feet, and the pain was excruciating. The whirlpool tub in my suite beckoned me.

"Okay. I guess you're not interested in what Benny said."

That woke me up instantly. "I'm sorry. Tell me before I beat you to death with these Louboutins. With what they cost, you'll die happy."

Gemma sniffed. "Don't you mean what they cost Violet? No way you had the bucks, partner of mine. Unless you're cooking the books."

She was right, of course. Violet had gotten them from an admirer and passed them on to me.

"Okay, okay. Calm down and spill. I got some scoop that might interest you, too."

We were joined by Kim, whose sparkling eyes told me that she had also made progress.

"Is this a private session, or do you have room for me?" Kim asked. "I just spoke to the housekeeping staff and got some interesting information."

"Don't be coy, Kim. Tell us." I hated being gruff, but aching feet and an anxious mind robbed me of all my party manners.

Kim's news validated what we already suspected. Mario had entertained in the fullest sense of the word that evening. Tangled sheets and contraceptive material were proof of that.

"And the lipstick?" I asked.

"Oh, I recognized it immediately. The police did a very sloppy job of clearing the room if I do say so myself. I found a tissue in the waste basket." Kim paused for dramatic effect. "Pink Dusk. Tom Ford's outrageously priced lipstick. Everyone loves it, and half the females in the conference use it."

Gemma piped up. "He charges almost sixty bucks a tube for that stuff. Can you believe it?"

I had no desire to debate cosmetic choices. Besides, just the thought of limping back to my suite brought out the mean girl in me. "I wonder who oversaw securing the scene, Gemma. Oh, wait. That was Benny's job, wasn't it?"

My partner and pal flushed with anger, but she kept a lid on her temper. "Hmm. Didn't I see your aunt wearing that shade of lipstick, Marky? I admit that Benny's no brain surgeon, but lay off him, will you? He may someday be the father of my children."

The thought of that induced a gag reflex that I could barely contain. Besides, Gemma was right about one thing. Violet did favor those subtle pink shades, and since she rarely had to pay for products, she could indulge in almost any of them. I had faith in Violet's taste and discretion. Her fling with Mario was ancient history, a musty relic of the past. Even a snootful of Krug was unlikely to revive that passion.

"Still interested in what Benny told me?" Gemma asked. Kim and I both nodded. I expected Gemma to indulge her passion for stagecraft and she didn't disappoint. "Okay. The night shift guys reported that someone was fiddling with the display of *Ricci Rich*. They had to restack it before Mario blew his top. You know how hot-tempered he was." She paused, saving the best for last. "Plus, they finally forced Nona Adams to fold. Technically, it was one of her minions but the result's the same. Remember that surprise she kept hinting at? They found a frozen hog's head in a cooler in Nona's room. Ugh! Disgusting thing. Even had the eyes still in it. She planned to wheel it out just when Mario did his big reveal. The FACE crowd had a big production staged."

"Maybe they tampered with the display, too," Kim said. "I wouldn't put anything past them. Fanatics. Reminds me of the Salem Witch trials, except Mario didn't get burned at the stake."

Maybe not, but he was just as dead. Until we knew the cause of death, our investigation was stymied. I realized that Violet hadn't reported yet, and I still had those poems to decipher. We parted and agreed to reconvene at breakfast the next morning. I limped to the elevator, praying that no one would notice my bare feet. That's where I saw Carla Standish. Her transformation from wan castoff to potential heiress was astonishing. No more ghastly pale for that girl. No sir. Her cheeks bloomed with youth; her complexion glowed with vitality. Despite those changes, there was one thing that transfixed me. Carla's lips were alight with a familiar shade. She wore that pricey product, *Pink Dusk*.

I tried to be subtle but ended up gaping at her. Everything about Carla screamed joy and happiness despite the untimely exit of her former spouse. Most people, especially a potential heir, would have feigned sorrow just to allay suspicion. If nothing else, Carla's carefree attitude proved that she was no hypocrite. "Feet hurt, don't they?" she said. "Stilettos are the ultimate beauty test." She stared down at her own exquisitely shod tootsies. "Mario insisted that I wear them, so I got used to the pain. Come to think of it, endurance was my trademark when we were together."

"Quite a character, wasn't he?"

Carla curled her lip. "Character? Mario was a monster. A user of women and anyone else who satisfied his needs. Don't make him something special just because he's dead." She lowered her voice and whispered. "Someone did the world a favor."

For once, I was speechless. If Mario had been murdered, Carla would zoom to the top of the suspect list, yet she seemed quite oblivious to the danger. "Aren't you worried?" I asked. "After all, you and my aunt stand to gain millions."

"So what? Instead of worrying, I plan to spend my time strategizing. A certain attorney has already offered to buy my share of Ricci Enterprises.

I haven't spoken to Violet about it yet, but I'm sure she'll agree. Any businessperson would jump at the opportunity, and your dear aunt is one shrewd operator."

I forgot my foot pain and glided onto the elevator. Was Killian Blaine the reason for Carla's youthful glow? I'd foolishly assumed that his interest in me was genuine, but it seemed that the man was a rogue who toyed with any reasonably attractive woman. Another strikeout for Marky Davis. Someday, before I reach my dotage, I might figure out the opposite sex. If I lived long enough.

I limped down the hallway to my room, so preoccupied that I ignored potential danger. Before I activated my key card, someone stepped from the shadows and confronted me. Sophia Lauren's usually lovely face was distorted by rage or something equally disturbing. Mascara ringed her eyes, making her resemble a rabid raccoon, and her lipstick—that familiar pink hue—was smeared. I sensed yet another emotion driving her, and it intrigued me. Fear. An almost feral scent contrasted with her exquisite perfume blend. Had guilt or remorse driven this woman into a frenzy?

"Where is she?" she sputtered, "Your aunt, the great artist."

She didn't frighten me because I carried a weapon. Louboutin stilettos were as lethal as a sharpened spike, and I was prepared to use them. Sophia glanced at me and hastily moved back. "I must see her. She murdered Mario."

"You're insane, lady. Violet never harmed anyone, especially Mario. He was her friend. Besides, she cared for him. She was never a gold digger like some." Even in her agitated state, it was impossible for Sophia to miss my meaning.

"How dare you," she huffed. "Mario took my youth. I was a mere child when he seduced me. I earned every penny that I got."

That tale might sell to the tabloids, but I knew better. There was an unflattering term for women who "earned" money from rich sponsors. Sophia was a succubus who had skipped childhood innocence entirely. Somehow, she had learned the terms of Mario's will, probably from Killian Blaine. I decided to chance things and play a hunch.

"Looks like your little interlude with Mario last night didn't work. Too bad. I suppose Chief Hall has already questioned you."

Sophia's eyes flashed, and she moved closer. "What? You don't know anything, and you'd better keep quiet if you know what's good for you."

I eased open the door and lobbed one parting shot. "I'll give my aunt your message. Don't count on seeing her anytime soon."

* * *

Lin Baugh heard the news first. Local contacts at the medical examiner's office leaked Mario's cause of death to him and the *Traverse City Herald*. Chief Hall was not pleased. According to Gemma, he had literally "blown his top" when the word spread.

"Gideon blamed Benny, but that wasn't fair. He never said a word to me about it." She grinned. "I'll bet that hot attorney bribed someone. He looks like he could charm the pants off almost anyone, male or female."

That bit of humor didn't please me, even though it had the ring of truth. When it came to Killian Blaine, esquire, I intended to keep my bloomers firmly in place no matter how charming he was. Besides, I had more important things to consider.

Violet convened a mini-conference with Gemma, Kim, and me to explain everything and plot our next steps. Little did I realize that the truth would give me the shock of my life. We sat sipping tea at a table festooned with pink napkins and a lovely view of the square. It seemed an unlikely spot to discuss cold-blooded murder, but that's what we did. What a curious quartet we made! My aunt was composed, although I noted that her usually flawless manicure was marred by several chips. Kim shivered despite the moderate temperature, and Gemma tapped her foot to a tune only she could hear. I forced myself to remain calm, sip my tea and listen. There was time for chatter later.

Violet took a deep breath before speaking. "First of all, the rumors are true. Mario was murdered. Gideon had that confirmed by the forensic team." She hesitated before continuing. "He was poisoned."

"No!" Kim sobbed, dabbing her eyes with her napkin.

"What?" Gemma couldn't contain herself any longer. "I thought he didn't eat or drink anything since the night before. How could that be?"

I put my hand on her arm. "Hush. Let Violet finish." I knew from my aunt's reaction that something was very wrong. No arrest had been made yet but that didn't mean one wasn't imminent.

"Someone mixed pure liquid nicotine into the *Ricci Rich* conditioner. The container I used was full of it. They tell me that the scalp is extremely porous and pure nicotine is extremely lethal. The other jars had it too. The killer wasn't taking any chances, I guess."

We listened in a state of stupefied silence. Liquid nicotine? Who ever heard of that, and how would you find it if you wanted it?

Kim pulled Violet's sleeve. "Couldn't you tell something was wrong? I mean, nicotine is that nasty brown color, isn't it? When everyone smoked, you could see it in cups or on saucers where they parked cigarette butts."

For once, Gemma zipped her lips and hunched over her computer. "Wait a minute. Listen to this. You can order liquid nicotine in flavors or colorless right on the internet! They use it in vaping. It's not even expensive."

I had never even considered vaping or smoking, but there were plenty of people around who had. A few of our participants hovered outside the conference center every day like lepers inhaling the pleasures of e-cigarettes. In fact, I had seen someone known to us all indulging in that nasty habit just yesterday. That wasn't surprising. Models and people in the fashion industry often vaped to avoid eating. As the saying goes, one can never be too thin or too rich.

"Benny Soto uses E-cigarettes," I said. "Did you know that?"

Gemma blanched. "Give him some credit. He's trying to quit smoking. Besides, his mother's always on him to stop, and you know how persuasive she can be."

Josephine Soto was a law unto herself, a solid wall of maternal energy devoted to all things Benny. I felt a momentary twinge of compassion for him that quickly dissipated. If anything implicated my aunt, I would fight to the bitter end to absolve her. Benny or anyone else who got in my way would simply be a casualty of war.

"Surely Gideon doesn't suspect you," Kim said to my aunt. "That's absurd."

She was right except for several inconvenient facts: Violet had a romantic history with Mario, she had applied the poison in question and stood to inherit a bundle of bucks if Killian's information was correct. For most lawmen, that would be enough to tighten the noose around her neck.

"What did Gideon say?" I asked cautiously. This was the kind of news I wasn't keen to hear, but I had to listen.

Violet lowered her eyes. "I don't know yet. Everything I learned came from Lin Baugh. I have a meeting in thirty minutes with Gideon to discuss the situation."

"Hold on," I said. "I'm going with you. Friend or not, he's still a cop, and you don't have an attorney yet. Not a criminal one anyway."

"I'll call Lionel," Kim said. "He can refer you to someone here."

Violet reached into her purse and found her lipstick. "Let's try not to overreact until I speak with Gideon." To my chagrin, I noticed that her choice of products was unfortunate. She skillfully applied Pink Dusk, Tom Ford's big bestseller, as if she hadn't a care in the world.

"Don't you have another shade?" I asked. "Remember Mario's late-night visitor. She used the same thing."

"Phooey," Violet said. "I'm not afraid of the truth, but you people can do a couple of things if you're willing."

"What?" Gemma asked. "Anything you want, Violet. Just ask."

"That goes double for me," Kim said. "I owe you so much."

"Circulate around the crowd and see how many smokers we have, especially E-smokers. I thought I saw Nona Adams lighting up or whatever they call it, and there may be others." Innocence was no defense against a mountain of motives, but Violet's composure didn't wilt. I shared my little contretemps with Sophia and that very illuminating chat with Carla. Both women had reasons to loathe the dearly departed and in Carla's case, financial and romantic betrayal applied. Killian Blaine added yet another part of the puzzle. In view of Mario's bizarre death, the value of his company probably declined. Competitors would be poised to scoop it up at a bargain price, with Killian leading the pack.

"I'm touched by your support," Violet said. "All of you. Friendship means a lot at times like this. Just so you know, I had nothing to do with Mario's murder. He was a lot of things—irritating, endearing and most of all a marketing genius. I'll miss him." My aunt wasn't the weepy type, but our reaction had obviously affected her. We linked arms and headed for our date with destiny.

* * *

The forty-person Traverse City Police force was housed in a no frills, non-descript cement structure that looked both sturdy and reliable much like our former police chief of Harbor Bay, Gideon Hall. I'd always considered him to be a fair and intelligent public servant who served his community well. As Violet and I entered his office I prayed that nothing would change that favorable opinion of him.

He looked like the same old Gideon—composed, exquisitely neat, and neutral. That's what bothered me. Every other time, he'd been openly friendly never neutral. I'd always believed that he nursed a secret passion for Violet, although Gideon had never betrayed that by word or deed. Now, he had shifted to a slightly adversarial stance, and that frightened me.

"Welcome, Ladies. Thanks for coming in."

Violet matched his grin with one of her own. "Frankly, I didn't think we had a choice. Benny said it was a command performance." She nodded toward his former deputy, who crouched in the background, ready to spring at us if we made a threatening move.

"We didn't bring an attorney," I said. "Do we need one?"

That made him chuckle. "Ah, yes. I recall now how familiar you are with detective fiction and television cops, Marky. I can advise you of your rights but you're not persons of interest at this time. This is merely an informal chat. Are you Violet's lawyer, now Marky?"

"Merely her witness, Chief."

I was troubled by part of his narrative. That "at this time" line was worrisome. Benny Soto stiffened like a hunting dog scenting prey giving

108

me renewed sympathy for poor woodland creatures under the gun barrel.

Violet leaned forward and placed both hands on his desk. "Okay, Gideon. Enough foreplay. I know Mario was poisoned by some substance, probably nicotine in the Ricci Rich conditioner that I applied. For the record, I had absolutely nothing to do with his murder, although I guess I was the unwitting instrument of his death."

Gideon sighed. "No doubt about it. Pure liquid nicotine killed him. Absorbed directly through his scalp and into his bloodstream. About how long did you leave it on?"

Violet thought about it. "Forty minutes or so. A bit longer than we'd planned, but the audience had so many questions that the segment ran over time."

"Why use that plastic cap?"

Violet dispensed with that immediately. "Routine procedure, Gideon. Ask any hair professional. Aids absorption and protects the stylist from dyes and other messes."

I remained silent and confined myself to analyzing every nuance of the conversation. Did he think that Violet used that plastic cap to protect herself from absorbing the poison? Gideon's face betrayed absolutely nothing, and Violet matched his every move. I felt like a spectator in an old western, watching worthy adversaries square off for a shootout. No one could predict the outcome. I didn't even try.

"You didn't notice anything out of the ordinary, I suppose."

Violet shook her head. "Not really. Mario thought the cream was a bit runny. You know, thin, but the color and consistency were fine otherwise. It covered his scalp without a problem."

She realized her gaff immediately. Since it caused Mario's death, there was indeed a problem. "Forgive me. That sounded insensitive. Mario was an old and valued friend and colleague. I'm still coming to terms with his death."

Gideon thumbed through some papers on his desk. "Seems like you were a bit more than his friend and colleague at one time. Is that a fair statement?"

"Many years ago, when we were both very young. That ended amicably, and we remained close friends."

He frowned. "I've been told that you took it hard. Told everyone around you that he'd broken your heart. Some things don't heal. Old sins cast long shadows, as the poet said."

I felt ready to burst. "Sounds like Sophia Lauren has been whispering in your ear. She's just a jealous, spoiled woman. Greedy too. She couldn't wait to get her talons on Mario's money. Just ask her why she spent the night before he died in his bed!"

"Marky! Be careful what you say." Violet was genuinely shocked. "We shouldn't implicate anyone else without proof."

Gideon gave me the side eye, and Benny openly snorted. "I'm told that Ms. Lauren replaced you in Mario's affections. Is that so, Violet?"

She nodded. "Yes. But that was almost twenty years ago. I'd hardly nurse a grudge that long before acting. We'd moved past any hard feelings ages ago."

"What about the disruption," I asked. "Did you find out who tampered with the Ricci Rich display? Perfect opportunity for someone to slip the poison in."

A muscle in Gideon's cheek moved. That spelled major annoyance in him and left me feeling sheepish. "Good point, Marky. We haven't identified the culprit yet, and unfortunately, there were no surveillance cameras in that part of the auditorium. The only fingerprints on the display jars were Mario's and your aunt's. Not unexpected, I suppose." His gaze sharpened as he continued. "Lin Baugh suggested it was a prank probably done by someone to agitate Mario. I'm told it wasn't difficult to rile him up."

Violet smiled. "That's true. He was somewhat volatile. Always losing his temper. It was temporary, though. Just a storm that quickly subsided. I suspect that advocacy group might have been responsible for that bit of mischief."

That made Gideon laugh out loud. "Ah, yes. The ladies of FACE. Guess they'd object to me calling them ladies. Women. Anyway, Benny already interviewed their leader, Nona Adams."

I swiveled around and watched Benny's reaction. "And how did that go?"

Benny was too insecure to admit defeat but, in any confrontation, I'd put my limited funds squarely on pugnacious Nona Adams. He cleared his throat and mumbled, "She denies any involvement. Had a slew of witnesses to her activities."

Nona was a seasoned player on the activist team, and I expected no less. If she poisoned that conditioner, she would have done so wearing gloves and without leaving any evidence. So far, the interview had been routine, but I steeled myself for what was to come. In most novels, the detective slowly and stealthily leads up to his main point before springing it on the unsuspecting prey. Violet probably read the same novels because she was ready when Gideon pounced.

"Mario's company was privately held, I understand. Worth a good deal."

My aunt nodded. Benny Soto went on high alert.

"Did you know you were one of his heirs along with Ms. Standish?"

"Not until recently when Mr. Blaine told us. Mario was superstitious. Never spoke of wills, heirs, or anything to do with death. A European thing, I think. He believed it brought bad luck."

A semi-smile from Gideon. "Seems he was right after all. You knew he was pressured to go public with his company. Handsome offer, so I've been told. Tempting."

Violet shook her head. "Not to Mario. Control meant everything to him. He obsessed over every little detail. That's why he insisted on modeling the Ricci Rich demonstration himself."

"I suppose you'll consider that offer now. Set you up for the rest of your life." Gideon nodded my way. "Nice legacy for your niece, too."

How I wished that feisty Killian Blaine were here to put Gideon in his place. Perhaps Violet was a suspect, after all, despite the Chief's bland assurances. He wasn't taping the interview or "chat," as he called it, but I was still wary. Benny Soto was surreptitiously taking notes in the back of the room. Who knew where that would lead? Good thing I'd switched on my iPhone the moment we'd settled in the office. Two can play that cat-and-mouse game, and we now had our own account of the proceedings.

"Ms. Standish was married to the deceased. Did they stay close afterwards? Friendly divorces are rare in my experience."

I knew that Gideon was divorced, and rumor had it that his ex-wife had cleaned him out. He never spoke of her, so most of what we heard was pure speculation. And why didn't he say Mario's name instead of calling him the deceased? It was dehumanizing, another devious cop game designed to throw Violet off her stride. In this instance, it was also a spectacular failure. My aunt was too wily to succumb to emotion. She folded her arms and said nothing.

"I asked you about Ms. Standish," Gideon said. It was obvious that his patience was wearing thin. That seemed like a victory and pleased me in an odd kind of way.

"I can't address that, Gideon. Ask Carla about it. She'll tell you anything you want to know. The beauty industry has very few secrets."

He withstood that rebuff without showing any emotion and immediately tried a different tact. "This next subject is rather personal, I'm afraid. Marky mentioned the guest in Mario's room. Was that you, Violet? Renewing old acquaintances or cementing your inheritance? We found traces of a lip color that looks an awful lot like yours."

I would have lost my composure, but Violet didn't turn a hair. "Sorry. I spent the evening in my suite. Alone." She grinned, "But just for the record, a sample of that shade was included in every attendee's guest bag. Sort of expands your suspect list, I fear."

I tried not to gloat, but the temptation was too much. "Can we leave now, Chief? My aunt has had a horrendous day and needs her rest."

As we rose, Violet added one final thought. "Something to consider, Gideon. Mario preferred young women who were awed by his position. The younger, the better. I'm afraid he considered me way past my sell-by date." She winked at him. "If he had an overnight guest, look for one of our younger participants."

Gideon wrote a note on his desk pad. "Thanks for the tip. Violet, if you haven't hired an attorney, I suggest you do so. You'll probably need one."

* * *

"Whew! That was quite an ordeal."

Violet's reaction surprised me. She'd been so self-possessed during that interrogation that I thought she took things in stride. Oh, wait. Gideon had called it an informal chat. Just another cop trick to lull a suspect into a sense of complacency. Either way, even as a witness, I was totally unnerved by the process.

"I suppose I should consult an attorney. What about this Killian Blaine? He seems up to the task."

"He doesn't practice criminal law, plus he may have a conflict of interest."

"Oh?" Violet gave me that piercing stare that I recognized from childhood. It had always stripped me bare and made me confess to any misdeed, either real or perceived.

"He acts awfully cozy with Sophia, and Carla practically drools all over him. He pretends that all clients get that type of treatment. What he calls personal attention. I just worry that he might be playing both sides of the street. Besides, isn't he a suspect himself?"

Violet raised an eyebrow. "How so?"

"Cui bono? Don't you see? His firm will make a tidy profit if he acquires Ricci Enterprises. I saw him arguing with Mario at the reception. Not a friendly conversation by any means. Lots of arm waving and raised voices."

"Hmm. Good to know. Guess I'd better keep my guard up then."

Sometimes, my aunt defines grace under pressure. It was admirable but also quite exasperating. I grasped her wrist to get her attention. "One thing more. Killian Blaine does that vaping thing. We saw him outside the building when we looked for Benny. He tried to hide it but couldn't. I call that downright suspicious."

Killian must use liquid nicotine to fuel his noxious habit, and he was shrewd enough to know just how dangerous the substance was. That elevated him to the top of my suspect list, but Violet was untroubled.

"Very interesting, dear. Keep an eye on him. That shouldn't be too much of a penance for you." Her saucy smile was particularly annoying. "Just to be sure, I will contact Mr. Blaine. One can never be too careful." With that, my aunt glided up the path to the hotel like a model strolling the catwalk.

No one would ever dream that she had been practically accused of murder.

* * *

Despite the murder, the conference rolled along without a hitch. People gossiped, of course, but they seemed curiously unaffected. Lin Baugh kept his emotions in check as he circulated among the various groups, projecting an air of good cheer and normalcy. If his smile was forced, one could hardly blame him. Kim did her best to assist, but Mario's death had taken a visible toll on her. Knowing how much this venture meant to her career, I totally understood. Naturally, there were the exceptions. Sophia Lauren had given a tearful account to a *USA TODAY* stringer about her devotion to her former lover and the thwarted prospects for them to reunite during the conference. Her skillfully applied makeup and artfully tousled hair also made great copy for television viewers. Even I had to admit that the woman was a superb actress. It was her script that infuriated me. Gemma's reaction was even more pronounced.

"Can you believe it?" she snarled. "That French phony practically accused Violet of murdering Mario. Can she say that? Aren't there laws against stuff like that?"

I shared her anger, but Sophia had been cagey enough to hint rather than openly accuse my aunt of any misdeed. That didn't keep me from confronting her when we met in the ladies' lounge. I wasn't expecting Sophia to flounce in while I freshened up, and I should have ignored her. Even though I value restraint, there are times when it just isn't enough.

"Nice photo of you in the paper," I said with a hearty dose of snark. "One would almost believe you were Mario's widow instead of the woman who dumped him."

Her eyes widened as she whirled around and faced me. "What do you mean? Mario and I reconnected at this meeting. We realized that our passion for each other had never died." She clutched her heart. "I had no reason to harm him. Not when his assets were going elsewhere. We planned to announce our engagement after his seminar."

She was lying. Proof positive that even a gifted actress can overplay her part. Sophia's version was strictly off, off-Broadway and it showed.

"That's unfortunate," I sneered. "You wasted all that effort in his bedroom the night before. Don't think Chief Hall doesn't know all about it. I told him so myself. And stop casting aspersions on my aunt if you know what's good for you."

Sophia lunged for me, but I was younger and more agile. I sped out the door at warp speed as she hurled several naughty French epithets my way.

* * *

I savored my petty triumph over the French strumpet. Davis women can give as good as they get when someone threatens us, and Sophia Lauren was now on notice. It probably wouldn't deter her, but defending my aunt made me feel less impotent. Fantasia had been sorely neglected during this drama, and I hastened to my room to free my princess from her prison. Fantasia never complained, but she had perfected what I termed her "Patrician Look," a wordless stare of utter disdain for thoughtless humans. I deserved her scorn but placated her by tossing several chicken treats her way and vigorously hugging her neck. The sunny day beckoned us, and I fastened her harness and sprinted out the door. As we rounded the corner outside the hotel, I noted a group smoking and vaping their little hearts out as they huddled around a nearby bench. One of them was none other than Nona Adams, who for once had abandoned her claque of admirers and stood alone. Having Fantasia by my side stiffened my resolve, so I girded my loins for battle and approached the irascible attorney.

"Enjoying your smoke?" I asked, summoning my sunniest smile.

My girlish high spirits didn't impress her, but when Fantasia nuzzled her hand, Nona reacted. "Such a lovely creature. Doesn't need any of your paint and creams to be beautiful, does she?"

I nodded in agreement. "Too bad about Mario, huh?"

She shrugged. "What does the Bible say about reaping what you sow? Looks like he got what he deserved. Someone finally stood up to that cretin."

"That's somewhat harsh, wouldn't you say? Mario was many things, but he had friends who loved him. My aunt, for one."

Nona blew out a vapor cloud. "Ah, yes. His little helper. Heard she'll do fine from his estate if they don't charge her with murder, that is."

I tensed up and was rendered temporarily speechless. "You're wrong. She's innocent. Someone else tampered with that conditioner." I leaned closer to her. "Maybe it was you. I'll bet you have a supply of liquid nicotine to feed your vile habit."

My words didn't dent Nona Adams. Not one bit. She laughed and shook her head. "Nope. I had my own plans for him, but they didn't include murder." Her eyes narrowed as her expression turned sly. "Tell your aunt I know she's not the one."

"How do you know that? Please tell me." Something, deep inside me turned my insides to ice. Nona was telling me something important, but would she reveal the truth?

Fantasia licked Nona's hand, evoking a more sincere reaction than I ever could.

"I saw the killer," Nona said.

"Tell me or tell Gideon Hall. Please. Innocent people might be hurt otherwise. You could be in danger, too."

Nona extinguished her e-cigarette and, with it, any hopes I had of hearing the truth. "Maybe I will, but first I'd need concessions."

"Concessions?" I deliberately lowered my voice. Otherwise, I might have screeched at this grinning excuse for a woman. "What kind of concessions? Money, fame? Make me understand."

Nona shrugged. "I'm used to negotiating tricky situations. After all, I'm an attorney."

"Did you send those poems?" I asked. I was desperate to keep her talking, hoping to glean even a small clue.

She looked quizzically at me. "Poems? I have no idea what you're talking about. Poetry means something special to me. Food of the gods, as they say. Mario Ricci was a philistine who wouldn't understand anything without a dollar sign. Why waste my time." Nona gathered her things and left me with one parting shot. "Oh yeah. Tell your aunt I really love her painting."

* * *

That encounter left me puzzled and perplexed. Nona Adams knew something that might clear Violet of suspicion. On the other hand, she may just have been messing with me. I'd recognized the contempt in Nona's eyes every time she glanced my way. Her final comment made me wonder if she had stolen my aunt's painting. That made no sense and merely jumbled my thought process. To Fantasia's delight, I lost my way and extended our walk well beyond our usual stopping point. That's where I stumbled into Killian Blaine. Literally.

"Whoa," he said, catching me when I tripped. "Women usually fall for me without the drama. Not that I'm complaining, you understand."

"Very droll. I had something on my mind and wasn't watching. Excuse me."

"Don't leave," he said. "I need to take a breather anyway."

I'd never seen Killian in casual clothes before, and I must say it was a sight worth seeing. Based on the way his outfit clung to him he had obviously been jogging for some time.

I described my frustrating conversation with Nona and Gideon Hall's low-key attempt to browbeat my aunt. As I finished, a look of horror and incredulity radiated from his eyes. Killian disapproved of my efforts in the strongest terms, and he made no attempt to hide it.

"I don't believe it. You let the cops interview her without having an attorney present? Not smart, Marky. I warned you and Violet about that before."

He ignored all my excuses and lectured me once again that in a homicide investigation, the authorities were not your friends. "Gideon probably has enough circumstantial evidence right now to charge your aunt with murder. You're lucky that he showed restraint."

I blurted out Nona Allen's comments, but Killian was not impressed. "Sounds like she saw someone messing with the *Ricci Rich* display. Might be significant, might not. Until she makes an official statement, it doesn't matter."

"I told her to be careful, not that she took me seriously. Nona treats me like I'm some sort of kewpie doll without a brain in my head."

"Nothing wrong with that. Personally, I like playing with dolls."

That flippant remark made my blood boil. "See here. I graduated from the Art Institute of Chicago. I own a successful business. Don't sell me short."

He raised his hands in a no harm, no foul gesture. "Sorry. How can I make amends?"

This was no time to hold a grudge, and Violet needed all the help she could get. "Okay. Tell me this. Do you still represent Carla and Sophia, and are you still trying to acquire Ricci Enterprises?"

His features hardened into a guarded, lawyerly look of caution. "What difference does that make? You know I won't disclose information about my clients."

"I think one or both had an excellent reason to eliminate Mario. Think about those threatening poems someone sent. Just an effort to spook him that failed. Poetry was not his thing, and he never took the warnings seriously." I glared at him. "And don't give me the trite line about a woman scorned. That fits Carla to a tee, but Sophia was the one who used Mario. I wouldn't put anything past that woman if she could turn a profit."

Killian looked confused. "What in the world are you talking about? Threatening poems?"

I explained about John Donne, Grey, and the final sonnet that I hadn't seen. "I think it's the key to the murder. Unfortunately, Mario ripped the thing up before even Violet could read it. No one knows what happened to the shreds of paper. Just my luck."

His response told me that Killian dismissed my theory. "It was probably just a prank. One of Mario's pals from the conference trying to get under his skin. Don't waste your time chasing after something that obscure. Even better, stay out of the whole mess. You're not a cop, and you could get hurt."

As we walked back to the hotel, I formulated a plan. Killian agreed to sound out Gideon on the murder and to counsel my aunt before any further encounters with the police. I decided to invite Carla to a girls' night out with Kim and Violet

. Carla was an admirable woman who had survived Mario's treachery and thrived. That didn't mean she forgave him, especially if she knew about her inheritance. Money was always a motivator, and Carla desperately needed an infusion of cash to save her business. Sophia was the avaricious type who craved money even if she didn't particularly need it. Time doesn't heal all wounds, particularly when they involve love and betrayal. In all the classic detective novels the character of the victim held the key to his murder. I believed that was true in this instance as well. Violet saw only the loveable side of her friend's character even though she should have known better. Mario's willfulness, ego, and callous treatment of women fueled someone's thirst for revenge. Perhaps he tried to atone for his behavior by willing his assets to two of his victims. Too little too late, as the saying went. Old sins cast long shadows.

* * *

After returning Fantasia to our room, I galloped over to the auditorium in time to catch a session on "Cosmetic Artistry for the Future." It was a popular topic that filled most of the available seats. Fortunately, I managed to snag a seat in the front row next to Gemma. Every savvy school child avoids the front row since it makes one visible and more likely to be called on by the instructor. Gemma was always fearless, and she ignored or forgot that stricture. I had no choice but to hope for the best. The presenter was none other than Sophia Laurent and she came equipped with a variety of new products featured by her company. Sophia herself was exquisitely garbed in a stunning black silk sheath that showed a peek of her abundant cleavage. With that outfit, she had no need to use additional visual aids. The glazed eyes of every male in the audience were glued to her chest. The distaff side was business oriented, more interested in the techniques and tools she used to transform her models. Go figure.

She was quite the showman. I admired that and enjoyed her presentation up until the point where she chose models from the audience. Gemma sprang up to volunteer, but I shrank into my seat, praying for a cloak of invisibility to shield me. When she called my name, I resigned myself to my fate. Sophia pasted a phony smile on her face and proceeded to apply a full range of cosmetics to our complexions. As she bent over, she hissed, "Stop asking Killian about me if you know what's good for you. That goes for your lovely aunt as well. Mario told me all about her that last night. Who knows what the police would think?"

I was dumbfounded, but Gemma leapt into the breach. "Buzz off, bimbo. Sounds like you're hiding something."

Sophia never lost her poise. She displayed her handiwork to the audience and fielded questions like the professional that she was. I dreaded the outcome but to my surprise both Gemma and I were transformed into glamorous versions of our former selves. Lin Baugh snapped publicity photos and we received a rousing hand of applause from the audience.

There were exceptions, of course. Nona Adams and her crew sneered at the results. Nona leapt to her feet and immediately launched a fiery denunciation of all things artificial. The boos and catcalls from the crowd did nothing to diminish her fervor. At the end of her diatribe FACE members marched out of the room with their unadorned faces proudly displayed and their heads held high.

"Thanks for being a good sport," Lin said. "Sophia does a lot of business in this area. Sometimes, I must swallow my pride and cater to her."

"Does that go for the FACE group, too? Nona was determined to make a scene."

Lin grimaced. "They won't be welcome at any future events. I can guarantee that."

"She says she saw someone fooling with Mario's display the night before he died. I'm not sure that I believe her, though. The woman is a born troublemaker."

Lin shrugged. "Let Gideon handle that. She might know something important." He ran his fingers through his hair. "Frankly, I'll be glad when this event ends. The national tabloids are buzzing around, trying to sniff out a story, and my bosses are less than thrilled about that. We sell luxury and serenity here, not murder and mayhem."

I commiserated with Lin as the crowd thinned and we were joined by Carla Standish. Her transformation since Mario's death had been truly remarkable. No longer the wan castoff spouse, Carla looked and spoke with the confidence born of success. She readily agreed to join our female fun fest that evening. Lin boosted our spirits by graciously offering to send a complimentary bottle of champagne.

"Not Krug, I suppose." That marvelous brew had the faint tinge of death attached to it since Mario's demise. Swilling it would appear insensitive.

Lin immediately understood. "We have some other fine brands in stock. I know just the thing. *Veuve Clicquot la Grande Dame* is perfect for a group of sophisticated ladies. I'll see to it."

He trotted off with spirits seemingly restored by his task.

"We have much to celebrate," Carla said. "Word already spread about our inheritance so no more worries about creditors for me. My company can remain a boutique brand." She clasped her hands together in what could only be described as ecstasy. "By the way, you handled Sophia just right. She's fuming about losing out on Mario's company. The woman is pure evil. A succubus, for sure. I even saw her buzzing around that awful FACE woman this morning. What do you suppose that was about?"

"Nona loves to stir the pot. She's hinting that she knows who sabotaged the Ricci Rich demo. I didn't get any details. No need to encourage her antics." For once, I restrained myself. Carla was a potential suspect, no matter how much I enjoyed her products. Better not to speculate about Nona or share any clues. I shook my head and immediately changed the subject. We chatted about the next seminar on using injectables and agreed to meet in Violet's room at eight o'clock.

Chapter Eight

I played hooky and took a much-needed nap. Fantasia curled up next to me, making me feel cosseted and safe. As I drifted into a haze of REM sleep, the form of a certain attorney popped into my dream. It was nothing romantic. Far from it. Killian Blaine starred as a sinister figure who uttered vile threats and menaced me. I awakened suddenly, feeling chilled and out of sorts. Someone was pounding relentlessly on my door, insisting on gaining admittance. Only one person would act that boldly. I thrust open the door and growled at Gemma.

"Thanks for disturbing my sleep. The entire hotel must have heard you."

Gemma shrugged. "Big deal. Don't be such a baby. Besides, you barely have time to get dressed for our ladies' night. Hop to it, princess."

I noted that Gemma had upped her personal glam factor by ten. Her exuberant red curls had been tamed by a healthy dose of pomade, and in place of her usual Goth garb, she wore a slinky slip dress in green velvet.

"Wow! If only Benny could see you now. That sex appeal will be wasted on us chickens."

"Huh. He's busy keeping everyone safe. Gideon has him patrolling the hallways."

That made me wonder. Was Chief Hall expecting trouble or merely being cautious? Perhaps it was merely a clever ruse to rid himself of Benny. I'm no seer, and I don't believe in ESP. Not totally. But a pall hung over the Beauty Expo, something that I couldn't or wouldn't explain to Gemma. I decided to focus on the positive, and in this case, it was the promise of clever chatter, and the *Veuve Clicquot la Grande Dame* that Lin Baugh mentioned. Forget murder, protests, and acrimony. Tonight was a time to party. I swept my hair into a chic top knot and donned a snazzy silk pantsuit straight from Paris. It came courtesy of Violet, of course, but I'd never worn it before. Formal occasions were scarce in Harbor Bay. Perhaps tonight was a rebirth, a time to discard my adolescent insecurities and emerge fully formed. On the other hand, it was probably just another evening out.

When we arrived at Violet's suite, a festive atmosphere prevailed. Kim was a vision of elegance in a sapphire cocktail dress with a touch of diamonds. A lovely broach with a matching ring complimented the diamond studs that graced her ears.

"Holy cow," Gemma said. "What'd Lionel do—rob a bank?"

Kim blushed and waved her off. "Nothing that dramatic. I seldom wear anything fancy anymore. Tonight seemed like the perfect occasion."

"Leave her alone," Violet teased. "She's gorgeous." My aunt was no slouch herself. She had chosen head-to-toe Chanel for her ensemble, and it suited her perfectly. Violet had a saying—one can never go wrong wearing Chanel. No argument there if one could afford to pay the freight.

One of our party was missing. By eight-thirty, Carla had yet to appear, and we were growing alarmed. That Spidey sense of gloom once again descended upon me. I exchanged glances with Violet, hoping to calm my fears. True to his promise, Lin delivered a magnum of champagne to complement our astounding appetizers. I adore caviar, although it is well beyond my budget. On this special evening, nothing was out of reach. Crab, lobster, and exquisite Scottish smoked salmon were on offer to accompany the morel mushroom soup for which the Traverse City area was famous. Dessert was more modest but no less delectable. Small lemon meringue tarts provided just the right sweet taste.

"What are we waiting for?" Gemma asked. "Let's dig in." My partner was practically drooling as she surveyed the tempting spread.

"Carla's not here yet," Kim fretted. "I hope nothing's wrong."

I shivered, not from the temperature but from my own fears. Fortunately, before we reached panic mode, our errant guest arrived full of apologies.

"Forgive me, ladies," Carla said. "I was on a trans-Atlantic call and could not get free."

"Good news, I trust," Violet said.

Carla's beaming face said it all. "You bet! Suddenly, suppliers can't get enough of my products. It's a miracle!"

No one mentioned that the miracle in question was a legacy of Mario's murder. Why spoil a festive evening with dreary details?

I noticed that the fabric of Carla's powder blue coat dress was marred by a smudge of dirt or some other dark substance. Kim saw it, too, and immediately dabbed sparkling water on the stain.

That flustered Carla. She looked down at the hem of her dress and sighed. "Just my luck. I must have brushed up against some of the planters in the lobby."

Kim patted her arm. "No worries. They have an on-site dry cleaner here. Tomorrow, it will all vanish. Poof!" She pointed to the champagne. "Come on, ladies. Let's toast to our future successes."

Violet popped the cork and poured each of us a flute of the heavenly wine. After several toasts and generous helpings of appetizers, our spirits were restored. Violet teased Gemma and me about our star turn as Sophia's models. "Very public-spirited of you two. She couldn't have found better representatives."

I stayed silent although my thoughts about Sophia verged on the obscene. Gemma felt no such restraints. "I detest that woman," she said. "Do you know she threatened us? Brought you into it, too, Violet. Wouldn't surprise me if she was on someone's hit list."

I shared my conversation with Killian and my suspicions about Nona Adams. Violet cautioned me about playing detective, but Gemma couldn't wait to join in.

"I'm part of the team too. Benny told me that hair conditioner had twice the lethal amount of pure nicotine in it. Lots of people around here vape, and that means they probably use liquid nicotine or know where to get it."

"Okay," Kim said, "who are our suspects?"

We compiled a list that included Killian Blaine, Nona Adams, and, despite Gemma's protests, even Benny Soto. I reluctantly excluded Sophia since she loathed any type of smoking and was quite vocal about it.

"That doesn't mean she didn't order nicotine. Anyone can do that." Carla narrowed her eyes and spit out Sophia's name. "Put nothing past that hussy."

By ten p.m., we had emptied that magnum and devoured most of the hors d' oeuvres. Before we left, Violet cautioned us one more time. "Please. I beg you. Stop snooping and speculating. Contact Gideon with any information, even if it's only a hunch. It may save someone's life. Even yours."

* * *

As usual, Violet was right on target. My cell phone buzzed at precisely four o'clock that next morning, rousting both Fantasia and me from a sound sleep. I expected to hear Gemma's dulcet tones, but I was wrong. Killian Blaine's deep baritone pierced the fog surrounding me and called my name.

"Get dressed, Marky. There's been an incident."

Sleep deprivation makes me cranky. "What kind of incident? Do you know what time it is?"

He wasn't penitent. In fact, he doubled down on attitude. "Forget that. There's been another murder. Stay there. I'm coming up."

Murder! Every nerve ending in my body wailed in protest. I thought of Violet and the other guests at our party. Had one of them fallen victim to this maniac? Killian hung up before I could ask the victim's name. That left me several minutes to splash water on my face, tame my tousled hair, and grab running clothes. Fantasia raised her head in mute protest of the disturbance. I tried to dial Violet's number, but my fumbling fingers wouldn't cooperate. I visualized Violet or Gemma, splayed across an unforgiving landscape of blood and guts. We'd left our party well before midnight, plenty of time for tragedy to strike. I sat on the edge of the bed, feeling too unsteady to rise. Violet's final words echoed in my brain: stop snooping or speculating. Had one of our merry band violated that edict?

When Killian rapped on the door, I flung it open without taking the precautions any rational being facing a potential murderer should have taken. His face was ashen, his mood somber. Somehow on him that looked good. The ice on those spectacular blue eyes had melted and for the first time he seemed almost human. He stepped inside and drew me to him.

"Tell me," I begged. "Who was killed? Not my aunt. Please say it wasn't Violet or Gemma." I loathe shows of emotion, particularly tears. They're stereotypical and reek of weakness and instability. Under these circumstances, however, I just didn't care. Let Killian consider me a weak vessel or a typical female. Murder left no time for posturing.

"Calm down, Marky. Violet and Gemma are fine. Unfortunately, Nona Adams was murdered sometime late last evening. Looks like blunt-force trauma. Someone bashed her head with one of those heavy wooden placards she paraded around with." He grimaced. "Not a pretty sight, I can assure you."

"You saw her?" It suddenly occurred to me that my suite was isolated, and I was face to face with a potential killer. Not my smartest move. I prayed it wasn't my final act. I backed up and stood next to Fantasia. If she sensed danger, it wasn't apparent. My stalwart protector stood there wagging her tail at Killian.

"Yeah. I went out for a drive and stopped by the auditorium, looking for Sophia. Something had upset her, and I thought I could comfort her."

Comfort? Huh! That kind of solace had another name—booty call. "You certainly jump every time Sophia beckons. Are you two an item?"

In retrospect I realized that it was neither the time nor place to delve into Killian's love life. My behavior was foolish and immature. Chalk it up to delayed shock. Anything but jealousy.

He squeezed his eyes shut as if to blot out an unbearable sight. "She was on the floor near the podium. I almost tripped over her body."

"Does Gideon know? I thought Benny Soto was patrolling the hallways to protect everyone." Come to think of it, Benny had a nasty temper that flared whenever he was challenged by a woman. Had he mixed things up with Nona and lost control? For Gemma's sake, I hoped that wasn't true.

"I warned her, but she wouldn't listen. Brushed me off like a piece of lint." I visualized Nona's face when I begged her to contact Gideon. She had zero respect for my advice and made that abundantly clear. Hubris can have

126

lethal consequences. In Nona's case, that proved to be true.

Killian put his arm around me. "Hey. You're trembling. You need to tell Gideon anything you know about this. If Nona confronted the killer, you could be in danger, too."

I insisted on phoning Violet and Gemma before leaving and giving Fantasia an immediate comfort break. Violet responded as she always did in calm, measured tones. "Stay where you are," she said. "I'll handle Fantasia and go with you to see Gideon."

Killian wasn't thrilled, but he wisely kept his own counsel while I contacted Gemma. Predictably, my volatile partner exploded once she awakened.

"What? Are you kidding me? Nona Adams dead? I can think of a hundred reasons to off that pest. The suspect list is endless." She paused. "Matter of fact, I thought of clobbering her a couple of times myself." Gemma insisted on getting dressed and joining our little party. I presumed that she was alone in bed since no sound was heard from Benny Soto.

Before Killian made any further protests, Violet arrived looking unflappable and perfectly composed. How she did it, I'll never understand. My hair was askew, and mascara tracks ringed my eyes. That surely banished any romantic notions Killian may have felt for me. When Gemma appeared, I felt less conspicuous. She must have dropped into bed without removing her makeup or hair pomade. My dear friend looked like forty miles of rough road.

My observations were frivolous, but they helped minimize the inner panic generated by Nona's murder. She was obnoxious and no great loss to the world. Still, as the saying went, *"...any man's death diminishes me."* That stray thought jolted me back to reality. It was yet another fragment from poet John Donne. Nona had rejected any link between the sonnets and Mario's death. I still believed they were the key to finding the killer.

* * *

"Do Kim and Carla know?" Gemma asked.

We shrugged and prepared to find the authorities. I recalled that Carla was late to our gathering and arrived with that dark spot staining her blue ensemble. It wasn't something I planned to tell Gideon. Not before Carla had a chance to explain. As an abused ex-spouse who now received a gigantic financial payoff, Carla had every reason to kill Mario. She was also a cosmetics expert who would know just how to poison that *Ricci Rich* conditioner. According to Violet, Carla had developed the original formula for that miracle product. How ironic if that same brew had ultimately led to Mario's death. Nona planned to gain concessions from the killer. In most states, those "concessions" were labeled by a less flattering term—blackmail.

With a maneuver that would do credit to a border collie, Killian herded us out the door and into the elevator. The hotel was deserted at that hour as most sensible beings were still snug in their beds. We approached the main conference room where Lin Baugh stood guard by the police tape. His appearance was impeccable, as always, but his air of defeat touched my heart. No reasonable person could blame him, and yet I knew that his corporate masters would do so. A scapegoat was needed, and Lin fit the bill perfectly.

"We need to see the Chief," Killian told him. "Marky has some information he'll want to know."

Lin made no move to stop us. I doubted that he had the energy to do so. "He's in there with the coroner's people," Lin said. "I promised him I'd head off that FACE contingent if they came this way. Or try at least."

Gemma grabbed Fantasia's lead and offered to take her for a walk. "Not alone, you won't," Violet said. "It's dark outside, and there's a killer roaming about. Come on. We'll both go." I handed them my flashlight as they headed off. I knew that Violet always packed Mace in her jacket pocket, so I felt confident they would stay safe. Fantasia would see to that.

"Remember," I said. "Trust no one. Come right back as soon as possible."

* * *

Trust no one. What a sad commentary on our situation. Most of the suspects were decent people, the kind of friends and neighbors we all appreciated. Yet one of them had killed not once but twice. Mario's murder had been carefully planned. Nona's was spur of the moment, a quick response to an unanticipated shock or a reaction to Nona's clumsy attempt at blackmail.

Although we entered the area cautiously, we were immediately confronted by Benny Soto. He stepped in front of Killian and blocked our path.

"Get out," said he. "No civilians. This is a crime scene."

Benny aroused the beast in me, and I couldn't resist taunting him. "Thank heaven you're patrolling the corridors, Benny. I feel so much safer. You've done a bang-up job protecting us."

Anger suffused his face, and he jabbed an accusing finger my way. "Get out, Marky. Leave while you still can, before I arrest the two of you for impeding a murder investigation."

Killian never raised his voice, but his tone conveyed enough menace to deflate Benny. "We have vital information for the Chief. I suggest you back off and let us deliver it. While you're at it, Deputy, you might check the Michigan statues on impeding an investigation. Very instructive."

Benny's eyes bulged and he fingered the handcuffs at his side. Before he exploded, we were joined by Gideon Hall, who quickly assessed the situation and defused it. "Marky, Killian, you have some information for me?" He turned to Benny. "Thank you, deputy. I believe the coroner could use some help removing the body." Benny was intelligent enough to grasp this face-saving opportunity and make a hasty exit.

Shadows underlined Gideon's eyes, and lines appeared around his mouth. Otherwise, his demeanor was unchanged from the calm, methodical officer I had grown to admire. "I didn't know Ms. Adams," he said, "although I understand she was a handful. What can you tell me about this?"

I swallowed twice before speaking to avoid giving a hysterical rant rather than a coherent recitation of facts.

"Nona spoke with me this afternoon. She claimed that she'd seen someone tampering with the *Ricci Rich* display before Mario's demonstration." Seeing the puzzled look on his face, I explained. "*Ricci Rich* was Mario's miracle product, an innovation that would revolutionize the hair industry."

"Or so he said." Killian couldn't resist that gibe at his former antagonist, a man who had frustrated him at every turn.

"Did she identify this person?" Gideon asked.

I wasn't sure that he believed me. That dented my credibility and my amor proprio. I wasn't some thrill seeker or fantasist. My record spoke for itself, at least I thought it did.

"She wouldn't say. I begged her to contact you. Told her it was dangerous to engage a murderer, but she scoffed at me. Can you believe it? Talk about hubris. Nona touted her legal credentials and said she was used to negotiating. Said she would demand concessions of some sort from whoever this person was."

Gideon sighed. "Everyone wants to play detective even If it kills them. Let that be a lesson to you, Ms. Davis. We can presume that this was an arranged meeting. I'll check her cell phone to see if we can identify any contacts."

I took a chance and raised the sonnet angle once more. "I still think the killer sent those threatening poems to Mario. Nona discounted it, but I think it's the solution. No one seems to know where the final one went. I don't suppose you found it, Gideon."

He was weary, and I regretted adding to that condition. "Not now, Marky. I have a full plate just interviewing those FACE people, let alone anyone in the vicinity when Nona died. If you have any more thoughts, save them for later." His eyes narrowed as he issued a warning. "No more snooping. I'm trying to save your life, young lady. Killian, if you have any control over her, use it." He stalked off toward the area that had been cordoned off by the forensic team. I'm no ghoul, and I respect the dead, but with a little effort, I was able to glimpse Nona's corpse before they zipped up the body bag. In death, as in life, Nona Adams was rather a mess. Her stringy hair stuck out in tufts matted with gore from her ruined skull. One blue eye was open, and it stared balefully at me as if to affix blame for her demise. Her killer had inflicted one final indignity on Nona. She, who abhorred any cosmetic touches, had her lips painted with that ubiquitous pale shade, dusty pink.

Killian caught me looking and hustled me out the door. "You heard Gideon. This is no time to play detective. I don't care about your previous triumphs. For once in your life, Marketta Davis, listen to reason."

"Her lips. Did you notice her lips?"

"What?" He glared at me as if I were unhinged.

"The killer put lipstick on her. That pink Tom Ford shade. It's ubiquitous."

Killian looked puzzled. "Big deal. Don't bother Gideon with that. Nona probably was trying to up her game. Maybe she was meeting a guy."

Hard to believe that a smart man could be so dense. Any woman would spot the inconsistency immediately. I very much doubted that Nona had ever worn lipstick. It conflicted with every belief she espoused. Far more likely the killer had applied that touch. It was a contemptuous gesture that spoke volumes about his or her personality.

Killian held out his hand. "Come on. Time to get dressed and ready for the day. Breakfast will be ready soon, and I'm starving."

My appetite vanished when I saw that corpse. Visions of Nona's sightless eye would probably haunt me for quite a while. The woman was someone I loathed, and she would not go gentle into that good night as the poet suggested. Poetry again. Nona scoffed at me when I mentioned those sonnets. She was certainly no fan of sentiment or schmaltz. I shuddered, visualizing how she had marched confidently toward her death, never fearing for one moment that she might not survive. She'd seen the killer poison the *Ricci Rich* but didn't fear whoever it was. What concessions could she possibly hope to extract, and did that reveal that the murderer was someone inoffensive? Two names leapt to mind—Carla and Kim. Sophia was ruthless enough to eliminate any threat to her survival, but Nona would be on alert around that French floozy. Another name popped into my head. One that I tried to ignore. Killian Blaine. Nona had hinted that the two had been more than mere strangers. She would have enjoyed matching wits with another attorney and flaunting her superior negotiating skills. She openly bragged about her ability to outwit opponents. But Killian was a strong male who could easily have overwhelmed Nona in a physical confrontation. Sometimes, brawn triumphed over brains.

He was staring at me. Waiting for my reaction.

"Go on ahead," I told Killian. "I'll catch you later."

"Okay. I told Sophia I'd ring her up anyway. Can't neglect my clients, you know." Killian's voice had a tinge of sarcasm and more than a measure of conceit.

I exercised forbearance and said nothing. After all, a grisly murder was far more important than the antics of a philanderer with a law degree.

I noticed that Violet and Gemma had returned unharmed from walking Fantasia, and I badly needed their company. They would understand the points that Killian dismissed and could help me to evaluate the evidence. We agreed to freshen up and reconnoiter in Violet's suite.

"What about Kim and Carla?" Gemma asked. "Should we call them too?"

Violet and I locked eyes. It was easy to communicate with my aunt without saying a word. "We'll get them later," Violet said. "Meanwhile, I'll call room service and order some breakfast for us."

Gemma rubbed her tummy. "Fine with me. Get coffee, too. Plenty of coffee."

I scurried up to my room before the lobby crowd thickened. Stragglers had gradually emerged, and conversation was already buzzing about the appearance of still more police tape. I wanted to avoid any awkward questions particularly from members of the fourth estate who might be lurking in the shadows.

A bracing shower helped to restore some sanity to my mind although had the option presented itself, I would have happily curled up in bed and snagged another hour of sleep. I chose a black pantsuit in partial tribute to the funereal atmosphere that was certain to prevail at the conference. Through the artful application of cosmetics, I emerged looking almost normal despite the grim start to the day. I presumed that the conference would limp on, even after the horrific loss of yet another participant. Nona wasn't part of the Expo crowd, not in the ways that mattered. While most would virtue signal by voicing pious platitudes, they would hardly mourn her loss. Nona had her supporters, of course. Lord only knew what the FACE contingent would do when they learned of their leader's demise. A full-scale riot was not beyond the pale.

When Gemma appeared at Violet's door, I was pleased to note that she had also made a remarkable recovery. She looked far more familiar in her typical Goth garb than in the finery of the previous evening. I detected a pronounced glow on her face which told me that she had also connected with Benny Soto in one of several ways.

True to type, Violet had assembled a tasty array of breakfast treats. Despite my protests that I couldn't eat a bite, I loaded my plate with eggs, wheat toast, and salmon and plunged right in. Food was life-affirming. At least, that's what I told myself as I downed my meal and ingested an alarming number of calories.

Gemma had no reservations about stuffing her face with carbs. Her first-rate metabolism allowed her to ingest a massive amount of food without gaining a pound. That was one of her least endearing traits, one that I openly envied. A decade after high school, she maintained the same svelte size six figure that she had as a teenager.

"Okay," she said while chewing a mouthful of eggs, "Spill. What did you find out about Nona?"

I shrugged. "Nothing much. Looks like death by blunt instrument. One of those sharp posters she insisted on carrying or maybe a club. Talk about hoist on your own petard!"

My aunt frowned at me. "No levity, Marky. A woman lost her life last night. Not a very nice person and a born troublemaker, but still human."

"Huh!" Gemma scoffed. "Barely." When my partner nursed a grudge, she held it with an iron grip. "Reap what you sow, I say. That woman looked for trouble and got more than she bargained for. Served her right."

Gemma made a valid point. Nona threatened to pressure Mario's killer for some concession known only to her. She made no secret of that. It was a foolish act for which she paid the ultimate price.

"There's no doubt that she saw something. Knew something. I warned her to contact Gideon, but she wouldn't back down." In my heart of hearts, I didn't mourn for Nona, but I was curious about her connection with Killian. Surely, it was nothing romantic. I closed my eyes, trying unsuccessfully to visualize the two of them in a passionate embrace. On second thought, perhaps it was some business matter.

Violet mulled that over. "So, it was someone she knew or at least didn't fear. Maybe a woman?"

We exchanged glances and said the name that immediately sprang to mind—Carla Standish. Who else had more motive, both financial and personal, to dispatch Mario? If Nona posed a threat, she, too, might have become a liability. Carla was a gentle soul and an unlikely killer, but, faced with threats to her own survival, even if she might have turned violent.

"These murders were different," Violet noted. "Mario's was carefully planned and flawlessly executed. Looks to me as if Nona's was a sudden explosion of anger. Even the weapon was one of chance. The killer didn't bring it to their meeting. I don't suppose Gideon found any fingerprints on that poster."

Gemma had a sly smile on her face. That told me that Benny had spilled some secrets.

"Okay," I said, hands on hips. "What did you find out?"

"Not much. Just that the placard was not the murder weapon. No prints or blood found anywhere."

"What!" Violet and I reacted immediately.

Gemma was a drama queen who enjoyed being the center of attention. She paused before sharing her news. "Nope. Gideon thinks it was something heavy and metal. Probably a wrench or hammer. No sign of it, of course. No killer is stupid enough to leave it in plain sight."

Speculation was useless, of course, but it was satisfying. We debated how much effort it would take to inflict a mortal blow. Could an average woman be the culprit, or would it require a man's strength? Nona was tall and wiry. She would have fought vigorously to defend herself.

"What if the killer took her by surprise?" Violet asked. "Nona was arrogant. Confident that she was the smartest person in the room. That made her vulnerable to a sudden attack."

"Maybe." Carla and Sophia were our primary female suspects. It seemed unlikely that either one carried a wrench on her person. I laughed, picturing Sophia with a weapon stuffed in her Bottega bag. How shameful to spoil the lines of that exquisite Italian leather.

Carla left our soiree at the same time the rest of us did, but she arrived thirty minutes later. That stain. I couldn't forget the dark stain on her powder blue sleeve.

"What's the word from Benny's end?" I asked. "Any pillow talk worth discussing." I saw the glint of mischief in Gemma's eyes and stopped her. "About the murders. Nothing salacious if you please."

"Spoilsport. Okay. Gideon's getting lots of pressure from the city bigwigs, and the crowd here is getting restless. They want to leave pronto, and you can hardly blame them. For all we know, the killer may be stalking another victim."

"Poor Lin," Violet said. "He and Kim worked so hard to make this a success."

Gemma nodded. "I bet they dump him when it's all over. Wash their hands of him even though it's not his fault. At least Kim has Lionel to lean on, not that I envy that."

Leaning on crotchety Lionel Stevens was an unappealing prospect, but his wealth and legal prowess might insulate Kim from any blowback. I wondered about the fate of *Ricci Rich*. How many customers would slather it over their heads now?

Violet had a different take on the situation. "Just think. People tend to have short memories. Years ago, when they had those Tylenol poisonings, the product had a temporary dip but recovered nicely. *Ricci Rich* could do the same. It's really a marvelous cream, and vanity triumphs over other considerations."

We agreed that a name change was in order. Carla had already suggested folding the conditioner into her *Hair Deluxe* product line. That seemed like a workable plan to me, especially since it had originally been her brainchild.

"Guess you two are business partners now," Gemma said as she buttered a muffin. "Unless you plan to sell the thing to Marky's guy. He's cozy with that Sophia, and she really wants Mario's stuff."

I knew very little about Sophia Laurent, other than the tidbits Violet had provided. It was easier to picture her as an assassin than upright Carla Standish, although I acknowledged my bias. Women who savaged other women made my skin crawl, and Sophia was as poisonous as a viper. Honesty compelled me to admit that I also felt intimidated by Sophia's beauty and aggressive use of sex appeal to control men. That was a skill set I'd never acquired and seemed unlikely to in the future.

"Maybe you could worm some information out of her," I told Violet. "She respects you. Maybe even fears you."

My aunt flashed one of her innocent looks my way. I wasn't deceived, and neither was Gemma. "I suppose I could contact Sophia about that stolen painting. She deserves restitution, of course."

"Okay, boss," Gemma said, saluting. "What's my assignment?"

"The FACE crowd seemed to accept you. Maybe Nona told one of them what she saw the night Mario's things were poisoned."

I'd watched Gemma, a natural grifter, worm information out of many unwary people. Her talent for duplicity astounded me and gave me pause.

"What about you?" Gemma asked. "You can't get away with doing nothing."

"Me?" I beamed my most innocent smile her way. "I'll be studying poetry."

* * *

Sometimes I can be stubborn. At least, that's what I've been told. My defense is simple but elegant: I am seldom obdurate, but when the occasion demands, I can be fiercely tenacious. That's a distinction I pride myself on. Several times, it has saved my life and brought criminals to justice. I was convinced that the fragments of poetry Mario received would like breadcrumbs lead a trail back to the killer. No one else shared my enthusiasm, however, so I was left to puzzle things out by myself. That's what led me to Traverse City's excellent library to ask for guidance from their information specialist. Malcolm Hadley defied the stereotype of librarians as bookish types whose eyes were firmly set in the past. Perhaps it was his ponytail, or the numerous tattoos that sprouted all over his body. No sober suit for this man. He wore a Def Leppard Hoodie and artfully faded jeans. Either way, his manner was approachable, and his depth of knowledge formidable. We spent a few minutes chatting about art, and to my surprise, I found that Malcolm was a museum freak, particularly attached to great European institutions.

"My dad was assigned to the US embassy in Rome," he said. "My brother Dan and I backpacked around Europe, visiting just about every museum on the Continent. The Louvre, Uffizi, Prado—never missed one of them. Great times."

"I'm an artist," I said. "Or at least I was. You probably know my aunt's work. Violet Davis."

Malcolm's eyes widened. "Unbelievable. She's one of my favorites. Dan absolutely adored her." When I asked if his brother was also an artist, Malcolm shook his head. "Things didn't work out for Dan. Woman trouble and drugs, you see. Every kind of drug. Messed him up big time. Some people are just too sensitive for this world. These days, he just drifts from place to place. He's homeless. Some people call him a vagrant, but I see only a gentle soul."

The memory pained him. I could tell by the look in his eyes and the grim set of his mouth. That prompted me to switch subjects and focus on poetry. I explained my dilemma as succinctly as possible without mentioning murder. Malcolm's eyes brightened as he sized me up and immediately cut to the chase.

"Aha! You're referencing the slaughter at the Conference Center I bet. Wasn't there an art theft, too? One of your aunt's works." He rubbed his hands together with such glee that I was astonished. "This is exciting for me. I'm a real crime buff. I met that guy Mario once or twice a while ago, but he wouldn't give me the time of day. Just a nosey kid to him, I suppose. Okay. How can I help? You're not the only one from that group who came nosing around here, you know. Sort of gave me a head start on the project." Malcolm's grin was infectious, and the freckles sprinkled across the bridge of his nose gave him a Huck Finn type of boyishness.

"I wouldn't call it a slaughter. And what's this about a project?" I opted for subtlety and nonchalance. "Who was it, I wonder?"

"A lady. That is, a woman." Malcolm grimaced. "Kind of brusque. Probably wouldn't like the term lady one bit."

That description made me shiver. Had Nona Adams followed the trail of sonnets, too? She'd brushed me off when I mentioned poetry, but Nona was cagey. Her pursuit of that clue may well have led to her death.

"Was she sort of …plain?" I fought to describe Nona without being unduly petty. "I'd hate to think it was someone from the Expo who beat me to the punch."

"You got it, sister. Even I figured that out." He grinned. "Not quite what I'd expect at a beauty conference, but hey, we serve all customers."

I leaned closer to Malcolm and spoke softly. "Did she come to any conclusions? It's important, Malcolm."

He scratched his head, looking puzzled. "Nope. I got her the full annotated text for John Donne's poems and Grey's elegy. There was one other, but I don't recall which one that was. When she read it, the lady got all excited. Went storming out of here without even saying goodbye or thank you. When I asked, she said I'd get the scoop for my newspaper if I kept my mouth shut." He grinned. "You know that was an offer I couldn't refuse."

I gulped, trying once again not to overreact. Nona's sleuthing was linked to the murder, but without that final stanza, I couldn't bridge the gap. I fished out my business card and presented it to Malcolm. "It's vital that we identify that final poem. Please, call me if you think of it. And you probably should alert Chief Hall, too."

The librarian's eyes bugged out. "The cops?"

I gathered my things and made a hasty exit. "You see, there's been another incident. I think your customer was murdered last night."

* * *

I scurried back to the hotel, more confused than ever. Gemma was conducting a session on eyebrow threading and lamination, and I'd promised to join the audience and provide moral support. The topic was a timely one for those in the beauty industry. Any woman who had endured monthly waxing knew just how painful that process could be. Most were thrilled to find an alternative. Business owners were pleased with the additional customers who were drawn to the salons offering the service and the added revenue it brought. After making introductory comments, Gemma did a demo using Kim as her model. She then fielded questions that generated a surprisingly spirited debate on the pros and cons of the various practices.

Kim helped by offering her perspective as a former model. Not one question was raised, or comment made about Nona's death. She was the invisible woman, forgotten and easily ignored. I suspected that they either didn't know or didn't care much about her absence.

By a stroke of good luck, I managed to find a seat next to Carla Standish. This was my chance to quiz her, and I intended to make the most of it.

"Too bad about Nona Adams," I said mendaciously. "Such a waste."

Carla lowered her glasses and stared at me. "Surely you're joking," she said. "That woman looked for trouble and found it. I ran into her last night on my way to join our party. She gave me one of those withering looks and made a nasty crack about Mario's death."

"No kidding?" I recalled that dark stain that marred Carla's pale blue outfit. Could it have been blood? Nona's blood?

"Any luck removing that stain?" I asked. "What a bummer. Your outfit was so lovely."

Carla nodded. "Yes. I was lucky. The cleaners removed most of it with no problem."

"So, what went on with Nona last night."

"Oh yeah," Carla said. "That woman was so snide. She said something about how fortunate I was to profit from his murder. I wanted to slap the smirk right off her homely face." Carla saw my look of horror and immediately corrected herself. "But of course, I didn't. I'm strictly a pacifist. Even when Mario was at his worst, I just ignored him. Matter of fact although I'm ashamed to admit it, most times I crawled into a corner and cried." She shook her head. "Never shed so many tears in my life as I did with that man. But that's ancient history now. I've got a chance to put that all behind me and make a success of my life."

I squeezed her hand. "You already are a success, Carla. Not many women could build a cosmetics empire single-handedly. Your products are awesome."

My praise seemed to mollify her. "You probably know that I was a chemist by trade before I hooked up with Mario. Earned a Ph.D., if you can believe it. Mixing potions was right up my line. I needed help, of course, on the business side. Without Killian Blaine's firm, I'm not sure I could have lasted six months. He's wonderful. A genius."

Another devoted fan. I wasn't jealous. After all, I had no reason to be. Even Nona Adams had some weird connection to Killian. He'd admitted as much, although he'd tried to downplay it. Carla's comments added yet another element to the mix. As a chemist she would be very conversant with nicotine and its deadly properties. Adding it to the conditioner would have been child's play for her.

"I was shocked that nicotine could be so lethal," I said. "Bad for the lungs, but who would believe that something so common could kill."

Carla jumped right in. "Absolutely. It doesn't take much, you know. A lethal dose of pure nicotine would work fast. Whoever mixed it with the *Ricci Rich* was one smart cookie. The scalp is so porous. Poor Mario just sat there like a dime-store dummy while it killed him. Ironic, wasn't it? Something he called his greatest triumph became the instrument of his death." Carla could barely conceal her glee. She might be innocent of Mario's murder, but she still nursed a grudge against him for his cavalier treatment of her. I liked and admired Carla, but in good conscience, I couldn't exclude her as a suspect. With this new information she had zoomed to the very top of my list.

After her seminar ended Gemma got a rousing hand of applause from the audience, took some bows, and joined us. She glanced my way and pointed toward the back of the room. "Have to see you," she said. "Boy, have I got news."

* * *

Gemma took her assignments seriously and had the tenacity of a pit bull when she was on the hunt. As requested, she had insinuated herself into the FACE group, taking careful notes on their reactions to losing Nona. The claque of two dozen or so genuinely mourned their leader, whom they described as a "committed and compassionate" advocate for women.

"They all looked pretty much the same," Gemma said. "No makeup or hair color, and a collection of clearly homemade clothes. No rivals for leadership or anything like that. Not yet, anyway. Lots of tears that seemed genuine, too." She hung her head. "They're not a bad bunch, and I felt kind of guilty spying on them. I still did it, though."

I longed to shake the information out of Gemma, but of course, I didn't. That would only delay things. "No need to feel guilt. It was all for a good cause."

"I guess so. Anyway, when I mentioned the lipstick on Nona's face, they went crazy. Swore she would never, ever defile herself that way." Gemma grinned. "By the way, those were their words, not mine. "

"Any clues about what she hoped to achieve with these so-called concessions?"

"Nah. But I did learn one thing. She worked hand in glove with some local reporter and planned to tip him off. Big project in the works exposing Mario for the crumb that he was and the hypocrisy of the beauty industry in general. No clue about the murderer, but she was working on it."

"Was she expecting money from this person? Something big that could fund FACE."

Gemma shook her head. "I don't think so. Nona had a whopping big trust fund, so she never worried about those kinds of things. Lucky girl, although I guess under the circumstances… Hey, I almost forgot. They're having a shindig tonight. They call it a celebration of Nona's life. Lin gave them a meeting room for free. Trying to curry favor, I imagine."

"Good work," I said. "It's a date."

Gemma whined about missing a date with Benny, but under the circumstances, she soon surrendered. We agreed to meet later and join the party such as it was. I dashed back to my room to rescue Fantasia and give that good girl a much-needed romp in the park. On the way out, I saw Kim and invited her to join us. She was also an animal lover, although until recently, her sour puss spouse had banned pets from their home. Now, they were the proud parents of a lovely grey cat, and a persnickety pup named Atticus.

"Remember how Lionel fought getting any animals," Kim asked. "Now that man is so bonded to Atticus that they're inseparable. Believe it or not, he's even chairing a charity auction for the local shelter." She beamed with pride and a newfound satisfaction with her life. Kim deserved that after suffering for far too long after the death of her son. She didn't often mention him, although I knew that memories of Patrick were never far from her mind.

"How is Lin doing?" I asked. "He looked very troubled this morning, not that I blame him one bit. He isn't ill, I hope."

"Okay, I guess. He's holding up remarkably well considering everything." Kim sighed. "He's such a fine man. Understands loss but doesn't dwell on his problems. I can discuss Patrick with him, and he shares things about his sister. Not many men can do that."

I told Kim about my visit to the library and the connection to Nona. "If only I knew how it linked up to the murders. As it is, the killer will probably waltz right out of here when the conference ends."

Kim leaned down and hugged Fantasia. "I have faith in Gideon. Don't give up on him just yet. I know for a fact that he's tracing the internet orders of nicotine. You wouldn't think that many people at a beauty expo would smoke, but I guess they do."

I laughed. "No, Kim, they vape. So much safer. As if that noxious stuff won't harm them. Anyway, I think they do it to keep off weight. Why eat when you can vape?"

"You know, even Killian indulges. I saw him last evening under the awning looking very guilty indeed. Probably doesn't want to admit to any vices, especially something as common as smoking."

I'd never seen him vaping or smoking, but Mr. Blaine was a man of many parts. He denied any connection with Nona, too. As to his other vices, anything was possible.

"I didn't realize that Carla was a chemist by profession," I said. "My omission. It's listed on her CV, and she never hides it. Not that she should. It's something to be proud of."

Kim gave me a quizzical look. "You think that's a link to Mario's death? Oh, I hope not. Carla has endured so much, and she's finally emerging from a rough period."

"She had no love for Nona. Only today, she mentioned that. On the other hand, Nona was an acquired taste, shall we say. Her followers idolized her, but the rest of us avoided her like the plague."

Kim bit her lip. "That stain on Carla's dress troubled me. I'm no expert, Marky, but I think it was blood. You don't think…"

Fantasia yawned, looking up at me with her bright eyes pleading for a treat. Naturally, I couldn't resist. That reminded me that it was time for her dinner and time for me to meet Gemma at the memorial service.

"If you had to guess, who would you tag as the killer?"

Kim's eyes widened, and she gave me a shocked look. "I'm no expert. If Nona saw the murderer tampering with Mario's things, that means it is someone here. I hate to think that. Lots of them are friends that I've known for years."

"Even Sophia?"

She coughed. "You caught me. There are exceptions to every rule, and Sophia is one. I can't stand the creature, but I just don't see how killing Mario would benefit her. Gideon says his murder was meticulously planned. If Sophia spent the evening with Mario that doesn't make sense. Why broadcast your involvement with him if you planned to kill him the next day? After all, Violet and Carla are both his heirs." Kim paused. "On the other hand, Sophia has a temper. She might strike out at someone like Nona if they had an argument. I guess I'm not being much help, am I? Everything's so complicated, and almost anyone could be the killer."

I couldn't disagree. Everything revolved around motive and the character of the victims. "Mario was volatile. Any recent feuds that you knew of?"

Kim shook her head. "Mostly, I let him rant and ignored him. Now I feel guilty, but it was easier to nod and agree with Mario than to debate anything with him. I do recall that he was fiercely opposed to boutique brands like his being absorbed into mega-companies. He was old fashioned that way."

That belief fueled his animosity toward Killian Blaine. I also suspected that Mario considered any male who stirred female emotions to be his enemy and rival. Killian was squarely in that category as any objective observer would be forced to admit. My own feelings about him were conflicted. He was gorgeous, and brainy but a bit too slick for my taste, the type of man who relentlessly pursued a woman until she yielded after which he discarded her. I had no desire to become another notch on his designer belt.

"Nona stirred up plenty of emotion with her antics. She was irritating enough to clobber but not important enough to kill." Kim flushed with embarrassment. "That sounds so cold. I'm ashamed of myself. I guess murder does that to you."

Kim and I parted company in the lobby while Fantasia and I scampered into the elevator and headed for our room. Considering Nona's crowd, I needed only to scrub my face clean of cosmetics and don a pair of worn jeans and a sweatshirt to fit in. Frankly, I felt weird and almost naked, facing the world without a hint of makeup. Was I insecure? That was something to ponder later. I was an artist with a genuine love for self-improvement and a passion for color. Customers left POPPET feeling good about themselves, and that made me happy. I enjoyed showcasing my products and sharing ways to face the world with confidence. If cosmetics helped with that, I had achieved my goal.

I shared the conflict with Gemma when she appeared at my door. Predictably, she took a totally different approach. "Are you nuts? What woman doesn't enjoy looking good? It has nothing to do with trapping some man, either. Nona's group are a bunch of unhappy souls plus some real loonies. Judge for yourself after you see them in action. Besides, no one forces them to use makeup. Half of our customers are only interested in skincare anyway. Nona led these pathetic women right into the lion's den, and they followed like lambs to the slaughter. What did they expect?"

They probably didn't expect that someone would murder Mario or Nona. That was a reasonable assumption, but I said no more to avoid further argument with Gemma. The room reserved for FACE was on the other side of the facility from the site of Nona's death. Lin Baugh was such a tactful man. I really hoped that he kept his job despite the unfortunate events that had marred the conference. I mentally chided myself for calling two brutal murders "unfortunate events." Had I become that insensitive to the loss of human life? Politicians typically papered over a disaster by using weasel words like that. Perhaps there was a career in public service in my future.

Gemma disregarded a discreet sign that said, "private function," and entered the conference room. Apparently, Nona's death hadn't affected their appetite. FACE members were milling about enjoying the open bar and snacks provided by management. There was a festive air to the proceedings that conflicted with the somber tone that Nona had encouraged. I was amazed at the many humorous anecdotes about Nona that were freely shared. She had seemed rather morose to me, but among her true believers, Nona was apparently regarded as quite the wit. One of the women, who introduced herself as Mala, approached us and asked if we were members. Her manner was wary but not hostile, and I responded in kind.

"Not officially. We didn't want to intrude, but we knew Nona and wanted to honor her."

"This must be a tough time for all of you," Gemma said. "I admire your courage."

Mala was tall and statuesque with no claim to beauty but a good deal of dignity. Her brown hair, threaded with grey streaks, was clipped back in a severe knot, and her complexion was weathered. I estimated her age at somewhere in the mid-fifties and briefly considered which of Poppet's products would suit her best. I wisely kept that thought to myself.

"Nona inspired that in all of us. We knew we would face scorn but wanted to make our case anyway." Mala folded her arms in front of her and said no more.

I used my most customer-friendly voice. "What precisely is your case? Nona spoke about the patriarchy, but as you can see, most of the participants at this conference are females."

She gave me a patient smile. "You're both so young. Life hasn't really touched you yet. Wait until you hit middle age. Women past fifty become invisible. Nona understood that and fought to change things."

I thought of my Aunt Violet, a woman whose beauty and presence knew no barriers, and Carla Standish, who forged ahead in a very competitive environment. They were scarcely invisible. Mala was so earnest that it would have been cruel to dispute her beliefs, however wrongheaded they seemed to be. I also considered the harsh reality that she sported major muscles and could probably deck me without raising a sweat. Wiser not to antagonize her.

"You're not from the press, are you? Nona had a newspaper contact," Mala said. "Someone who was ready to expose the truth about this shindig. Mario Ricci and his kind were at the root of societal injustice. Someone did the world a favor by eliminating him."

Now I understood what Gemma meant about loonies in this crowd. If Mala typified this group, heaven help us. I accepted a glass of wine from one of the waiters and slowly sipped it. Fortunately, my partner jumped into the conversation.

"Yeah, you got that right. Mario was kind of a crumb. What kind of work do you do, Mala?"

"Oh, I thought you knew. I'm a therapist specializing in women's issues. Healing societal wounds is most fulfilling. Most of our group devotes themselves to the cause. Nona had an entire dossier on that vile Mario Ricci that she shared with her journalist friend. His treatment of women was abominable. Young or old, it didn't matter to him. He used them and abused them."

"And what do you two do?" Marla gazed at us with sharp eyes that saw right through us.

"We're shopkeepers," I said. "From Harbor Bay. When we heard about this conference, it seemed like a chance to make some contacts. You know, press the flesh."

Gemma sensed danger and quickly changed the subject. "Nona told us that she saw the murderer, or at least someone who tampered with the display. She had the guts to face off with a killer. Too bad it didn't work out." Gemma returned the hard stare Mala threw our way. "Maybe you should have gone with her. Might have saved her life."

Mala's expression slowly changed from benevolent to bellicose. Her voice rose. "She didn't say who it was, but she wasn't frightened. We talked it over, and she decided to go mano a mano with him. I offered to come too, but Nona wanted a scandal that would end this charade for once and for all. She let me accompany her to the room but made me leave her alone." She edged closer to us, way beyond my comfort level. "Wait a minute. I recognize you. You're one of them. You and your aunt, the artist. You have no business being here."

My fight-or-flight response was suddenly activated. There was a hush in the room as the other FACE participants formed a ring around us and stared us down. Visions of the Salem witch trials and several Steven King horror tales made me cringe. We had no weapons except our quick wits with which to defend ourselves. Mala turned and addressed the group. Her voice had an almost hysterical edge to it now.

"We have intruders here. Spies." She lifted her arms and frowned. "Why are you here? You don't share our beliefs."

I was known for quick thinking, and it came in handy now. "Hold on! We're not your enemies. We're trying to find Nona's killer. She knew who it was, and you might have a clue too. Help us."

My words hit their mark. Mala grew misty-eyed at the thought of her friend. "If I knew who hurt Nona, believe me, I'd handle things myself. Maybe you should ask that dark-haired Jezebel what she was doing lurking around the corridor at the same time. Not sure of her name but Nona despised her I know that much. Any woman who flaunts herself that way is an enemy of decent females everywhere."

I turned toward Mala, confused by her words. The only other woman who was likely to be in the mix was Sophia Lauren, but this was news to me. "Think hard, Mala. It had something to do with those poems Mario got. I'm almost positive of that. Did Nona say anything to you about them?"

"Poems?" she scoffed. "Nona never mentioned poems. We deal with serious things. Concrete issues that we can resolve. Nothing fanciful."

A tiny blonde woman with opaque blue eyes interrupted her. Her features were as delicate as a child's, and she was garbed from head to toe in a white tunic that virtually swallowed her small frame. An unkind thought popped immediately to mind since, with her pink-tipped nose twitching, she resembled an angora rabbit I had loved as a youth. Her voice was timid as she spoke up. "Wait a minute. Nona told me about them. I write poetry, you see, so she asked for my opinion."

Mala gave her colleague a bemused smile. "Typical. She's being modest. Althea is a published poet and a university professor. We call her our muse at FACE."

I made eye contact with the poet, hoping to pursue our conversation before Mala ejected us. "What did Nona say? Tell us."

After Mala nodded her approval, Althea told her tale. "Nona loathed those old white male poets. We all do. But she loved the way those verses got under Mario's skin. All that talk about death. He didn't understand them, but the theme was unavoidable. The final one was a dead giveaway, if you pardon the pun. Nona identified the sender right away. Mario Ricci was a philistine, certainly no intellectual. It meant nothing to him, so he just crumpled it up and threw it away. We laughed because the shoe was on the other foot for a change. The predator became the prey."

The other FACE members cheered lustily, but Mala intervened. "Don't think for a moment that we had anything to do with that nicotine stuff. We're strictly non-violent. We wanted that monster humiliated and twisting in the wind. Not dead. That way was an easy out for the cretin. Public scorn. Expulsion from society. That was our goal."

"Good to know," I said, edging toward the door. "Who wrote that verse? It's an important link to Nona's killer."

Mala shrugged. "No clue. See, she picked it up from the wastebasket and kept it. Never discussed it with me."

"She mentioned it in passing, but I can't recall it off-hand." Althea looked ready to weep. "I'll try to remember, but everything's a big blur."

"Holy moly," Gemma yelped. "Is it still with her stuff?"

Mala grimaced. "How would we know? That lawman locked her room down right away, and he had one of his creepy henchmen guarding it. What a joke! He tried to intimidate us, but we never flinched."

I grinned picturing Benny Soto, the henchman in question, standing toe to toe with Mala. In a fair fight, he stood absolutely no chance of prevailing. As we edged toward the door, I left them with my best exit line. "Please contact Chief Hall. He needs your help." Mala's closing comment put me squarely in my place. "Huh! That'll be the day."

* * *

"We have to search Nona's room." Gemma raised her eyebrows and scoffed. "Are you nuts? Police tape, guards, etc. Do you want a ticket to the pokey, or is this a way to get that hot lawyer to defend you?"

She had a point. Not about Killian Blaine but about the need for a plan. Accessing Nona's room wouldn't be easy. There were obstacles to overcome, but we had a good track record. Besides, if the guard in question was her dearly beloved, I knew I could rely upon Gemma's superior seduction skills. Sex trumped duty every time for that boy.

"Get real. Benny is putty in your hands. I'll bet you can lure him away from his post if you try." An appeal to her vanity usually worked with Gemma. "You always brag about your acting skills, don't you? Well, here's your chance. Put up or shut up. All in a good cause."

I could see those wheels churning in my partner's mind. When it came to hatching schemes, Gemma was a world class player.

"I suppose I could think of something, but you wouldn't have long. An hour at most." Gemma smirked. "Like the song says, I like a man with a slow hand."

"Ugh! Must you be so graphic? I get it. Of course, you'll have to change into something more alluring and pile on the paint." I gave her an evil grin. "Unless Benny prefers a minimalist look these days. He might be turned on by the FACE members."

"Very funny. Give me thirty minutes to primp before you try anything. If the coast is clear, you can take your chances. Keep your phone on, though. I'll call you when he leaves."

I winked at her to seal the deal before dashing back to my suite. I hadn't gotten far when I felt someone plucking at my sleeve. To my surprise, it was Althea, the poet muse of FACE.

She drew me behind a large potted plant and glanced furtively around her. "I remembered something that might be important. Please don't tell Mala or the others that I told you."

"Of course not. You can trust me." I beamed my most angelic smile, always prepared to lie for a good cause.

"It's about Nona's press contact. I don't think he's employed by the newspapers, but he is a stringer. You know, he writes local features and tries to sell them to editors."

I glanced at my watch and panicked. This endless tale was consuming an inordinate amount of time. Gemma would soon be calling to launch our operation. I gave Althea what I hoped was a sign of encouragement. "Yes?"

She spoke so softly I could barely hear her. "He works at the town library. His name is Malcolm something."

That was news worth mentioning. "Malcolm Hadley?"

"Yes, that's it. I never met him, but Nona seemed to trust him. He wanted a big scoop and promised to work with her."

Recalling that unconventional librarian, I could understand his appeal to Nona. This merited another trip to his lair. Who knew what that scribe had squirreled away on his computer? I thanked Althea, and she scurried back to her home base without saying another word.

When I tiptoed into my suite, Fantasia gave me a hopeful look that I tried to ignore. In desperation, I called Violet and begged her to babysit that good girl. Anyone else might have agreed, but my aunt has a suspicious nature. She immediately wondered where I was going and why. I never could deceive her, even when I tried my best. She wouldn't approve of rifling Nona's room and Violet certainly didn't buy my excuse about running errands.

"Okay, Marky. What are you up to now? Tell me, or I'll refuse to help."

Violet knocked on my door five minutes later and immediately gave me the evil eye. "This is a very bad idea. Perhaps it's even illegal. What can you possibly hope to gain other than a criminal record?"

I provided a quick synopsis of my plan which caused Violet to reluctantly agree. "I still think you'd be better off having Gideon handle this. He's probably already made a preliminary search of Nona's room anyway. Besides how are you going to get into the room? I'm sure its locked."

That's where another co-conspirator came in. As co-host of the event Kim

Stevens had access to a master pass key. When I explained my idea to her, she was initially wary but ultimately persuadable.

"Lionel would have a fit if I got arrested," she said. "You know what a stuffed shirt he is about respectability."

I folded my arms and gave Kim my steeliest glare. "You're an adult, Kim. Take a chance for once. Besides, it's for a good cause. You'd be avenging Mario's murder and maybe saving Lin's job in the bargain."

Using pressure tactics on Kim was distasteful but necessary. Ultimately, she folded and produced the master key. Although she denied it, I detected a gleam of excitement in her eyes at participating in a caper. She had only one caveat: Kim insisted on accompanying me into Nona's room. If necessary, we could fabricate some excuse for our possibly illegal entry. It wasn't a foolproof scheme, but it worked for me.

Chapter Nine

Nerves almost overtook me while I awaited Gemma's call. I changed into my version of a cat burglar's attire, black leggings, hoodie, and shoes ala the inimitable Emma Peel of *Avengers* fame, and counted all the ways this scheme could backfire. Kim's arrival did nothing whatsoever to bolster my morale. She shredded her previously pristine manicure while pacing back and forth and biting her lip. Her attire— a vivid purple caftan— was more sultry than sinister. She hadn't gotten the message about blending into her surroundings, and it showed.

"What if they catch us?" she wailed. "I swear I'll take the blame even if Lionel divorces me." She lowered her head. "I've never done anything like this before, so please forgive me for being a wimp. Never even got a speeding ticket. Dull and reliable Kim. That's what they call me."

"Nonsense," I said with false heartiness. "Just opening night jitters. You'll be perfect. No one would ever suspect you of skirting the law. Say, why don't you stand outside the door while I search the room? That way, you can be the lookout rather than the accomplice. Much safer that way but practical, too. You can head off anybody who comes near."

Her reaction surprised me. In an unexpected show of spirit, Kim insisted on playing her part. "Things will go quicker if there are two of us searching. I doubt that Gideon would arrest us if we do get caught. He respects you even if he doesn't always show it."

I must have gaped in amazement because Kim started laughing. "Besides, I looked it up, and according to Michigan statutes, I'm still what they call 'an accessory after the fact' if I aid and bet your crime." She shrugged. "As they say, in for a penny, in for a pound. Okay, partner?"

"You've got it!" We slapped hands just as Gemma rang.

"You're on, kiddo. Everything's under control here."

* * *

My hands felt clammy as we climbed the stairs toward Nona's floor. Taking the elevator was too risky, but climbing those steep stairs left me huffing and puffing. More gym time was advisable if I expected to survive these types of encounters. In view of Kim's fragile state, I kept my misgivings to myself. Suppose we discovered that missing stanza? We might also unveil a double murderer, and that posed some ethical dilemmas. Should we implicate someone we liked or respected? Carla's name was once again on the tip of my tongue. Both Mario and Nona had provoked plenty of people. Several times, I had longed to strangle Nona myself. I hesitated and stumbled on the top step, almost causing Kim to lose her balance. Hardly an auspicious start to our caper.

"Hey, partner," she whispered. "Steady as she goes. This is so exciting! Just like that police show on ACORN television." Kim was an avid armchair detective who solved crimes vicariously. Was she prepared to embrace the real thing? I feared that the answer was no.

Nona's room was at the end of the corridor, almost directly abutting the exit door. That was a bit of luck I hadn't counted on. Worst case scenario, we had an easy escape route at hand. The garish police tape warning unauthorized persons like us to keep out didn't deter me. Benny had done his usual sloppy job of fastening it, and once Kim opened the door, it was easy to slip under the tape without causing too much disruption. I winked at Kim and helped her into the room. We agreed to each search one half of the suite. I took the living room while Kim tiptoed into the bedroom and started work. Despite her initial misgivings, Kim had the presence of mind to supply both of us with plastic gloves. Score one for fantasy television. No fingerprints to implicate us, just in case Gideon got curious, or Benny got lucky. Just as I expected, the most obvious spots— baskets, drawers, and suitcases, had already been searched. But I told myself that men might not look in less traditional places. Nona was a minimalist who had brought very few articles of clothing with her. I probed the pockets of her jacket and robe, scrutinized the lining of her satchel, and examined the toes of her boots. Inside the toe of her slippers, I hit gold. Eureka! It was a printed note containing the following message: **eight pm, grand ballroom. Come alone.** I shuddered, realizing that these were the words of her killer. It didn't identify the sender but at least the message helped to pinpoint the probable time of death. Eight pm. So many fictional detectives relied upon a shattered watch crystal to affix TOD. That was strictly amateur hour because any killer worth his salt could fabricate that. An actual note was far more indicative. Allowing for a few moments of discussion, Nona had probably been bludgeoned no later than 8:15 p.m.... Carla had arrived at our party thirty minutes after that, sporting that unsightly dark stain on her cuff. Maybe it was coincidence. Maybe not. Carla wasn't the only person of interest. Nona's pal Mala had referenced a "dark-haired floozy" who was prowling about the area at the same time. There were many brunettes at the conference, but no one fit the floozy descriptor better than Sophia Lauren. I wasn't as certain as Violet was that the French femme lacked motive. If Mario had told her about the provisions of his will, she might well have plotted revenge. The subtlety of his death suited her perfectly. It had a quality of feline menace that Sophia positively radiated.

I lost track of time until Kim's shrill cry alerted me. "Come here, Marky. Wait 'til you see this." In my haste to join her, I stumbled over a bench and sprawled headfirst on the floor. No one had ever called me graceful despite my poor mother's efforts to transform me from duckling to swan. Ballet lessons and a stint at martial arts had largely been a waste of money. After assessing the damage, I picked myself up and joined Kim. Her finger shook as she pointed to the wall behind the bed. There, hiding in plain sight, was a painting, the missing painting by Violet Davis.

* * *

154

"Unbelievable," I yelped. "Nona stole my aunt's painting! Who would have suspected her of being the thief? It makes no sense."

"I'll tell you what makes no sense," Kim said. "How could the cops have searched this room and failed to find the painting? Talk about inept public servants! I'm surprised at Gideon."

Nothing surprised me when it involved that bungling bureaucrat, Benny Soto. No doubt, he had been charged with the task of searching Nona's room. Instead of being thorough, he had focused on the obvious and missed crucial evidence. Had his mama never taught him that haste made waste? Every hotel room I'd ever seen featured the usual bland decor and banal paintings. A person of taste would have immediately noted how inconsistent Violet's lovely oil was with the rest of the suite. Poor Gemma! I prayed for the sake of her prospective children that she would never dip a toe into Benny's gene pool.

"What should we do?" Kim asked. "This is serious stuff that Gideon should know about."

We decided that our first move was to leave the painting intact and vacate the premises immediately. Maybe an anonymous phone call could alert Gideon to the painting. I seldom believed in coincidences, but Nona's criminal act might even be irrelevant to the murders. I was less certain of how to share the note without implicating myself or my cohort. Suddenly, I longed for Violet's good counsel. She had an uncanny ability to diffuse unpleasant situations and find the perfect solution. When my cell phone dinged, I saw Gemma's distinctive message. "Scram right now or get caught." My partner had a unique talent for cutting to the chase. With Kim following close behind, I made my escape.

* * *

Violet listened to our story without interrupting. I admit our account was overheated and somewhat incoherent but between Kim and me we managed to eke out the main details. Patience was one of my aunt's strong suites, and it was on open display at that moment.

155

"Interesting," she said calmly. "Perhaps we should wait for Gemma before we go any further. How about sharing some brandy while we wait?"

Kim and I nodded in tandem. I seldom drink alcohol, but now the urge to drown myself in spirits was overwhelming. Successful cat burglars were supposed to be calm and methodical. We didn't fit that mold at all. My teeth chattered, and Kim shivered uncontrollably. A more unlikely criminal duo was hard to imagine. Fortunately, a snifter of brandy did its work. Ten minutes later when Gemma pounded at the door, we had regained some semblance of dignity.

My partner arrived dressed for seduction. The slit in her pencil skirt verged on illegal, and her plunging neckline left little to the imagination. From her exuberant red curls to her slightly smeared lipstick, Gemma epitomized a fictional femme fatale. Small wonder that Benny Soto had been lured from his post.

"Mission accomplished," she crowed, giving a smart salute. "Fill me in."

I managed a reasonably concise account of our exploits, with Kim adding occasional tidbits. Either way, our words hit the mark. Gemma was flabbergasted.

"You found Violet's painting? No way! You mean it was just hanging there in plain sight? Score one for the boys in blue." In typical Gemma fashion, she managed to avoid the unpleasant fact that her fiancé was the chief blunderer.

Violet's frown told me that something troubled her. "I just find it hard to believe that Nona Adams stole my painting. She hardly seemed like an art lover, and she was far too intelligent to openly display stolen goods. I suspect that someone—probably the killer—is responsible."

"Maybe Nona did it to anger Sophia," Kim said. "They were polar opposites, you know."

"Perhaps. It seems rather pointless, though. Nona wanted public displays, plenty of publicity. This feels like an act of private revenge. Someone took a big risk hanging it in plain sight."

I agreed with Violet. Nona was an extremist, but she was also an attorney who was far too savvy to risk her reputation and freedom in such a puerile scheme. Violet's scenario was far more likely. Had the murderer placed the purloined painting in Nona's room as a final act of contempt?

"What should we do about that painting?" Kim asked. "I worry that someone might sneak in and dispose of it. You're famous, Violet, and that work would fetch quite a price. How do we alert Gideon without implicating ourselves?" She was nibbling on her nails again and taking very deep breaths. Kim had little talent for deception and even less for withstanding pressure. She would crack like an egg under the mildest interrogation.

Violet smiled. "Leave it to me. Now, hush while I make this call." She plucked her iPhone from her pocket and selected a number from speed dial. Gideon Hall answered immediately, which told me that was a private number not accessible to the public. That gave me pause for thought. Just how close was my aunt to the top cop? His blend of machismo and sophistication might attract a worldly woman like Violet Davis. Another time, another place. I would quiz her when we were alone.

"Gideon," Violet said, "I just received a puzzling message. Someone said that my painting is hanging in the bedroom of Nona Adams's suite. Could that be possible? I realize that you searched the room, so it was probably just some crank."

Her words galvanized the Chief into taking immediate action. Violet made a few desultory comments, ending with a promise to meet him in front of Nona's room right away.

"You're a marvel, Violet," said Kim. "I could never have pulled that off."

"Nonsense. I didn't lie, although I must admit that I skirted the truth just a tad." She fluffed her hair and freshened her lipstick before leaving. "Stay right here, ladies," she said. "I'll be back in a flash." And with that, my wily relative flounced out the door.

I realized that the note I'd found was still nestled in my pocket. Confession was supposedly a tonic for the soul, but silence was also golden. Like Scarlett O'Hara, I'd think about it later. After all, tomorrow was another day.

* * *

We were somewhat shell-shocked and said very little until I recalled my encounter with Althea, the poet muse of FACE. I decided to confront Malcolm, the secret scribe, that very next day. If I grilled him, he might reveal the pact he had made with Nona. We had very little time left, and a killer was still at large. Any reporter worth his salt would sell his credentials for the chance to crack two murders.

Gemma scoffed at my plan. "Forget it. You're too much of a lady to do that alone. Too refined. I know how to handle a guy like this, Malcolm. A librarian! Huh! Easy peasy. We'll both go." She gave us a wicked grin. "I may have to rough him up a bit, but so what."

Kim exhaled sharply. "Oh, Gemma, you wouldn't."

My dear friend and valued partner sneered. "How do you think I survived all this time? You two never came from the wrong side of the tracks and had to claw for everything you ever got. It's a jungle out there, baby. Own it."

"Okay. How can I help?" Kim asked. She squared her shoulders and faced us. "Don't think I can't be tough. Remember, I was a model at one time. There's no more vicious and competitive business than that. Deception was everywhere, and I learned plenty."

She made a valid point. Because of her elegance and beauty, I had discounted Kim's other assets. She was much more than just a pretty face.

"How about confronting Sophia? She meets Mala's description of the woman lurking outside around the time Nona died. And remember, she held a grudge against Mario for refusing to sell his company?"

Gemma snickered. "Yeah, Kim. Time to flex those model muscles."

"Sounds like a plan." Kim hesitated. "This is a bit delicate. I think we should consider the possibility that Killian Blaine might be involved. He could have easily overpowered Nona, and he's certainly smart enough to plot Mario's final exit. Nona wouldn't have feared him. After all, they spoke the same language and had the same training."

I shifted uncomfortably in my seat as two pair of eyes swiveled toward me. I'd tried to avoid discussing the elephant in the room although in this instance that pachyderm was an alluring attorney with charm aplenty.

"I suppose I could try," I said. "Killian did ask if I'd have a drink with him. Not that I have any intention of letting things get out of hand."

Gemma hooted quite rudely. "I'd let that guy put his hands wherever he wanted. So, what if he's a killer? The ride would be worth it."

Fine talk from an engaged woman. Maybe Gemma was rethinking her alliance with Benny Soto, and that was a good thing. Despite my reservations, I reluctantly agreed to do my part. I'd approach Killian and casually discuss the situation. He might have some interesting theories to share, especially if his tongue was loosened by alcohol. I shuddered as I considered what Gemma would make of that double entendre. I'd never mastered the fine art of flirting and had no desire to learn at this stage of my life. Killian would see right through me if I tried any feminine wiles. Far better to confront him directly and ask for his advice.

Violet returned soon afterward, sporting a look of supreme satisfaction. She took her time before speaking, slowly unwinding her pashmina, patting Fantasia, and kicking off her Louboutins. It was a maddening exercise that left us sitting on the edge of our seats. Predictably, Gemma was the one who ended it.

"Okay, Violet. Spill. You're killing us here."

Our plan had worked perfectly. Chief Gideon had arrived accompanied by Lin Baugh. After shielding Violet from possible danger, the intrepid lawman edged his way into Nona's bedroom and claimed the painting. He asked Violet to identify the work and Lin to sign as a witness. Gideon offered no excuses or explanations for a major blunder by his team. That was his way, and I respected him for it. After the forensic people dusted it for possible prints, the painting would be returned to its rightful owner, Sophia Lauran. I hated to think of my aunt's beautiful work resting in the claws of such a woman, but fair was fair. It was far more intriguing to wonder how it got into Nona's room in the first place.

"For Lin's sake, I'm glad you found it. One less worry for the poor guy to handle." Kim sighed. "The top corporate honcho is meeting with him next week, and Lin fears the worst."

I recalled the note in my pocket. Perhaps Killian could suggest a clever way to get it to the police without risking my freedom. The contents didn't really change anything, but validating the time of death was important.

After agreeing to reconvene that next morning at breakfast, we headed for our rooms. Nothing kept Gemma from a sound sleep, and she was soon snoring softly. I was restless, unable to feel the slightest bit drowsy. There was one sure cure for my problem. I fished my iPhone from the bedside table and dialed an unfamiliar number.

"Ready for that drink?" I asked.

Killian Blaine didn't hesitate. "Absolutely."

Chapter Ten

The hotel bar was still awash with convention goers. I was glad about that since being part of a crowd buoyed my confidence. When I arrived, Killian was already seated at a table for two. His look of cool appraisal temporarily flustered me, but I forced myself to be brave. After all, this was an assignment, not an assignation. He stood and pulled out my chair, a show of manners that was most welcome. No doubt about it. From the top of his lush brown hair to the toes of his polished loafers, Attorney Blaine was one class act. That didn't mean he wasn't a killer, however.

"What's going on?" He asked. "Not that you ever need an excuse to phone me."

"I need advice. Something you can provide in your professional capacity." I explained my excursion to Nona's room but kept Kim's name out of it. As they say in the British shows, "I don't grass."

Killian slowly sipped his martini. I had opted for Perrier to keep a clear head.

"That was brave of you," he said, "but also unwise. Police take a dim view of disturbing a crime scene."

His patronizing attitude irked me. "Nona wasn't killed there, so it wasn't a crime scene. And who cares about some tacky police tape anyway? It was just a technicality."

Instead of speaking, he laughed. Big, hearty guffaws that caused several other patrons to turn our way. "Hey. No harm, no foul. That's the spirit." He stared me down. "Now. What haven't you told me?"

Slowly, with exquisite care, I mentioned the note in Nona's boot. "I intended to leave it there. I really did. but I got distracted by the painting." Before he spoke, I held up my hand. "No sermons, please. Solutions. That's what I need."

"Do you have it with you?" Killian asked. "I suppose your fingerprints are all over it."

"Think again. We wore gloves."

His eyes glinted with amusement. "We? I thought you said you went by yourself. Never mind. Hand it over. I'll think of some way to get it to Gideon. Unless, of course, you prefer Benny Soto." He scrutinized the note before gingerly placing it in his billfold. "Now, where were we? Your stint as a cat burglar wasn't very fruitful after all."

"Very droll. Since you're a suspect, you might want to bow out."

For once, I held the upper hand. The look in his eyes said it all. "Me? Why in the world would I kill not one but two people? Do I look like a mass murderer to you? Lawyers use words as their weapons."

Like it or not, money was one of the oldest motives in the book, and Killian had it in spades. Acquiring Mario's empire would give his firm a financial jolt that would only increase his power. Nona might have deduced enough to implicate him and demanded a share. Who knew what her mysterious concessions were, but they were probably sizable. Confidence surged through me. He didn't frighten me, not in a roomful of people. I put both elbows on the table and dared him to contradict me.

"You quarreled with Mario. I was right there when you two mixed it up. And Nona hinted that at one time, you two had been more than colleagues. Much more."

He gulped down his drink. "Now, just one minute. Call me a killer, but please give me credit for some taste. I assure you that Nona Adams was never once on my radar screen. Jeez! Where did you ever get that crazy idea?"

Now, it was my chance to be smug. "Straight from the source. Nona Adams, herself."

It took him only a minute to calm down and speak rationally. "You don't really believe that, but for the record, I had no part in either murder. Since you fancy yourself as a detective, let me provide you with two rock-solid alibis. According to this note, Nona was attacked somewhere around 8 p.m., and whoever tampered with Mario's product must have done so early that morning. I wasn't alone either time. A very lovely lady will verify that if need be."

That wasn't quite what I'd hoped to hear. Something told me that the lovely lass in question was none other than Sophia Lauran. What a strumpet! She certainly kept busy jumping from one man's arms to another. First Mario, then Killian. I wasn't jealous. Not for a minute. Killian never pretended to be interested in me. Not really. That man probably had more notches on his bedpost than I could ever imagine. I managed to shrug off my surprise with an ease that would rival Violet's Parisian sang-froid.

"Fine. Any guesses about who stole my aunt's painting? We think it was the killer's gesture of bravado, and putting in Nona's room was pure contempt. You know, an in-your-face thing."

If Killian had any suggestions, he kept them to himself. He was probably still miffed by my accusations and preferred sulking to sleuthing. After signaling to the server for the check, he rose and bid me goodnight. "I trust you'll sleep well, Ms. Davis. The sleep of the just as the saying goes."

I faked a yawn and smiled sweetly. "You got that right."

* * *

Lin Baugh met me at the elevator. His harried look told me that he, too, needed a good rest. He'd aged a bit since I'd first met him, but that was scarcely a surprise. Theft and double murder will take a toll on almost anyone.

"It's been quite a night," he said sheepishly. "Gideon was cool, but I'm not thrilled with my staff at this point. They're trained to spot anything out of order. I guess we blew it big time."

I wanted to comfort him, but words seemed inadequate. "The police searched that room, too, and they missed it. You're in good company."

"Won't impress my boss, though, when he gets here next week." Lin waved goodbye and sauntered off down the corridor. He walked like a beaten man, although I hoped that was only temporary. Something Killian said niggled at the back of my mind. Sophia couldn't have been the woman Mala had seen. Prejudice had blinded me, and I made that assumption because of my loathing for Sophia. There was yet another woman who fit that description. One who was unaccounted for at the time of the murder and had acquired a suspicious stain on her clothing. Carla. I didn't want it to be her, even though she had the most compelling motive of all my suspects. Mario had betrayed her in so many ways. She openly rejoiced in his death and had reaped a financial bonanza as his heir. By almost anyone's standards, Carla was suspect number one. Was she capable of throttling Nona? Possibly. Probably. Nona incited violence wherever she went. I'd never once been in a physical fight, but her antics provoked me to give it a try. Time was closing in, and the beauty expo would soon be history. With those glum thoughts uppermost in my mind, I slipped noiselessly into our suite and went to sleep.

* * *

"Someone has to brace Carla," I said. "No more nicey -nice. Take off the kid gloves and work her over." Such aggressive tactics were totally out of character for a goody-two-shoes like me. I could tell by the faces of my breakfast mates that they didn't take me seriously. Their reactions ranged from blank expressions to open scorn, with Gemma taking the lead.

"Tough talk from Miss Congeniality. Wasn't that the title you won in high school, Marky?"

Raking up the past was unproductive and annoying. I'd left high school a decade ago and learned a lot since then. Violet sensed that a kerfuffle was brewing and acted swiftly to diffuse it. "Explain yourself, Marky. Then we might be able to help."

I shared Mala's comments and Killian's alibi for the nights in question. Gemma immediately pounced on that pearl of wisdom.

"Aha! Very interesting. How did you worm that info out of him—or dare I ask?"

Kim told her to hush. "I could probably handle it. Carla and I are doing a session on exfoliating creams this morning. No one ever suspects me of having an ulterior motive." She grinned. "I'm not sure if that's a plus or minus—a reputation for being dumb or devious."

We decided that she would warn Carla about unspecified rumors. It was a perfect ploy guaranteed to camouflage her real purpose and get at the truth. Meanwhile, Gemma and I set off for the town library to confront Malcolm. Since the building was dog-friendly we included Fantasia in our trip.

He was at his post, busily previewing a fresh batch of audiobooks. Gemma gazed at the tattoos covering his long, lanky frame with a decidedly carnal interest. I pinched her arm and whispered, "Down, girl. Remember why we're here. Besides, you're an engaged woman."

"Engaged, but not dead. No harm in looking, is there?"

We took Malcolm by surprise. His eyes, partially hidden behind aviator glasses, held a mixture of uncertainty and guilt. "Back so soon?" he said. "Not another murder up there, I trust." To my surprise, he stared uneasily at Fantasia as if my beautiful girl was poised to attack him. Any man who feared a gentle collie was immediately expunged from my list of potential pals. He must have skipped those wonderful novels by Albert Payson Terhune that had gladdened my childhood with tales of *Lad a Dog*.

I leaned over his desk and glared at him. "You misled me, Malcolm. Don't play the innocent. This is too serious."

Gemma finally chimed in. "Yeah. Come clean, book boy, or our next chat is with the cops."

He stood up and looked around the room. No chance of being overheard. The library was deserted at this early hour. I must admit that he was poised. Perhaps a bit too cool to pass the litmus test. Malcolm was no country rube. He scratched his ear and asked, "What do you want to know?"

"You knew more about Nona Adams than you admitted. Don't deny it. Our informant said that you two were conspiring together. Developing an expose on Mario and the entire conference. Tell us everything, and maybe we can help you too."

He hesitated, as if he were weighing his options. In the end, either my steely glare or Gemma's lascivious one convinced him to cooperate. "You know I'm a newsman," he said. "My sources are confidential."

"Really? We heard you were just a stringer." His face fell at Gemma's derisive comment.

I stomped on her toe. "Not helpful," I hissed. "Let the man speak."

Malcolm regained his dignity and plowed ahead with his tale. "For your information, I have a journalism degree from the University of Michigan. Jobs are scarce for newcomers. Everyone must start somewhere. The news business is tough."

I nodded in agreement. "Don't mind Gemma. She loves to goad people. Now, you were saying…"

Malcolm cleared his throat. "Nona approached me with a proposal. We'd work together to reveal the truth about Mario Ricci and the beauty industry. All the dirt. She knew some shady dealings that he had with women." He smirked. "In this 'Me-too' era, editors would eat it up."

"How far did she get? We know about her stunt with the hog's head."

Malcolm lowered his head. "I admit that creeped me out. Not my idea at all. I'm a vegan, for heaven's sake. Wouldn't you know my one chance to hit the big time, and look what happened? My source gets murdered."

Those comments revealed a cynical side to his character that was off-putting. How inconsiderate of Nona to die before bringing their plan to fruition. She certainly paid a heavy price for her crime.

"Not so fast," I said. "All may not be lost. If we crack the case, it could still work out for you. Now, what were Nona's theories about Mario's murder?"

His eyes brightened. I realized now that this was no aspiring bookworm. Malcolm was committed to his career goals and probably a tad ruthless. That made him the perfect match for our own goal of solving the murders.

"Normally, I wouldn't reveal my sources," he said piously. "But since she's dead, it can't do any harm. Nona detested Mario Ricci and everything he stood for. You probably figured that out. She certainly didn't grieve when he died. In fact, it rather proved her point. She believed the murder was personal, not a hit or anything related to the beauty business. I guess he'd messed up a lot of lives."

"You can say that again," Gemma chirped. "Tell me this. Why did Nona grab that painting? Seemed like a dumb thing to do under the circumstances."

"Huh?" His puzzled look confirmed what I already believed. Nona did not steal my aunt's painting. Doing that made no sense for a woman so committed to achieving her mission. Sophia bought the painting. She was the target of Nona's contempt but not her wrath.

"Nona saw the killer tampering with Mario's display. At least that's what she hinted. We think she planned to either blackmail or expose that person."

Malcolm shook his head. "She didn't care about money. Everything was about her cause. Hubris. It might have saved her life if she trusted me. She did say that she saw the killer. Someone with a great motive, she said. Wouldn't say if it was a man or woman. Nona dangled that tidbit in my face but wouldn't share anymore. Just like the ancient Greeks said. It led to Nemesis."

He was right, of course. Those old Greeks were preternaturally wise. Human nature hadn't changed that much since the days of Aristotle and his band of philosophers roamed the earth. As the proverb warned, pride did indeed goth before a fall. Finding the identity of Nemesis was trickier than I'd anticipated. My thoughts reverted to the poems once more. The murderer teased Mario and probably revealed his or her identity in that final verse. "You're sure Nona didn't mention those snippets of poetry? I still feel they hold the key to this whole tragedy."

Gemma hit her head with her hand. "Poetry again. I'm sick of hearing about it. Probably just some crank or an enemy trying to pull Mario's chain. He annoyed plenty of people. All he thought of was that *Ricci Rich* nonsense."

Malcolm offered to trace any poetry volumes that Nona used. Since the killer may well have avoided the library and found the poems on the internet it was a long shot. But it was still worth trying. Meanwhile, at my suggestion he agreed to interview Sophia Lauran and Carla Standish for a feature story. Sophia would devour any bit of attention and as an astute businesswoman, Carla would welcome the publicity.

"I'll focus on the human-interest angle," he said, rubbing his hands together. "A nice juicy story. I can see it now. How was each lady affected by Mario's murder? The pathos, the trauma. After all, both were his paramours at one time."

I advised him to tread carefully, especially since Carla had been Mario's long-suffering wife, not merely a girlfriend.

"Don't forget the financial aspect, either. Qui bono, you know."

Gemma was so reluctant to leave that I practically had to drag her from the library. Never a dull moment when she was involved. My pal's sudden interest in literary pursuits was another facet of the ever-changing saga of Gemma Reid.

"Watch out for that French floozy," Gemma teased as we left. "She might think you're a snack and gobble you up."

"Hmm. Maybe you should go with me. I could use some protection." Malcolm winked at her and bid us goodbye.

* * *

"Are all librarians like him?" Gemma asked. "Remind me to check ours out."

I reminded her to focus on our mission, not men. We hadn't learned much from Malcolm, but a press contact was still useful. I knew that by excluding any mention of Violet's involvement, I had been less than candid with him. That didn't bother me one bit. Protecting my aunt was my top priority, and any hot-shot reporter worth his salt could dig up those details without any help from me. We entered the hotel lobby amidst a swirl of activity. Sophia Lauran was distributing full-size samples of her brand's newest offerings to an eager and somewhat greedy bunch of conventioneers. I had to admit that the woman looked lovely in a confection of gauzy pink chiffon that highlighted her lustrous raven locks. Obviously, it was a case of exterior beauty masking a shallow soul. Gemma made a gagging sound that perfectly reflected my own sentiments. That didn't stop us from gathering our share of the samples for Poppet. Customers loved freebies and we made sure to fill our bags with samples galore. As I scooped up the products, Sophia confronted me.

"Still playing detective, I see," she said with a malicious grin. "Your aunt returned my painting thanks to you." She leaned over and whispered. "Unless you stole it in the first place. I wouldn't be at all surprised. Killian said you had a vindictive streak."

That surprise attack left me flustered and momentarily speechless. I mouthed several unprintable words that no lady should even know but exercised my right to remain silent. Killian Blaine must have engaged in a spate of pillow talk about me with this vixen. So much for his discretion. Good thing I no longer cared what that lusty lawyer said or thought about me.

"Too bad Mario excluded you from his will," I said with a saccharine smile. "After all the effort you put into it that last evening. Champagne, caviar, sex. It's a shame. Men can be so fickle."

Sophia puffed up like a giant cobra spewing venom. "How dare you! Mario and I hadn't been together in years. I spent my evenings reconnecting with him and sharing old memories. Mario hadn't forgotten." She sneered at me as she made this parting shot. "You're not the type to understand, but some women are unforgettable. They fascinate their men. Killian knows all about it."

I decided to risk a scene and go for broke. "So why were you rifling Mario's display? Nona Adams saw you there. I'm sure Chief Hall has already quizzed you about it, although, unfortunately, poor Nona can no longer testify."

No weapon was at hand, or else Sophia would surely have flung it at me. Anger mottled her complexion, spoiling the perfect matte finish of her makeup. Before we were treated to a Vesuvius-style eruption, Lin Baugh magically intervened.

"Ladies, I trust everything is going well." Poor Lin. He had aged a decade since the Beauty Expo started. Lines under his eyes suggested a troubled sleep, and the set of his mouth was strained. Sophia immediately unleashed a series of complaints mixing English and French epithets. Lin nodded sympathetically and guided Sophia toward a secluded spot. Soothing outraged customers was part of his everyday business life, one I did not envy. Since I was my own boss, no one could discharge me if a customer at Poppet complained. Lin was not as fortunate. He was subject to the slings and arrows of outrageous fortune, as the Bard so aptly termed it.

"Trouble in paradise?" Killian Blaine glided up behind me. "I trust you didn't upset my client too much. Sophia has quite a temper, or so I'm told."

"I'm sure you know all about that. Frankly, I think she has something to hide. She lied about being with Mario and had every reason to hate him." I sniffed. "As for Nona, she had nothing but contempt for Sophia. Called her a strumpet and worse."

Killian laughed. "Sticks and stones, my girl. Sophia is one smart businesswoman. Never gives up on a deal even though she loves the strum and drag of a good scrap." His eyes were alight with mischief. "Seems like you do too."

He knew an awful lot about Sophia. Intimate details are more suited to a lover than an advisor. I thrust those thoughts aside, recalling that I had a more important task—protecting my aunt. "What do you hear from Gideon? He must have his hands full with two murders to solve."

Killian wasn't diverted by my sudden change of topics. He seemed amused by my efforts to entrap him. "You're the one with the police contacts, Marky. Benny Soto must have the last word on everything. I'm just here on business for my firm."

I resolved to take this bull by his horns. "Okay. Give me a straight answer for a change. Were you really with Sophia the entire night when Nona was murdered?"

He gave me that evil grin once more. "A gentleman never tells."

"Huh! I'm trying to solve a murder, and you're pretending to be chivalrous. You're no knight in shining armor, believe me."

"Whoa!" This time, Killian was serious. His eyes were narrowed, his speech brusque. "You are neither a cop nor a detective. Back off, Marky. Lives are at stake—yours, for one. A double murderer is no one to trifle with. Get this straight. If I knew anything about either murder, I'd notify Gideon directly, not you." He turned on his heels and strode away without saying goodbye. So much for manners.

"What was that all about?" Gemma appeared out of nowhere, looking very pleased with herself. I was ready for some good news, so I indulged her need for drama.

"Okay. What did you find out?"

She fluttered her eyelashes, giving a very poor impression of a coquette. "Benny just happened to pass by, and I put some pressure on him."

"And..."

"Gideon found something big. He's almost ready to make an arrest."

Random thoughts, none of them pleasant, ran through my mind. Was Violet imperiled? She was on the scene of Mario's murder, had applied the nicotine-laced conditioner, and had a previous relationship with him.

Plus, she stood to gain a financial windfall. Her stake in Mario's empire was probably somewhere in the millions. There was one saving grace: Violet had an alibi for the time of Nona's death. We were in her suite sipping champagne and nibbling snacks. Three of us could vouch for that. I discounted Carla since she had become my prime suspect. No matter what, she claimed that noxious stain on her hem could not be explained away. Unfortunately, Sophia had a gilt-edged alibi. It would have been so satisfying to nail her elegant hide to the wall, even though she'd probably look great in prison orange. On the other hand, suppose both Killian and Sophia were involved. That would explain their mutual alibis and what appeared to be a very close alliance.

"Hello? Marky, are you in a trance or having a fit?" Gemma was never one to mince words. "Don't you want to hear the rest?"

I nodded.

"Gideon tracked down orders for that colorless liquid nicotine. You wouldn't believe how many in this crowd vape. Anyway, a bulk order was sent in the care of this hotel, probably for the convenience of the guests. No name attached. The local smoke shop sold some to Killian Blaine, Carla, and get this—our local librarian Malcolm." She wrinkled her nose. "Guess he's into more than just books."

That was interesting, but hardly a smoking gun. One thing I knew for sure: Violet Davis hadn't ordered that nasty substance. She avoided anything like tobacco. Always had. When I was a teenager, she had lectured me constantly about the dangers of tobacco. Bad for your complexion and your lungs.

"Okay. How does that lead to an arrest?"

"Don't you get it?" Gemma became impatient. "Everything points to Carla. If they ever found out about that stain on her dress, she's cooked."

We agreed to keep that tidbit to ourselves unless it was necessary. I realized that Fantasia needed a walk, and I badly needed time alone to think. Was Killian right? After all, if Violet was no longer a suspect, I had little to gain and plenty to lose by pursuing this. Maybe I should back off and allow those with a badge to do their job. On second thought—no. Our amateur squad had found more clues than the so-called professionals. I dialed Violet's number and asked her to arrange a meeting. A strategy session was in order.

* * *

"Make this quick," Gemma squawked. "Some of us have a social life, you know."

Kim shook her head, but Violet quelled rebellion with one stern look. "We each had a task, Gemma. Personally, I'd like to learn the results. I'll go first. As you know, I agreed to liaise with Sophia when I returned her painting."

Gemma interrupted. "Marky mixed it up with that hussy too. You probably came out of it a lot better."

I reminded myself that Gemma was my partner and best friend. As such her frequent outbursts could be tolerated or ignored. She deserved a thorough shaking, but I exercised self-control and chose the better part of valor.

Violet poured herself a tumbler of Perrier and sipped. "Sophia and I had quite a pleasant chat. Remember, she's interested in acquiring Mario's business, and by now, she knows my status. Don't underestimate her. She's quite a canny businesswoman who's determined to get her way."

At what cost, I wondered. Surely even Sophia wouldn't pulverize two people just to meet her goal. On the other hand, she might be ruthless enough to do just that. There was a fanatical gleam in her eyes that made me very wary.

"We didn't discuss specifics, of course. Not dollars and cents or anything remotely like that. Each of us was taking the measure of the other." Violet paused, "I've dealt with people like her before. They probe for an adversary's soft spots then press their advantage."

Even Kim was getting anxious. "Then what did you talk about?"

"Mario. Both of us knew him well. Intimately. We reminisced about the man and the times, good and bad, that we'd had with him. I'd like to think that wherever his soul resides, it pleased him to once again be the center of attention." Violet had a smile on her face as she thought about her friend. "In his own way, he loved women."

I seldom contradicted my aunt, but her version of Mario Ricci was colored by time and distance. My own view was more objective: I considered him a monster whose actions precipitated his own doom. "Did you reach any conclusions?" I asked.

Violet hesitated. She reached over and hugged Fantasia as though that furry embrace had brought her comfort. "No conclusions, just speculation. We agreed that this was a very personal murder, probably related to Mario's treatment of others. Women, of course. He was careless and often hurtful. Never deliberately, perhaps, but he disregarded the impact of his actions. In many ways, he was still an impulsive little boy who'd never learned to curb his behavior."

Kim nodded. "I saw that too many times. Mario was willful, quite childlike, but charming at the same time. He hurt people but always got forgiven."

"Not always. Carla told me herself that she still loathed Mario. I'll bet she didn't shed many tears when he died." I sympathized with Carla's feelings. After what he did no way would I have forgiven Mario or any man who treated me so shabbily. "You spoke to her, Kim. What did Carla tell you?"

Kim rose gracefully and paced around the room. Although she was self-effacing by nature, on this occasion, she seemed to crave the limelight. "I was rather pleased with myself. Almost as if I was playing a role." She ducked her head. "I acted in our high school play, you know. Desdemona. She was a fascinating character."

Gemma was getting impatient. She tapped her feet and rocked back and forth. Her behavior was rude, but luckily, Kim was oblivious to it.

"I remembered what we discussed. You know, pretending to warn Carla about the police. That was the line I took. I mentioned the stain on her hem. Then I hinted that someone saw her quarreling with Nona that evening."

That caught our attention. "No way," Gemma said. "Girl, you've got guts! Suppose she's the killer? She could have snapped your neck like a twig."

Kim cleared her throat and continued. "I doubt that. Anyhow, Carla got so pale I thought she might faint. She clutched her chest and backed up against the wall. Then she confessed."

"Confessed!" Gemma's shriek could have penetrated a bank vault. "Unbelievable!"

"Hold on." Violet held out her arm. "Let's get this straight. Did Carla confess to murdering Mario and Nona?"

Kim looked astonished. "Oh no. Of course not. She had an argument with Nona that evening. A real imbroglio. Nona made unpleasant remarks, and Carla threw a drink right at her. That's how she got that stain. It was burgundy wine, not blood."

My head was spinning. I forced myself to calm down and analyze the situation. Carla was at or near the ballroom right before Nona's murder. Had she noticed anything or anyone who appeared out of place? "Anything else?"

"She didn't say. Before things turned violent, Lin and Killian Blaine walked up. That diffused the situation. Carla felt humiliated, but she said Nona was ecstatic, as if she were bragging. She looked those fellows straight in the eye and claimed to have solved Mario's murder. Called it a big victory for FACE."

One word reverberated in my head as Kim spoke. Hubris! Nona was so sure of herself that she announced her discovery to the world. Lord only knew how many people she had crowed to. One of them killed her. One of them was Nemesis.

"Gideon must be told. This conference ends in two days and everyone will disperse. He'll lose his chance to find the murderer." I'd never seen my aunt so distressed. Normally she faced adversity without turning a hair.

Gemma shrugged. "So what? I can live with that. Neither one was any big loss."

As usual, Gemma missed the subtleties of the situation. An unresolved double murder left a stigma on everyone involved. In this instance, Carla and my aunt would always be tainted by their perceived role in the tragedy. Gideon's career would be haunted, as would Lin Baugh's. Killian would sail through it without a scratch, but that wily fellow could probably wiggle out of almost any unpleasant situation. The same could be said for the sultry Sophia.

I didn't even consider abstract concepts like justice and equity. Hercule Poirot one of my favorite literary icons often said that he did not approve of murder. Neither did I. It was disquieting to think that any criminal could evade punishment for such foul deeds. I shivered as I pictured the final moments of Mario and Nona. Neither one was an exemplary being, but both deserved a different fate.

"What should we do?" Kim said. "Carla didn't murder anyone. Why involve her?"

Violet's lips were set in a firm line. "That's not our decision to make. Someone must tell Gideon."

Chapter Eleven

My aunt conferred with Carla and accompanied her to the police station. Their discussion wasn't an easy one. I could tell by the grim expression on Violet's face and the haunted look in Carla's eyes. My nerves were shattered by the entire experience. When Gemma suggested that we join the group for a beauty trivia contest, I reluctantly agreed. Any diversion from the topic of murder was a plus.

The lounge area was jammed with avid conference goers who were eager to display their knowledge of the beauty biz. Winning conferred prestige, plus the chance to snag a prize from the treasure trove of gift baskets on the stage. Gemma and I edged through the throng and found space at the bar. Both Kim and Lin served as quizmasters for the event. A general air of hilarity prevailed despite the shadow of death that lingered like a noxious cloud over the proceedings. I was probably being fanciful. Everyone else seemed transfixed by greed and the possibility of free swag. Gemma tapped me on the shoulder and pointed. There, to my surprise, was Malcolm, the librarian clad in his party duds and looking every inch the professional. He waved when he spied us and hastened to our side.

"Reporting for duty, ladies." Malcolm gave us a smart salute and bowed.

"Cut the clowning," Gemma said. "What did you find out?"

"Patience, my lady." He was such a tease that even I yearned to slap him silly. "Sophia was a doll to interview until I mentioned Mario. Then she clammed up and sent me packing. I haven't found Carla yet. I got the idea that Sophia planned something big with Mario. Like a wedding, maybe."

"Okay," Gemma said. "What else did you find out?"

Malcolm checked the notes on his phone. "I interviewed the guy at the local smoke shop. He's been flooded with customers wanting liquid nicotine. Most wanted the flavored kind, you know, like the kids buy. But one stood out." He paused theatrically as if awaiting applause. One look at my curled lip and Gemma's murderous frown convinced Malcolm to speed things up. "Okay, okay. I showed him headshots of our leading suspects, and he pointed out Carla Standish."

"No way," Gemma gasped. "She doesn't even smoke."

Malcolm shrugged. "What can I tell you? He was one hundred percent certain. I guess she made a big deal about wanting the colorless kind. Maybe that's the point. A woman who doesn't vape buys liquid nicotine." He smirked. "Highly suspicious, I'd say."

I wouldn't condemn Carla without questioning her first. "What about those poems? Any luck there?"

"Not much. But I checked the internet search history on our library computers and found that someone was terribly fond of old English poets. Not much interest in John Donne or Grey these days, so it stood out."

I took a deep breath. Perhaps my hunch was finally paying off. "Could you identify the person?"

"Sorry. They're available to the public with no password required. Guess that's a dead end if you'll pardon the pun."

I thanked Malcolm and urged him to keep digging. Suddenly, my Cosmopolitan tasted flat, and my mood darkened. Carla had every hallmark of the murderer except one. She was a tenacious woman who achieved success through her own efforts. Why risk her freedom and empire over a cad like Mario Ricci? It simply didn't compute. Furthermore, murdering Nona was simply not Carla's style. She was far more likely to compromise or succumb to bribery than become violent.

"What's your problem? Stop being a gloomy Gus for a change." Gemma said. "This is fun." Her response to the question about which conglomerate owned *Bobby Brown Cosmetics* had netted her a huge basket overflowing with Oribe products. That would immediately serve as a raffle prize for Poppet's customers even if I had to wrestle it from Gemma's clutches.

177

"Nice move," a cheerful male voice said. Killian had maneuvered into a spot uncomfortably close to me, generating a wave of feeling in my most private parts. Something about this man threatened my resistance. I knew he was a rogue, possibly a bounder, but those icy eyes seared into my very being. Once again, Gemma was right. I badly needed a social life or male companionship.

Nothing deterred Killian Blaine from his appointed rounds. Perhaps he was a postman at heart. He gave us a saucy smile and asked, "How goes the sleuthing game, ladies?"

"We gave that up," I said firmly. "Leaving it to the police where it belongs."

His raised brows told me he didn't believe my story. Gemma turned away in an unconvincing effort to hide her expression.

"Too bad," Killian cooed. "Just when you managed to agitate your suspects. Sophia was quite put out by your snooping. Used some strong language to describe you, Marky. Her sentiments, not mine. I admire a woman with tenacity. Very alluring."

"You're still a suspect, you know," I said, giving him my fiercest scowl. "Without Mario around, you stand to make a tidy profit. Everyone heard the two of you arguing and who's to say it didn't go farther?"

Instead of showing guilt, the big lug laughed heartily. "I'd be devasted if you dismissed me. But remember, your dear aunt also profited by poor Mario's passing. In fact, I'm meeting with her and Carla this evening to finalize our arrangements." He rubbed his hands together. "Should mean sizable profit all around."

For some reason, Violet hadn't mentioned that. It made business sense to explore her options, but she still felt unfeeling to dispose of Ricci Enterprises so soon after Mario's death. Killian's smug, self-righteous manner was infuriating. He patronized me, acting as if I were a neophyte needing guidance instead of an astute businesswoman. That's not the way he acted around Sophia, and I resented it.

"Looks like everyone comes out a winner," Gemma said. "Except Mario, of course, and Nona. I feel sorry for poor Lin Baugh, too. Bet his bosses will bounce him right out of his job."

Killian shrugged. "Too bad. Fortunes of war, as they say. Mario ruined several lives. Dead or alive, he's still going at it." He shrugged. "As for Nona...she was a born troublemaker. No one will miss her much."

Before I gave him the rebuke he so richly deserved, Gemma hushed us. Kim announced the grand prize in the trivia contest, a five-hundred-dollar gift certificate for Ricci Products. It was a final tribute to the fallen beauty scion, one that he would have heartily endorsed. Mario subscribed to the theory that publicity was better than obscurity. No doubt he expected to enjoy it while he was still breathing.

"Here it is, folks," Kim said. "Listen closely. Name two beauty enhancers used by Cleopatra and her court."

My hand shot up, but before I could answer, another voice rang out. "Kohl and henna."

The lucky winner was unexpected. It was Althea, the poet from Nona's FACE group. She pranced up to claim her prize, beaming all the way. Unless my eyes deceived me, Althea also sported a hint of blush, a glimmer of gloss, and a touch of mascara. Something magical had transformed this drab poet into a glamour girl. Killian Blaine noticed it, too. He leered at her and whispered, "Who is that? Haven't seen her before."

"Down, boy," Gemma said. "She's a member of FACE. Newly converted, it seems. Way too innocent for the likes of you."

"You wound me," he said. The glimmer in Killian's eyes betrayed him, and I could tell that he enjoyed playing the role of bad boy. "Perhaps I should go over and congratulate her."

He sped toward Althea, all smiles and oily promise, abandoning both Gemma and me to our own devices.

"Well," Gemma huffed. "How do you like that? What a snake. Poor Althea won't know how to handle him."

I was indifferent to Killian's antics. Besides, Althea was no ingenue, and bad boys loved to flaunt their prowess whenever an opportunity presented itself. What bothered me was the meeting between him and my aunt that evening. Violet didn't need my help. I knew that. She could take care of herself and handle Killian Blaine without any interference from me. But why plan something without telling me? I could help her strategize or at least offer some advice. Gemma saw the pout on my face and immediately pounced.

"Aha! Violet's keeping secrets, isn't she? Grow up, Marky. Let's find Malcolm and see if he has any other scoop."

"You go ahead. I'm tired. Time to walk my dog and go to bed. Maybe a good night's rest will refresh my mind." Gemma looked doubtful, but she nodded. "Go on, shoo. You're just a party pooper anyway."

I realized that she probably was right. It seemed that my days of frivolity were far behind me. My mindset at twenty-eight closely mirrored that of my mother. She was a vibrant woman of fifty-five, but unlike me, she had a husband who adored her and a successful career behind her. A far cry from her work-obsessed offspring whose romantic adventures had all fizzled along with dreams of artistic mastery.

"Whoa, Marky, watch out." Carla Standish steadied herself by grasping the arm of a nearby wing chair. She gave me a look that mixed concern with caution. "What's going on? You're usually so upbeat. Maybe I can help you."

Carla was lively enough for both of us. Had her meeting with Killian caused the flush in her cheeks and the spring in her step? Who could blame her? The prospect of receiving a financial windfall was enough to gladden any business owner, especially one with a mountain of debts.

"I suppose you're meeting Killian and my aunt. Good luck with that."

"Thanks. Violet is twice the businesswoman that I am, and she's very optimistic. I was always the drudge when Mario and I were together. Working night and day, developing new products. Look what it got me." Her comments were tinged with bitterness, the understandable residue of a most unhappy marriage.

"People respect you personally and professionally. That means a lot in any business."

Carla blinked back tears. "Very kind of you to say that. At least Mario did the right thing in the end, whether he intended to or not. You realize that he planned to marry Sophia." Carla bit her lip. "If it happened, all bets were off. That vulture would swoop down and grab everything in the Ricci empire.

There wouldn't even be crumbs for Violet and me."

That bit of news stunned me. "I had no idea. No wonder Sophia spent personal time with Mario. She's quite a beautiful woman, and Mario was susceptible to that."

"Tell me about it," Carla said. "Sophia was a bit long in the tooth now for Mario's taste, but he still pursued her. The one who got away, I guess. That man couldn't stand rejection. No wonder he preferred young girls like Linette Baugh, who sat at his feet and thought he was a god." Carla checked her watch and excused herself. "Oops! Don't want to be late. This could be the answer to my prayers." She whisked away, leaving a cloud of expensive scent in her wake.

If true, Carla's comments eliminated Sophia from my list of suspects. Why would she kill Mario before he changed his will? It simply wouldn't happen. Unless…suppose Mario's eyes had turned to Althea or another nubile candidate. In my opinion, Sophia was perfectly equipped to wreak revenge on any man who disappointed her, especially Mario. If Nona interfered, Sophia would swat her down like an errant fly.

When I reached my room, Fantasia leapt up from her crate. Guilt suffused me when I saw her beautiful eyes dance with hope and delight. I fastened her lead, grabbed my flashlight, and placed pepper spray in my pocket. Vigorous exercise was the antidote I needed to blast away the doldrums. I checked my cell phone in case Violet had left a text. No such luck. There was a cryptic message from Gideon, though urging me to contact him "at my earliest convenience," whatever that meant. I decided that he could wait. I wasn't up to a lecture from the police chief even one as engaging as Gideon Hall. With my luck, Benny Soto would be staffing the office, issuing commands and meaningless threats. Gemma knew how to deal with him, but I didn't even try. Besides, my princess was prancing around, eager to claim her walk time. I hugged Fantasia, drawing comfort from her soft fur and sweet kisses. I understood animals and easily returned their love. Too bad that didn't transfer to my relationships with men.

We jogged up the hill and circled around the park, doing a very creditable two miles of exercise. Fantasia's ears perked up as she charged ahead, yearning to repeat that performance. Alas, I was not equal to the task. I spied a bench, made a beeline for it, and plopped down to rest. Before long, I was joined by Lin Baugh. He was decked out in a handsome jogging suit that seemed too large for his wiry frame. Although his manner was pleasant, his face looked fatigued. Small wonder. The man had endured enough during the last week of the Beauty Expo to curb anyone's appetite.

"I bet you're glad it's almost over," I said. "Not that anyone should blame you."

Lin chuckled. "Murder and mayhem do take their toll. Mario's death was bad enough, but the guy had enemies everywhere. He ruined a lot of lives."

"What about Nona? She was annoying but hardly a candidate for murder."

Lin sighed. "I agree that it's puzzling. Have any theories about it? Maybe she pushed the killer's buttons and paid the price. From what little I knew of her, she enjoyed needling people."

I'd given that a good deal of thought. Nona must have seen something that implicated Mario's killer. She'd bragged to anyone who would listen that she knew who it was. Not a smart move by such an intelligent woman. Her friends said she had plenty of money so blackmail seemed an unlikely motive. But she might have sought a concession, something that would advance the cause of FACE and humiliate the beauty industry. Or, she might have relished the idea of taunting a murderer and proving her superiority.

"Nona was arrogant. She didn't fear the murderer. According to Malcolm, the librarian, Nona enjoyed having power over others."

He ran his fingers through his thick crop of hair. "Hard to predict what a woman like that wanted. I meet plenty of difficult clients in this job, but she was a real challenge."

"Mario was no picnic to deal with either. His killer was meticulous—planned everything so perfectly. That took precision and determination. I think Nona's murder was spontaneous. A sudden act of passion. You knew Mario from before, didn't you? Think of how humiliated he would have been to expose himself at his moment of greatest triumph."

Lin grimaced. "I suppose you're right. I didn't really know either one of them. Not really. Nona was a stranger, although I'd read enough about her antics to be wary. I met Mario briefly in Italy when I went to bring my sister home. That was a tough period for my family. Linette was a gentle creature, almost ethereal. Too fine for this world. My mother never recovered from her death. Just faded away until finally, she passed last year."

I squeezed his hand. "Oh, forgive me. I didn't mean to pry. Linette's obituary was such a lovely tribute that I felt like I knew her. Especially the line from Lord Byron."

He patted Fantasia and rose from the bench. "He was one of Linette's favorites. She was such a romantic that she saw the world through literature and poetry. Don't worry about hurting me. I've learned to live with their loss, but I still miss them every day. My family. I try to remember the good times we had and not dwell on the loss. That's the secret to survival, I'm told. Carla knows how it feels. She told me that she thought of committing suicide after Mario left her, but something pulled her through. Sophia is another story entirely. Tough as an old boot, that one. When she heard about Mario's will, she exploded. Went ballistic. I heard her screaming all kinds of curses at that attorney. Good thing she didn't have a weapon handy, or he would have been toast. Then we'd have another death on our hands."

"Killian Blaine?" I asked. Thinking of that scenario pleased me. Killian thought he could manipulate any woman, but Sophia taught him otherwise. Score one for the French spitfire.

"It's getting late," Lin said. "I'll walk with you back to the hotel." He anticipated my protest. "No arguments, now. Need I remind you that there's a killer on the loose."

It was easier to acquiesce than to argue. Lin was a kind man whose intentions were honorable. That was rare enough in these turbulent times and I had to admit it was comforting to have additional backup.

I checked my phone on the way to my room and found a text from Violet. She urged me—no, ordered me—to join her in her suite ASAP. Like an obedient niece, I sped down the corridor without combing my hair or disposing of my jacket. An official summons from my aunt could not be ignored. I crossed my fingers, hoping that she had gleaned some useful information from Killian. Time was running out, and the identity of the killer was still unknown. Until it was, the reputations of both Carla and my aunt would be tainted. I'd seen the looks and heard the whispers of the conference-goers. Like most industries, the beauty world was incredibly close and occasionally vicious.

As I approached Violet's suite, a chorus of female voices wafted out. They were joyous sounds, laughter, and general merriment combined with strains of Nina Simone's distinctive music. Violet answered the door with a flute of champagne pressed to her lips. This time the brand was Cristal, not up to the Krug standard but still quite respectable. Violet was swathed in sumptuous silk pajamas in her signature shade and her guests looked suitably festive as well. My running togs were woefully inadequate for the occasion, and I held back using Fantasia as a shield. "Come on in," said my aunt. "Join the party. We're celebrating."

"I'm not dressed for a party. Nobody told me." I seldom whined but this time I didn't hold back. The other guests put me to shame: Carla, resplendent in a Valentino slip dress, Kim elegant as ever in an Armani jumpsuit, and Gemma, garbed in a floor-length concoction of patchwork velvet. I could tell by their high spirits that the Crystal had been flowing for some time. Trays of tempting crudites were placed around the room and Violet had even splurged for a mound of my favorite indulgence, Beluga caviar. At that rate, any profits from the big merger would soon evaporate along with those Russian fish eggs!

Carla glided over and handed me a flute. Although her words were slurred, the message was abundantly clear. "Come on, Marky. Don't be a party pooper! Today marked the start of a brand-new adventure for us. For once in my life, I'm free from the yoke of debt." She raised her glass in a mock salute. "Thanks to Mario Ricci, the vilest villain who ever sold shampoo! That man finally did something decent for me, even if he had to die to do it."

Violet put her arm around her new business partner and hugged her. "You deserve all the good luck in the world, Carla. In the end, I think Mario was truly sorry for the way he treated you."

"Huh! You're a trip, Violet. So smart yet so naïve. Mario cornered me the night before he died and told me he planned to marry Sophia and change his will. I'll never forget his words. He laughed. Can you believe it, that slimy snake laughed in my face? Told me he'd planned to make things right, but he'd reconsidered. Then he made a low-ball offer to buy my business. Said it would be his wedding gift for Sophia."

The room grew quiet as we listened in stunned silence to Carla's tale. Everyone, even Violet, who knew him best, seemed shocked by Mario's perfidy. Carla gulped as tears ran down her face. "I swear, someone saved me the trouble of killing him on the spot. I planned to spoil his Ricci Rich reveal by using this—Carla reached into her purse and produced a pearl-handled derringer."

Kim blanched. "Oh Carla, no. You couldn't murder someone. Even a monster like Mario. He wasn't worth ruining your life over."

Carla's eyes filled with tears. "You still don't get it, Kim. Until today, my business—the thing I'd worked and slaved for—was doomed. Without *Hair Deluxe,* my life was already ruined. You bet your life I planned to kill Mario. I don't have a rich husband to pay my bills like some of you do."

Kim reeled back as if she had been slapped. On Sirius XM, Nina Simone warbled about "The Other Woman," a song that seemed particularly apropos under the circumstances. Even Gemma was momentarily dumbstruck. Fantasia, ever sensitive to the atmosphere, dispelled the tension by putting her head in Carla's lap. Meanwhile, I took a moment to process things. Had my ears deceived me, or had Carla just confessed to Mario's murder? I kept my head down, fearful of reading my friends' faces. As usual, Aunt Violet saved the day.

"It's been an emotional day for both of us, Carla, but you must be careful about your language. The killer is still free, and Gideon regards both of us as potential suspects. Don't make it easy for him. Sophia has been whispering all kinds of things into his ear."

Gemma spooned a taste of Beluga on a cracker and spoke up. "Come on. Forget about this doom and gloom. You two were just about to fill us in when Marky showed up. What did Killian Blaine say?"

Violet took her cue and immediately treated us to a faithful account of the business meeting. Naturally, Mario's will still had to go into probate, but the provisions were surprisingly simple. After discharging all debts, the balance of the Ricci empire would be evenly split between Violet and Carla. At that time, both legatees agreed to sell their interests to the international conglomerate represented by Blaine's firm. I was curious about the sum involved but too constrained by good manners to inquire. Fortunately, Gemma felt no such qualms. "How much money are we talking about here?" she asked. "Mario was pretty tight with a buck, but was it all talk, or did he have a lot of dough?"

Violet shrugged and laughed at my pushy partner. Then, she named a staggering sum that comprised the legacy. It ensured that neither Carla nor Violet would ever again worry about money. I hadn't taken him seriously, but Mario's emotional volatility did not extend to his business dealings. They were crisp, well-reasoned, and very shrewd. Small wonder that Sophia had agreed to his marriage proposal.

Contemplating her new financial status helped Carla to recover her poise. She dried her tears, apologized to Kim, and faced the group with a triumphant look on her face. "I refuse to dwell on the past, ladies. The weak woman moping over Mario is long gone. Let him rot in hell where he belongs."

"What about Nona," Kim asked. "She didn't deserve to die. I admit she was a troublemaker, but nothing worth murdering over."

Carla shrugged. "Collateral damage. Frankly I don't care about her one way or the other. Focus on the future, I say. It's looking mighty bright."

Gemma and I exchanged glances. This was certainly a new side of Carla Standish that we hadn't seen before. The woman standing before us was quite unapologetic about murder. She had the skill to poison the Ricci Rich and a simmering hatred for her former husband. Eliminating Nona would have been a regrettable but necessary act. I shivered and turned my attention to Kim.

"Are we sure that Mario intended to marry Sophia? No offense, but he may have been taunting Carla just to hurt her. I really misjudged him. Never realized that he enjoyed inflicting pain."

Kim chose her words carefully. "Mario was focused on comfort—his. He was a realist who understood what a rough ride Sophia would have given him. After all, she'd done it before. With that volcanic temper, she could easily erupt and make his life miserable. If he was toying with her, Mário was playing a dangerous game. I could see her febrile brain plotting to destroy him and enjoying every minute."

Violet sipped her wine cautiously. "Okay, ladies. Time to turn in our detective badges. Leave everything to the professionals. We're not equipped to deal with a double murderer. Gideon knows what he's doing, and he has the establishment behind him. Let's back off and let him do it."

That pleased Gemma. "Don't forget, he has Benny to help him too. At least for a few days more. You know, they found a couple of vials of liquid nicotine in the trash. No prints, of course, but still…"

I bit my tongue to avoid starting an argument with her. We already knew that fully fifty or more participants vaped. Most of them used unflavored nicotine, so that got us nowhere.

"What else did Benny tell you?" I asked.

For once, Gemma took a measured approach. Instead of using superlatives to describe her fiancé's exploits, she downplayed everything. "There isn't much to tell. Benny said that Gideon can't seem to get anywhere with this. All the town bigwigs are pressuring him to do something, anything. I think he'd arrest his own mother at this point."

Even more reason to be wary. During the first five days of the conference, we'd had a major theft and two murders, all unsolved. The Chief hadn't exactly covered himself in glory. Traverse City billed itself as the ideal American resort town, and the powers that be were determined to keep that reputation untarnished at any cost.

Violet closed her eyes and grimaced. "All the more reason to be very cautious. Remember that old World War two slogan, 'loose lips sink ships'? In this case, one careless comment might torpedo everything for all of us."

"I heard one of the big network shows is interested in the case," Kim said. "*Dateline,* or maybe *48 Hours.* You must admit there's a lot of drama involved. Poisoned hair conditioner—not your typical murder weapon, and Nona's death adds more drama to the mix."

Gemma jumped up and twirled. "Wow-wee. We'd be famous. Think of the publicity for POPPET. You can't buy that kind of advertising. Maybe they'd even interview us."

"Hardly an endorsement for our beauty products, Gemma. Our best bet is to hope the attention fades away without doing too much damage." Violet's repressive frown proved that she had considered all the angles and was genuinely concerned.

I thought of our local news stringer Malcolm and wondered if he was stirring the pot. This might be his only chance to leave the library and connect with big city outlets. He wouldn't think twice about scuttling our deal to advance his own interests. I could hardly blame him for seizing the opportunity, but that left Violet and Carla vulnerable. Killian Blaine's name also popped into my head. He wouldn't hesitate to dangle information in front of the national media. I could just picture his handsome mug gracing the television screen or leading a podcast as a celebrity lawyer or commentator.

Much of the gaiety deserted our little party as we contemplated the worst possible case. Normally our group bubbled over with plans and ideas, but this evening was the exception. Violet and Carla had gotten a tremendous windfall but the downside of that might well be disastrous. A sudden pounding on the door stopped everyone in place. It was reminiscent of the game Freeze that we had often played as children. In this instance, as the last to freeze, I was forced to answer the door.

"Go on, Marky. Don't be a scaredy cat. Answer the darn door, for heaven's sake." Gemma turned my way but remained stationary. I wobbled a bit but edged toward the door, managing to complete my task. Why were my nerves so fraught and my legs so weak? I had nothing to fear, and neither did my colleagues. At least, I hoped that was true. Violet's face showed no trace of emotion, but Kim and Carla looked panicky. No sense in overreacting. Our caller was probably the room service guy or an especially officious member of hotel security. The mystery was solved when a familiar voice rang out.

"Police, ladies, open the door now." I stumbled as the stentorian tones of Benny Soto filled the air. With him in attack mode, this encounter was

188

destined to be unpleasant. I summoned every vestige of calm that I possessed and slowly turned the doorknob. Benny would have relished the chance to satisfy his macho fantasies by breaking down the door. I refused to oblige him.

"What is it, Benny? Noise complaint about our party?"

He barged in past me, accompanied by an older deputy I had not seen before. "It's Officer Soto to you, Ms. Davis. We're here on official business with an arrest warrant. Stand aside, or you'll be joining us downtown."

My mouth felt dry as I croaked out a response. "What are you doing? Have you gone mad?" My friends did little to help the situation: Carla shivered, Gemma's eyes bugged out, and Kim supported herself by leaning against the table. Even Violet was temporarily rendered speechless.

Soto dangled handcuffs as he strode up to Carla and pointed. "She's the one. Carla Standish, you're under arrest for murder."

Her face lost all color as Carla collapsed in an ungainly heap.

Chapter Twelve

"Help her up, Benny, you big oaf. Don't just let her lie there." Gemma left no room for refusal. Somewhat reluctantly, Benny and his colleague each took one of Carla's arms and helped her to the couch. Violet sprang into action and dabbed Carla's face with a wet napkin. "What's this all about, Benny? Where's Gideon?"

Soto folded his arms and glared. "That's none of your concern, ma'am. Stand aside or face charges for impeding an arrest." That highhanded behavior, so typical of Benny, was designed to intimidate. Fortunately, it had the opposite effect on me. Despite mighty efforts to control myself, I laughed in his face.

"Let's see the warrant," I said, holding out my hand. "I presume you do have one."

Benny's normally olive complexion grew scarlet with either rage or embarrassment. I couldn't tell which one. He fumbled in his back pocket but came up empty. "I don't need one, smarty. Exigent circumstances."

Gemma regained her senses and stood toe to toe with her fiancé. "Oh, give it a rest. We've all been here most of the night, and no one got murdered. Explain yourself."

"Chief Hall wants to interrogate this suspect." He pointed at Carla. "That's why we're here."

Carla had regained consciousness, although she still looked a bit green around the gills. "I didn't kill anyone," she whimpered. Violet put her arm around Carla's shoulder and confronted Benny. "If Gideon wants to speak with her, Carla will cooperate in every way. She'll need to call her attorney, of course, and I urge her to say nothing more until she consults with him."

I doubted that Carla had a criminal attorney, but one name immediately sprang to mind. Killian Blaine would know how to handle this situation, and he'd have no fear of Benny and his minions. As I checked the pocket of my jogging suit for my iPhone, Benny vaulted into a crouch as if daring me to draw a weapon.

"No worries." I dangled the phone in front of his nose. "Non-lethal weapon." I had the number on speed dial and as luck would have it, Killian answered immediately. "We have a situation here," I said. "Need your help ASAP."

I moved to a far corner of the room and summarized Carla's dilemma. He remained cool and collected despite the hour and the unexpected nature of my request. If Killian had any female company, I couldn't hear any other voices. He spoke briefly to Carla, telling her not to worry and to button her lips. Meanwhile, Violet gathered her belongings and whispered softly to Carla.

"No problem, officer. We'll go with you to see Gideon." She shook her head when Kim, Gemma, and I tried to join the group. "Stay here. We won't be gone long."

Benny snorted but had the good sense to remain silent. My aunt's glare deterred him from cuffing Carla, although I knew he was itching to do so. As a minor concession, Benny agreed to take the service elevator to the lobby, thus saving Carla some of the adverse publicity that was certain to follow.

After they left, I poured myself a snifter of brandy and swallowed it in one gulp. Kim and Gemma did the same although I noticed that my partner doubled her dosage.

"Hey," she groused as I gave her the eye, "it's medicinal. I'm still in shock." Kim shook her head. "I don't understand it. Why arrest Carla now? They can't possibly have any evidence against her. At least nothing new."

Gemma shrugged. "Something must have happened. Even Benny wouldn't cook up an arrest without having something behind it. I know that boy can be impetuous, but he values his job too much to risk it."

Once again, I chose to exercise discretion. Gemma's view of Benny clashed violently with reality, but she clung to it with the ferocity of a mama bear. If Gideon Hall had enough evidence to arrest Carla, then we had every reason to worry. He was cautious by nature and thoroughly professional. Benny— not so much. I poured myself a glass of Pellegrino and leaned back on the recliner. Perhaps if I just closed my eyes, inspiration might come to me. Kim and Gemma lounged on the couch, their voices lulling me into a fugue state. When my aunt returned, I was shocked to see that two hours had passed. Violet stowed her things and immediately poured herself a brandy. It suddenly dawned on me that she was alone. Carla was either in custody or in her own suite. Kim and Gemma, who had also been napping, rubbed their eyes and leapt up from the couch.

"What happened," Gemma asked. "Where's Carla?"

Kim's eyes searched my aunt's face as though expecting to hear some very bad news. She looked very close to tears.

Violet waved them off and lowered herself into a wing chair. "Don't panic. Carla wasn't charged. She was exhausted, and I insisted that she get into bed and rest."

Although I longed to pepper her with questions, I forced myself to wait patiently. My aunt would share everything in her own good time. She did so after removing her heels and finishing her drink.

"Okay. Here's the story. Benny overstated when he threatened to arrest Carla. Gideon did caution her but only as a person of interest. He was his usual low-key self, but he zeroed in on Carla's hatred for Mario and her unfortunate public comments."

Kim heaved a sigh of relief, but Gemma's expression was far from pleased. Had Benny's overblown performance once again cast doubt on their relationship? As Gemma's best friend and business partner, I secretly hoped so. It couldn't be easy knowing you were engaged to a dolt.

"Why question Carla now?" I asked. "In the middle of the night. What could be so urgent?"

Violet nodded. "Precisely what Killian asked. I think the time factor forced Gideon to act. When the conference ends, so does any real chance to find the killer. Killian's performance was magnificent. He was firm with Gideon

192

but respectful, too. Carla couldn't have been in better hands."

We absorbed that information and waited for more. It appeared that an anonymous tipster had notified the police that Carla Standish, a non-smoker, had purchased a large quantity of liquid nicotine on the day preceding Mario's murder. Carla had motives aplenty for hating Mario, as she had made abundantly clear to any number of people. The financial incentive only upped the ante.

"Gideon had done his homework," Violet said. "Can't fault the man for suspecting Carla. She had access to the Ricci Rich conditioner and the knowledge of how it was used. Recall, Carla was a chemist by trade before branching off into cosmetics. She knew the poison would be absorbed into the scalp while Mario sat patiently unaware of what awaited him."

"Why would Carla order that nicotine?" Kim asked. "She's too intelligent to leave such an open trail if she planned to kill Mario with it."

"She denied it, of course," Violet said. "But the purchase was charged to her credit card. Killian insisted that since her information was on file, anyone could have used it. Gideon wasn't convinced, however."

There was more to come. I dreaded hearing it but felt compelled to ask. "What else?"

"One of the FACE crowd heard Carla quarreling with Nona on the evening she was murdered. Not a polite exchange of views either. Angry words and threats. Remember Carla was late for our gathering."

The expressions on our faces said it all. We remembered every detail, including the stain on Carla's beautiful outfit. She said it was wine, but it could well have been blood. Nona's blood.

Violet's next words confirmed my worst fears. "It gets worse. Gideon was very well-informed. He commandeered Carla's silk garment from the dry cleaners and sent it to forensics. If they find blood evidence or Nona's DNA, look out. Even Killian won't be able to forestall her arrest."

Kim shuddered. "I can't believe it. I've known Carla for years, and she's one of the least violent people I've ever met." She sensed our skepticism and quickly backtracked. "I know she talks tough, but believe me, it's all talk. Carla collects any stray animal she sees and finds it a home. She donates her products to women's shelters, too, and helps them transition into jobs. The woman has a big heart."

"Bet I know who dropped a dime on Carla," said Gemma. "Malcolm. Wait till I get my hands on that boy. He'll hide in the library stacks forever, the little traitor."

I urged Gemma to calm down until we got all the facts. Malcolm could still be useful to us if he wasn't too terrified to talk. I didn't discount Sophia as the source of the leak either. She knew that if Carla was convicted of murder, she'd be unable to inherit her share of Mario's estate. Guess who would be first in line to claim some of the spoils or to try negotiating a settlement.

It was almost midnight when our group disbursed. Despite my exhaustion, I owed Fantasia one final potty break before turning in. I could have asked Gemma to join me, but I hated to show weakness. Pride had been my downfall in the past. My mother had called me pig-headed on more than one occasion, but with a pinch of luck, nothing bad would happen this time.

The silence in the deserted lobby was tomblike, and despite the abundant outside lighting, I felt a premonition of danger. Devotion to my pup compelled me to dispel such fantasies and fulfill my duties as a responsible pet parent. It didn't banish my fears, however even though the whistle and pepper spray were still nestled in the pocket of my jacket, and Fantasia herself was a formidable ally. Only a coward or a sensible woman would resist taking a brisk walk in the dark while a double murderer roamed free. I recalled my favorite Shakespeare quote from *Julius Caesar*. "Cowards die many times before their death. The valiant never taste of death but once." I wasn't particularly valiant. I tried to be brave whenever possible, even when good common sense dictated otherwise. Despite his brave words, Julius Caesar hadn't fared too well when confronted by assailants. I hoped to do better.

The walking path was illuminated by overhead streetlights. They didn't stop the thick shrubbery surrounding the area from casting ominous shadows, but they provided some degree of comfort. I urged Fantasia into a brisk trot and hummed a catchy tune to buoy my spirits. When she suddenly stopped and growled, I went into full panic mode. My heart thudded, and adrenalin flowed freely. Maybe I screeched in terror, although that was pure speculation. Either way, I fled the scene in full gallop. I could hear footsteps behind me, and that spurred me on. When a man's voice called my name, I stopped, gasped for breath, and turned to confront him using every technique I'd mastered in self-defense training.

"Wow," said Killian Blaine. "You're like a gazelle. Didn't mean to frighten you, Marky."

"What did you expect in the middle of the night with a killer on the loose?" When I'm flustered, I sometimes become surly. In this case, Killian Blaine deserved every bit of ire I could muster. I gathered Fantasia's lead and collapsed on a bench that was conveniently located in my path. The smirk on his face told me that Killian was enjoying this scene way too much.

"Ah come on. Give me a break. I just saved your pal Carla from spending the night in the hoosegow and had to have a smoke." He pulled out a vape pen. "See. No weapon."

I searched his face for signs of guilt but found none. Lawyers were skilled in deception, so that meant very little. "You never said you vaped. What else have you been keeping secret?"

Killian must have found me amusing because, once again, he guffawed. "Let's see—several murdered wives, Ponzi schemes, and massive unpaid debts. Forgive me, my lady. I also confess to the sin of occasionally using e-cigarettes. Last time I checked, that wasn't illegal."

"Not unless you use the nicotine to murder someone. Is that flavored or plain?"

Killian's composure finally cracked. His glare was so menacing that Fantasia blocked his path and growled. "You have really lost your senses. For the record, I did not kill Mario, although he richly deserved his untimely end. As for Nona Adams, it was only a matter of time before someone bopped that woman on her head. She was truly unpleasant. There, does that satisfy you?"

I didn't apologize, but I turned the conversation to other matters. "My aunt sang your praises tonight. Said you handled things perfectly."

He bowed his head in faux humility. "Glad to hear it. Violet is a woman of taste and discernment."

"Cut out the clowning. Just how much trouble is Carla in? For the record, I don't think she's a killer. Mario's death was exquisitely plotted but Carla's emotional by nature. She would strike out in anger and make a mess of things. I can't see her sending threatening poems, either. She knew Mario was scarcely the literary type, so the effort would be wasted."

Killian crossed his long legs and shrugged. "So, I guess that leaves us back at square one. Unless, of course, you still cast me as the villain of the piece."

My ferocious frown stopped him in his tracks. He agreed that Carla was the prime suspect but added that my aunt was still in the mix as well.

"That's absurd. She didn't need his money and certainly didn't hate him. If anything, Violet was far too generous with that egomaniac. She forgave his bad behavior. Coddled him even. Besides, I doubt that she even had a conversation with Nona, let alone a brawl. My aunt simply doesn't do that kind of thing. She rises above it."

The strong lake breeze caused me to shiver. That prompted Killian to do the gallant thing and put his arm around me. "You're really something, Marky Davis. Spunky and smart. Just the type of woman I'd want in my corner if I were ever in a tight spot."

He meant it as a compliment, although spunky was hardly a term of endearment. Sexy or alluring would have been preferable. Killian tilted my chin toward him and kissed my forehead. It was still a more brotherly kiss than I had hoped for, but at least it showed some progress.

"Someday soon, when this mess is cleared up, you and I need to have a serious talk."

"About what?" I held my breath, waiting for his answer.

"Us."

"There is no us. We barely know each other."

Killian chuckled. "I plan to remedy that as soon as possible. Believe it or not, I can be very persuasive."

I held my ground, but it wasn't easy. "I wouldn't put anything past you. But right now, romance is the least of my concerns. My aunt needs my help. Carla too. Mario wasn't much, but he deserved to live. As for Nona, I admit she was a major pain. That woman had ego issues that wouldn't quit. No wonder she confronted a killer. Trying to prove her superiority once again."

"Okay. Who's your primary suspect? You and Gemma have been snooping around since the first murder. You must have come to some conclusions."

He was humoring me. I knew that but didn't care. Truth be told, I had no suspect in mind although Sophia was my preferred villain. If Mario told her about his will, she would have gladly eliminated him just for spite. Proof was difficult to come by and the conference was almost at an end. Gemma and I weren't trained investigators just talented amateurs.

Killian gave my shoulders a little shake. "Listen to me, Marky. Back off. Let the police handle the investigation. You and Gemma go back to Harbor Bay and run your business. Beautify the women of Michigan, or the entire country, for that matter. I don't want you to get hurt."

His suggestion was tempting, but I had that stubborn Davis gene. Who knew what might be accomplished in two more days? Instead of answering, I punted. "Makes sense. Let me speak with Gemma first. I know Benny has been bugging her about doing the same thing."

We walked back to the hotel in silence, both of us absorbed in our thoughts. Killian insisted upon walking me to my door even though Fantasia was by my side. Was it a gallant gesture or another example of his patronizing behavior? Either way romance was off the menu that night since he made no attempt to join me. Even if he had, I was too exhausted to debate the issue. I brushed my teeth, curled up in bed with my dog, and slipped into a deep, dreamless sleep.

* * *

Violet texted me early the next morning. Way too early in my book. She'd scheduled a breakfast meeting in her suite, and my attendance was compulsory. That immediately galvanized me into action. I glanced in the mirror and saw, to my horror, that last evening's activities had taken a toll on my hair and complexion. Self-improvement had absolutely nothing to do with Killian Blaine or any faux rivalry with Sophia Lauren. It was my obligation as a purveyor of beauty products to always look my best. Customers, and especially my Aunt Violet, expected nothing less. That was my story, and I stuck to it. After using Oribe's excellent dry shampoo and a judicious application of foundation and blush, I was finally ready to face my colleagues. I stepped into a delicious yellow confection that elevated my spirits and flattered my figure. Fantasia approved and we made a jaunty pair as we exited the hotel. Our morning walk was brief, but it served the purpose. We managed to avoid predators of every stripe or lotharios on the make and returned to Violet's suite before the eggs cooled.

"Aren't you a little ray of sunshine," Gemma said. Her waspish tone clearly indicated that my buddy had not had a good evening. Trouble with Benny always translated into sour comments and frowns. Rather than surrender to her bad mood, I chose to rise above it by smiling broadly and chirping a greeting. That drove her mad.

Violet ignored our little drama. "Help yourself to some eggs, ladies. Protein is essential before a busy day. Besides, Carla will be joining us, and we need to show our support."

I wasn't hungry, but the sight of perfectly turned cheese omelets tempted me anyway. Gemma, who seldom missed a meal, dove into the buffet with her customary zeal. Food and sex were her top pursuits, and she gave both her full attention. Violet filled her plate with eggs and fruit but avoided starch. Surely, whole wheat toast could pass muster even if it was a dreaded carbohydrate. I convinced myself of that as I chowed down.

"Is Carla in the clear?" Gemma asked. She buttered a bagel and took a big bite.

"Put it this way," Violet said. "Gideon doesn't have enough evidence to charge her—yet. Keep your fingers crossed that the stain on her dress was not blood."

At that point, Kim and Carla joined us. Kim looked elegant in a ruby red pantsuit, but despite her vivid mint green dress, Carla's face reflected the travail she had just suffered. Both women headed immediately for the espresso machine and poured a generous serving of that magic brew.

"I know you're dying to quiz me about last night," Carla said. "Oops! Not a great time to speak about dying. Forgive the gallows humor, ladies."

Kim put her arm around Carla's shoulders and hugged her friend. "We're just glad you're here."

"Was Gideon hard on you?" Gemma asked. "He can be tough even though he's always a good guy." Fortunately, she elected not to ask about Benny's behavior. We'd seen enough to know the answer to that.

Carla straightened her shoulders and showed some spirit. "It was nothing new. Let them test my dress. They're just wasting time and money. And for the record, I didn't order that nicotine, no matter what the sales slip said. Anyone could have charged it to my room. Smoking is a vile habit that I have always avoided."

"People heard you say you hated Mario," Gemma said. "Naturally, you had every reason to loathe the little creep, but your timing was bad."

Carla shrugged. "Perhaps. I didn't mention everything to the police. Killian advised me to answer truthfully but not volunteer anything extraneous."

I had to admit that hearing his name lifted my spirits. Killian's comments echoed those that my idol Perry Mason would have made. Sweet!

"I'll bet Sophia dropped the dime on you," Gemma said. "Trying to excuse herself. Or maybe it was Malcolm, after all. He'd do anything to curry favor with the cops. Never did trust him. Marky can tell you that."

"I don't even know this, Malcolm," Carla said. "Why would he implicate me?"

Violet looked pensive. "We shouldn't accuse anyone at this point. They don't have much time to act. Once the conference ends, everyone will scatter. Linn Baugh told me that the town council wants to call in the State police if they don't make an arrest. That's a big blow to Gideon if they do so."

I refused to speculate and kept my thoughts to myself. The character of the victims still bothered me. Mario had blithely disregarded the pain he inflicted on so many people, mostly women. He was a willful child who grabbed what he liked and discarded anything that bored him. Nona Adams had courted controversy with a vengeance. She was cocky and unpleasant, two qualities that helped seal her fate. Despite their prominence and a wide circle of acquaintances, neither victim had truly been mourned. That was a sad commentary on their lives. It also suggested that any number of people could have nursed a grudge against Mario that finally resulted in his murder.

"The hair styling competition is today," Kim said. "I'm one of the judges, and it promises to be a lot of fun. Linn recruited some of the local high school kids to serve as models. Most teens still have a decent head of hair, and they tend to be adventurous."

Carla brightened at the prospect of displaying her products. Hair *Deluxe* featured some truly remarkable items that were cruelty free and packed with protein. She had every reason to be proud of them. Violet had agreed to showcase the Ricci line, excluding the infamous *Ricci Rich* conditioner of course.

"Too bad," she mused. "Mario was on to something with that product. I tried it and had amazing results. We've decided to repackage and rename it as soon as we start up the business. I considered dubbing it 'Mario's Magic Masque,' as a tribute to him."

Gemma wrinkled her nose. "Yeah, but who would even try that stuff, no matter what you call it? I certainly wouldn't."

Violet laughed. "People have very short memories. As I said before, Tylenol is still on the shelf and very popular. Seven people died in that wave of poisonings."

I recalled reading about the incidents in the Chicago area in the 1980s. I also recalled that the evil perpetrator was never identified. Would the same thing happen in our case?

We agreed not to dwell on the negative and to try to enjoy the festivities instead. Some of the nation's top haircutters were featured on the program. They'd named it "Makeover Madness," always a popular draw. The afternoon session featured one of the biggest dilemmas facing beauty professionals: color correction. I pitied the patrons who tried at-home color and ended up slinking into a salon begging for help. The price of failure was enormous since most women still regarded luscious locks as their "crowning glory." Extensions and straighteners had only exacerbated the horrors faced by the hair obsessed. That didn't count the many women whose hair thinned as they aged, either.

"I don't expect that FACE crowd to show up," Gemma said. "They have a real bee in their bonnets about anything smacking of self-improvement. You should hear the things they say. I still wonder if they weren't involved in wiping out Mario. He called Nona ugly right to her face, if you recall. Nobody likes hearing that."

Violet dismissed the theory. "To each her own. Besides, one of their group, I think her name is Althea, has signed up for my demo. Surely that suggests that not all their members loathe what we stand for."

The poet of FACE? That was interesting. Althea had also nabbed one of the beauty prizes at last evening's raffle. Had we made cosmetics convert, or was this part of some bizarre ritual? I pictured the FACE members burning those pricey hair products at stake in a reversal of the Salem witch trials. Another thought struck me. Althea was a poet. She had to be conversant with John Donne, Grey, and all the others, even if she abhorred everything they stood for. Perhaps Mario's poison pen pal was not his murderer, just an adversary who wished to taunt him. As I considered that theory, my colleagues droned on about forthcoming seminars. It wasn't courteous but I admit to zoning out while they babbled on.

Kim mentioned that the evening session featured a seminar on wigs with high-end representatives giving lectures, doing demos, and promoting their products. "We'd gotten a ton of inquiries about hair replacement for cancer patients," she explained. "You wouldn't believe how realistic the products are these days."

Violet nodded. "A necessary adaptation to the market. Illness hits hard at every level, but there's something particularly cruel about losing one's hair at a time when morale is low."

The conference agenda intrigued me, but I was still plagued by doubt. Would we ever find those responsible for Mario and Nona's deaths? The final day included awards, speeches, and plenty of hugs but by evening, most of the participants would vanish.

"Quarter for your thoughts," Gemma said. "Inflation, you know."

She'd caught me wool-gathering, and I couldn't deny it. "Any additional insights from Benny on where the investigation stands?" Talk about sinking to the depths of desperation! I was now probing for ideas in the thought processes of bumbling Benny Soto. It was a sad commentary on my detective skills, or lack thereof.

Gemma rolled her eyes and looked coy. "Well...Benny's been kind of secretive, but I can tell you this much. Gideon has a suspect. A hot prospect we haven't thought of before." She grinned. "Isn't that exciting?"

Carla jumped into the conversation. "What? You mean someone besides me? Hallelujah! Maybe I'll be able to leave this place without losing my reputation after all."

We gave Gemma a hard stare. Even Kim, who typically played peacemaker, frowned at my partner. "Come on, Gemma. Give us a hint. We're supposed to be a team."

Gemma hung her head and admitted that Benny hadn't revealed a name, although she was confident that he soon would. "Don't stress. As soon as I know, you guys will know, too."

We left things at that and scrambled for the elevator. I pledged to become a sponge, absorbing every morsel of beauty and wisdom. Let Gideon and Benny deal with killers and handle the tough stuff. After all, that's what they were paid to do.

* * *

Killian Blaine was nowhere to be found, and that was fine with me. My feelings about him were complicated. On one hand, I was attracted to the man, but on the other, I distrusted him. It was a conundrum that demanded some serious thought, and I had no time for it now. The session was ready to start, and most of my colleagues had queued up in the aisles, laughing and gossiping with friends. As I entered the crowded auditorium looking for a seat, I got a nasty shock. The only available spot was a front-row space next to the odious Sophia Lauren. She glared when she saw me, and I briefly considered making a hasty exit. Courage prevailed, however, and I pasted a hammy grin on my face and sat down.

"Still playing detective?" she sneered. "Maybe you should give up and focus on your business instead. So many small operations fail."

"Funny thing," I said. "Someone told me you're still on the suspect list." I shrugged. "Probably just a rumor. You know how gossip spreads at this kind of event."

Sophia's reaction was priceless. Her mouth dropped open, and she sputtered something vile. Confession—I assume that it was, but since my knowledge of French curses is limited, I might be mistaken. She didn't attack me, so that was a plus. We spent the next fifty minutes sitting in stony silence while a trio of talented haircutters entertained us. Just as the session ended, I received an urgent text from Gemma. The wording was brief, but the message was clear. It read, "Emergency! Arrest made." I leapt up, tumbled out of my seat, and loped up the aisle, anxious to avoid the crowd. My thoughts were confused, and I prayed that Carla and Violet were both safe. Gemma was stationed outside, ready to intercept me. Her eyes were wild, and she clutched my arm so tightly that I yelped.

"Can you believe it?" she asked. "When Benny told me, I almost fainted. Who would ever have believed it?"

I guided Gemma toward a deserted alcove and shook her. "Stop! I have no idea what you're talking about. Who was arrested?" I closed my eyes, praying that some itinerant vagrant would be named.

Gemma paused. "Oh, I thought I told you. They arrested Malcolm Hadley."

Chapter Thirteen

"Malcolm? The librarian?" I heard the words but still couldn't believe them. "What possible motive could he have to murder two people? You got it wrong."

Gemma shook her head. "Afraid not. Benny told me so to my face. I couldn't believe it either. Malcolm didn't seem like the type to me. All talk."

"Does Violet know? We need to tell her and Carla right away. Come on." I rushed toward the elevator in a blind panic and collided with the man himself, Killian Blaine.

"Whoa," he said. "Where's the fire?"

Gemma was never at a loss for words. "You've heard about the arrest, I suppose."

"Chief Hall notified me as a courtesy. He wanted Carla to know."

I was still baffled. "But what motive could Malcolm possibly have?"

Killian hurried away, promising to get more details as soon as possible. I decided that the best antidote to anxiety was taking Fantasia for a long walk. I texted Violet and asked her to join us. If the murders were indeed solved, there was no reason to fear any violence. Besides, my beautiful Fantasia would keep us safe.

My aunt already knew about Malcolm's arrest. Of course, she did! Violet Davis had more sources than a small-town switchboard. She had never met Malcolm, however, so I shared my impressions of the tattooed librarian.

"He doesn't seem like the type to murder someone," I said.

Violet rolled her eyes. "Marky, there is no type, at least not in most cases. Think how charming Theodore Bundy supposedly was. I'm certain if Gideon arrested Malcolm, there must be credible evidence. Be glad that Carla is in the clear."

My faith in Gideon was immense, but he wasn't infallible. And he was under pressure to serve up a suspect—anyone— even if the evidence was scant. We paused after a mile and sat on a bench. That's where Killian found us.

"Oh good," he said. "Both of you are here. I promised to get more details, and I have. The Chief couldn't tell me everything, but he shared enough."

I was puzzled. "Why pick on Malcolm? We hardly saw him around the conference center, and I doubt that he knew Mario very well."

According to Killian, they had booked Malcolm on suspicion of murder/.

"Why?" Gemma squawked. "That doesn't make any sense."

Killian's eyes twinkled, and he gave us a bow. "You can take credit for that. You and Gemma. It seems Malcolm and Nona had a violent quarrel. Your librarian pal acknowledged it when Gideon pressed him."

It still didn't make any sense. That didn't equate to a double homicide, did it? I put my hands on my hips and confronted Killian. "Okay. There's more. I know there's more to this."

Malcolm may have murdered Nona in a frenzy, but why eliminate Mario? It was a big jump from manslaughter to homicidal maniac, and I didn't believe he'd made that leap. There was more to this story, and I intended to find it out.

"I think you should hear the story from Gideon. He's waiting for you in his office."

I jumped up. "Gemma and I have been on this case from the beginning. I'll call her right away. We should both hear the story."

Killian wasn't surprised. He sighed and turned back toward Main Street. "I'm sure he expects no less, Marky. Let's go."

* * *

Gideon Hall's genial smile faded into a grimace when he saw me and Gemma, but he retained the façade of the professional lawman. I suspected that the presence of Aunt Violet and Killian Blaine helped to keep his temper in check. Gideon ushered us into his conference room, where that stalwart deputy Benny Soto stood guard.

"Again, thanks for coming," Gideon said. "This shouldn't take too long. You probably heard that we've made an arrest."

I couldn't control myself, so I plunged into the conversation. "It was quite a shock. I understand that you charged Malcolm with Nona's death. Or has that changed?"

Violet squeezed my arm and faced the Chief, turning on the charm. "Forgive my niece, Gideon. She can be impetuous sometimes. We appreciate your hard work but can't help being surprised."

I've always believed that Gideon nursed a secret passion for my aunt that had not dissipated through the years. His reaction confirmed my suspicion. They exchanged smiles and shared plenty of eye contact before he spoke.

"Malcolm admitted that he quarreled with Nona, Violet. The law makes no distinction like that. He has not admitted to the murders, however. We're still working on that angle."

Killian's eyes had that predatory look again. Behold the handsome hawk, ready to seize his prey. "I must admit that this doesn't seem to connect with double murder. How were Mario and Nona on Malcolm's radar?"

Gideon exhaled loudly but kept his composure. "We're still working on that. For the record, Malcolm denies any involvement in the murders."

A loud snort from Benny Soto voiced his opinion of Malcolm's claims.

"May I speak with him?" I asked. "We got to know each other during the conference. He might feel more comfortable speaking with me."

That suggestion evoked a strong response from both Killian and the Chief.

"You're delusional," Killian said. "Stop playing detective and go back to the conference."

Gideon's reaction was milder but more emphatic. He folded his arms and gave me a hard stare. "No way, Marky. I won't let you compromise my case. Malcolm can speak with his lawyer when he gets one, but no one else."

Soto didn't even try to hide his glee. The little twit's smirk lit up the room. I was bloodied but unbowed. With nothing to lose, I tossed another question into the mix.

"Does Malcolm vape? I've never seen him do that. Besides, he was partnering with Nona on a hit piece about the conference, you know. One that might get him a permanent slot as an investigative reporter. Why kill her when she was sort of the golden goose?"

Violet flashed me an approving smile. "Her questions make sense, Gideon."

The big man reached into his desk drawer and pulled out a sheet of paper. "Okay. Here's one thing I can share with you. Maybe then you'll back off and let the professionals go to work. Our librarian ordered a full case of liquid nicotine. Unflavored. Oh, he claimed it was for his brother, who vapes to relieve anxiety, but that seems awfully suspicious. A jury would question the amount and the timing of his action. I'm sure of that."

My thoughts whirled with several possible retorts, but I confined them to myself. I had to face the real possibility that Gideon was right.

"We'll be on our way," Killian said. Violet thanked the Chief and herded Gemma and me out the door.

"Come on, girls. We still have work to do before the conference wraps up. I assume Killian will notify Carla. We'll let Kim know the good news."

Killian nodded. He should have been jubilant since Carla and Violet were no longer under suspicion, but his manner was curiously subdued.

I said very little on our walk back to the hotel. I was way too busy making plans. Someway somehow, I must convince Gideon to change his mind and allow me access to Malcolm. I was certain that the librarian was innocent of murder and that he held the key to solving the case. Feminine wiles had no effect on the Chief, and girlish charm was a wasted effort. Guile and stealth were my only weapons, and they relied heavily on finding the weak link in Gideon's operation. That meant luring Benny Soto into deserting his post. Gemma, my stealth weapon, would have to immediately be pressed into service.

When I broached the subject, Gemma's eyes brightened. She leapt up from her seat and did a little dance. "Count me in, Marky. I'll have Benny so confused he won't know what day it is, let alone where they stashed Malcolm."

Violet raised her eyebrows and put out a cautionary hand. "Stop right there, ladies. If this is going to work, it requires planning. You can't just storm the police station and expect to find Malcolm. Finesse. That's what we need. Don't underestimate Gideon Hall. He's wily, and in this instance, his reputation and job are on the line." She bowed her head and gave a sly smile. "Of course, I'll be glad to do my part. Gideon is my date for the closing ceremonies this evening. I'll get the particulars from Kim and ensure that we both keep the Chief fully occupied during the festivities."

Gemma and I exchanged glances. I could tell that she was already plotting her strategy, and I almost felt sorry for Benny. Almost. I knew from checking the website that the Traverse City Jail could house over 120 miscreants at a time. Fortunately, this was the off-season, and according to blabbermouth Benny, only a fraction of those cells was currently occupied. Our task was to reach Malcolm before he was charged with double homicide and placed in a higher security area. Gideon couldn't hold him forever. Ultimately, bail would be set, and Malcolm would be freed. There was only one problem. By then, the conference would be over, and all its potential suspects would vanish. Unacceptable!

Gideon planned to meet my aunt at eight o'clock. After sharing a revoltingly vivid text with Benny, Gemma confirmed that he would be in charge that evening and interested in having company. It wasn't difficult for her to entice her fiancé into meeting her there, especially since she failed to mention that I would accompany her.

"I told him I'd bring some snacks from the buffet," Gemma said with a lascivious wink. "That boy does like his food."

"Remember," I said. "Both of us must fawn all over him. Pretend to be impressed by what an important job he has and ask for a tour of the jail. Save the snacks for later."

Gemma tossed her russet curls and struck a pose. "Don't worry. I'll think of something. Benny can't resist." She frowned. "Did he really do the deed? Nona looked stronger than Malcolm, and she wouldn't go down easy."

I shook my head. "Nah., I think that was a case of wrong place, wrong time coupled with her nasty habit of antagonizing people. Everything revolves around Mario Ricci. That murder was meticulously planned, and even though Malcolm is plenty smart, I don't read him as a cold-blooded killer."

We linked arms before readying ourselves for the big caper. Neither one of us was a stranger to intrigue, although, in several instances, our plans had gone awry, placing us in mortal danger. We'd learned a lot since then. Malcolm was no killer, and he was safely behind bars. Right now, our biggest obstacle was Deputy Benny Soto.

Later, when Gemma tapped on my door, I was flabbergasted by her transformation. She had abandoned her usual Goth attire for a sleek, slightly scandalous slip dress that offered a peak of cleavage and loads of leg. Her glammed-up makeup added just the right cosmetic touch.

"Wow," I said as I gave her the once over. "Hope Benny has a strong heart. You don't think he'll suspect anything, do you?"

"Nope. The poor sod doesn't stand a chance." She winked as she opened a carry-all from Whole Foods that was jammed with savory squares of pizza and lemon tarts. "See. It's a full-service operation designed to satisfy all a man's appetites."

By contrast, I looked totally forgettable in a simple shift and sandals. My goal was to blend into the woodwork and avoid scrutiny. Judging from Gemma's curled lip I had exceeded that goal. We took the stairs and scurried down the corridor being mindful that Violet and Gideon might appear at any moment. We eluded them but not our host, Lin Baugh.

"Ladies, what's the rush?" Lin asked, giving us his genial smile. "You don't want to miss the closing ceremonies, I hope. I guess you heard about the arrest. Quite a shock."

I felt obliged to respond. "Don't believe for one moment that Malcolm is a double murderer. We understand that he was only booked for assault."

Lin gave a cautious response. "Oh yes. I didn't mean to suggest..."

I looked him straight in the eyes, daring him to say more. "Malcolm is innocent. Trust me on that."

Gemma piled on. "Who's his brother, Daniel? Do you know him?"

Lin's polished demeanor frayed. "Gideon asked me not to comment. Just until this conference ends. I don't believe Malcolm is guilty either. Of course, his fingerprints were found on Violet's painting."

Gemma stepped toe to toe with him. Her temper flared, and she narrowed her eyes. "Poppycock! Who cares about that when a killer's on the loose? You should be focusing on that and not Violet's painting."

Lin took a few steps back, made some excuses, and escaped before we got any more inquisitive. The poor man looked close to the breaking point, a far cry from the elegant hotelier we had first met. Perhaps his future would be secure now that Gideon was focused on a suspect.

"Come on, Cerberus," I said. "Hackles down."

"What in the world are you saying?" Gemma looked puzzled. "Sometimes you just don't make sense."

"Oh, nothing. Cerberus was the attack dog, the hound of Hades. That's how you struck me just now. Poor Lin has enough troubles without us adding to them. He doesn't look healthy."

"Stop trying to save the world," Gemma groused. "Focus on the task ahead. Benny might smell a rat if you start babbling."

She was right, of course. Until I spoke with Malcolm, trivial details were unimportant. As we exited the lobby I caught a glimpse of Killian, looking splendid in a bespoke tuxedo. That vision was spoiled when I saw his date—the equally toothsome Sophia Lauren in an elegant white gown. Obviously not chosen to represent purity, I thought without a scintilla of guilt. Sometimes, being petty is its own reward.

Main Street in Traverse City was deserted at this time of night. We slipped into the police station without encountering any obstacles and came face to face with Deputy Soto. More precisely, as he made clear, tonight Benny was Acting Chief of Police and Sheriff of Traverse City Soto. Gemma threw her arms around him, batted her eyelashes, and gave her fiancé a kiss. She also opened her satchel, letting Benny have a whiff of the delectables inside.

"We can't stay long," she trilled. "Any chance you can give us a tour? I've never been in a real jail before."

I did my part by summoning a weak smile of encouragement and an expression of awe. "Do you have many prisoners this time of year?" I asked. "You must worry about security arrangements."

Benny scoffed at the notion. "Mostly drunks sleeping it off. There are over 100 cells here, but they're usually vacant. Of course, we do have one major catch." He inclined his head toward the back row of cells.

"Who?" Gemma asked, all wide-eyed.

"Can't say for sure, but I believe we finally bagged the murderer. The same one who stole Violet's painting."

More shock and awe from Gemma and me. "I haven't felt safe at night since it happened." She edged closer to Benny. "Except for those nights you were with me."

That cringe-worthy display was almost more than I could stand. Any sensible man would have seen right through us, but Benny was a man in love, and he was anything but sensible.

"Who is it?" I finally asked. "Don't keep us guessing."

He frowned as if my presence was a major annoyance. "Malcolm, the librarian. Says he's a member of the press too but I don't believe that."

"So, he actually confessed?"

Benny brushed that little obstacle aside. "Not yet, but he will. We'll get the truth out of the little twerp before long."

I dreaded Malcolm's fate if Benny was in charge. Gideon would never use excessive force on a prisoner, so that was a comfort.

"Come on," Gemma coaxed. "Let us peek. I've never seen a real jail cell before. Just the ones on TV."

"We don't want to get you in any trouble," I said mendaciously. "Gideon might not like it."

Benny's chest swelled with indignation. "Sheriff Hall leaves those decisions to me. I'm in charge while he's away." He motioned to a deputy who was hunched over his desk eating an apple.

"Sherman, watch the shop for me. I've got something to do." The young man leapt to attention and saluted. "Yes, sir. Right on it."

With Gemma clutching his arm, Benny strutted toward the jail cells. He brandished the keys to the main door and ushered us into the row of individual cells. Most were empty. They were sterile structures that conformed to standard prison fare. Furnishings were sparse: a single bed, chair, sink, and toilet. If I'd hoped for drama, I was disappointed. Benny pointed to the cell at the very end of the row. "Be careful there. That's where we stashed our killer."

Gemma and I exchanged glances. She knew the drill and began to ooh and ah. "Imagine being locked up, helpless. Anyone could take advantage of me. I suppose the bed isn't comfortable at all. Barely big enough for one."

While they bantered back and forth, I edged around them and slipped down the hall toward Malcolm's cell. If I'd envisioned seeing a beaten man, desperate for company, I was mistaken. Malcolm was seated on his bed leisurely reading Proust and looking quite at ease. I tapped on the bars to catch his attention.

"Marky," he said. "What in the world…"

"Quick," I whispered. "We don't have much time." I noticed that Gemma and Benny had disappeared into one of the empty cells. "Why did they arrest you?"

Malcolm laughed. "It was a mistake. No big deal. They found my fingerprint on the picture frame in Nona's room. Right away, I admitted to borrowing your aunt's painting. Not stealing, just borrowing. You see, my brother adored her work, and I hoped it would help snap him out of the depression he's been in. He's been on and off like that for years. Between the drugs and his other problems, Daniel just couldn't cope. I thought the painting might remind him of Paris. I returned it, though, so it wasn't stealing."

I checked the corridor. Time was short, and Malcolm wasn't helping much. "What caused his problem?"

"Oh! I thought I told you. He fell madly in love with a girl in Paris. Wrote her poems, exchanged love sonnets, the whole thing, but she dumped him for Mario Ricci. That shattered Daniel. Then Mario used her up and went on to someone else. That guy was particularly callous toward women. Discarded them like used tissues."

"Didn't Daniel try to win her back?"

"No luck. Mario destroyed her will to live. She disappeared, and Daniel went downhill from there."

I was still confused. "You seem awfully complacent. I'd be terrified in your place."

Malcolm closed his book and grinned. "Trust me. I didn't kill anyone, and I have an iron-clad alibi. I'm just using this experience as background for an article on unjust incarceration."

A cell door clanged, freeing the happy couple from their passion pit.

"Got to go," I said. "Stop screwing around and tell Gideon the truth before things get out of hand."

Malcolm shrugged. "Good advice." He reopened his book and continued reading. Ironically the volume in his hand was on of Proust's best—"The Fugitive."

From the flushed looks on their faces, I assumed that Gemma's assignation had gone well. Benny hitched up his pants and endeavored to assert his authority once again. He hustled us out of the jail area and back to the main lobby. "Time for you to scoot," he said with a last look at Gemma. He growled as he faced me. "No need to tell Gideon anything."

"I wouldn't think of it."

Gemma quizzed me about my chat with Malcolm, but I asked nothing about her time with Benny. Some things are better left unsaid.

"What's this iron-clad alibi he's got? Not Sophia. That hussy was busy with Mario and Killian, if we can believe her." Gemma folded her arms and huffed.

"He wouldn't say. It must be bulletproof if he's holding it in reserve. Not a strategy I'd recommend but Malcolm is determined to get a big story."

The conference was almost over, and Gideon's dilemma remained un-solved. After the attendees scattered, the chances of naming the killer would evaporate. Mario's murder would go unavenged. Nona's demise would go unmounted. Worst of all, the stain of suspicion would still blemish Carla. Violet's involvement was never really a factor. Even the odious Benny Soto acknowledged that my aunt was blameless.

The soiree was still in full swing when we returned to the hotel. Gemma plunged into the crowd and immediately started to mingle. I tiptoed to the elevator and fled to my room to upgrade my attire and make some cosmetic changes. Violet had left a splendid Prada pantsuit on my bed with a note urging me to enjoy myself. With a little bit of luck, I planned to do just that. Forget about sleuthing. I'd tried my best and failed miserably.

When I entered the ballroom, Killian suddenly appeared at my side. He looked me up and down with a rakish grin, a technique he had obviously perfected. Most men would leer, but Killian Blaine was far too sophisticated for that. The wily lawyer ranked somewhere between those irresistible film stars Sean Connery and Cary Grant. He was one hot ticket, and he knew it.

"Wow! Quite a change from your earlier look."

I played innocent. "What do you mean?"

Killian was unperturbed. "I saw you slink off with Gemma a while ago. You were either incognito or slumming. Which was it?"

That man pushed every one of my anger buttons. "It just so happens that I was making inquiries. You know, the kind of things the police used to do."

He didn't scoff, but I could tell he wanted to. "And what, pray tell, did you discover?"

I should have ignored him, but I couldn't resist flaunting my success. "For one thing, Malcolm is innocent. He has a cast iron alibi for the nights in question. Gideon will have to release him unless he wants to look either incompetent or foolish."

Killian raised one eyebrow. "You verified this alibi, I presume."

"That's not my job. Gideon will do it. Malcolm was only trying to help his brother. That's why he borrowed Violet's painting."

The smirk on his face infuriated me. "Borrowed? Funny thing. My criminal law Prof called that type of action theft. In this case, felony grand theft. Sophia is quite livid about it, you know."

"I'll just bet you can change her mind. You're very persuasive, and Sophia seems to dote on your every word."

He gave me a look that defined smugness. "Feeling jealous, are we? Don't worry. I'm still true blue. Devoted to only you." I slapped away the hand he placed over his heart.

"Very droll. You're supposed to be helping us solve the murders, not clowning around."

"You won't admit it, will you?" Killian said. "This charade ends tomorrow. The whole thing. If the police don't make an arrest, so be it. I don't see the public clamoring for anyone's hide. Even the FACE crowd seems to have moved on. Perhaps Malcolm can still write an expose or make a name for himself on one of those true crime shows."

There were several tart retorts on the tip of my tongue, but the appearance of Kim and Carla stifled them. Both ladies were in high spirits, whether alcohol induced or natural I couldn't say. Their linked arms and flushed cheeks suggested the former.

"Why so glum?" Kim asked. "Time to celebrate the end of this extravaganza. It's almost over, and no one else has been murdered."

Carla added. "Not that we know of, at least." Their jovial tone aggravated me.

"What about poor Malcolm? He's still rotting in a jail cell for something he didn't do."

Carla waved me off. "Oh pooh. For one thing, a few days in Gideon's jail hardly constitutes rotting. Besides, Malcolm deserves some punishment for stealing that painting."

Kim nodded in agreement. "They'll release him by tomorrow. Trust me on that. Once they check out his alibi, Malcolm will be a free man."

I realized that I was missing something. Killian, Kim, and Carla were acting nonchalant, as if they had inside information. "Okay, you guys. Level with me. Who is Malcolm's alibi?"

Carla couldn't resist teasing me a bit more. "It's someone you already know. Our local scribe has been a very busy boy."

I wracked my brain for clues but came up empty. They exchanged glances before finally taking pity on me. "Marky," Kim said. "Remember Althea, the FACE poet? Apparently, she and Malcolm were composing love poems both nights. She'll vouch for him even if they rescind her membership in FACE."

Althea? I visualized the vapid poet, astonished that Malcolm or anyone else could find her interesting. On the other hand, Malcolm was no Adonis himself. Maybe they were a good match, after all.

Carla added more. "And believe it or not, Sophia has withdrawn her complaint. Now she says she lent him the painting. Nonsense, of course, and a total lie, but that lets Malcolm off the hook."

I detected the fine hand of Violet Davis in that maneuver. No doubt, my dear aunt had used either flattery, bribery, or veiled threats to influence Sophia. That resolved most issues except for the pesky problem of two unsolved murders. Was I the only one who cared about that?

* * *

Everything went smoothly at the closing ceremony the next day. Kim and Lin received accolades, and a general spirit of bonhomie prevailed. Amid the handshakes, hugs, and passing of business cards, the names of Mario Ricci and Nona Adams were ignored or forgotten. Maybe it was better that way. Gemma found out that Malcolm had been released that morning when all charges had been dismissed.

"That Altea person marched right into Gideon's office and signed a statement. Benny said they made goo-goo eyes at each other and kissed." Gemma made a retching noise before adding. "And get this. Althea highlighted her hair and was wearing makeup! Nona Adams must be spinning in her grave or whatever passes for it in the bowels of hell."

That tired cliché, "Love conquers all," had prevailed in Traverse City. I was happy for Malcolm but disheartened by the outcome. As usual, Aunt Violet was philosophical. She put her arms around me and administered a strong dose of common sense.

"Gideon won't give up on solving the murders, Marky. Don't sell him short. Besides, you and Gemma aren't detectives, even though you try your best. Let justice prevail. It usually does in the end."

She was right, of course. Aunt Violet always was. It was time to return to Harbor Bay and pour our energies into Poppet. I'd jotted down several promotional ideas and couldn't wait to try them. We'd ordered a slew of products from the reconfigured Ricci Enterprises at a generous discount. Carla and Violet promised to conduct an in-person seminar to coincide with the launch of their new venture. As for Killian Blaine—that was still a work in progress. We'd started slowly with lunches, intimate dinners, and a constant spate of texts and emails. Gemma said I was the original slow mover, but sometimes a steady flame was preferable to a raging inferno.

Several months later, Kim came into our shop looking somber. My first thought was that her crotchety spouse Lionel had once again harangued his wife for some perceived misdeed. As it turned out the truth was far more disturbing.

"I have a favor to ask," Kim said. She bit her lip and took a deep breath.

"Of course. Anything I can do to help."

"Lin Baugh is leaving his job and I've agreed to substitute until they find his replacement."

I was speechless. The powers that be must have blamed Lin for the debacle at the conference after all. It was outrageous. The poor man had done a fine job under impossible circumstances.

"That's so unfair," I said. "How could they?"

Kim reached into her purse and found a tissue. She dabbed at her eyes as she spoke. "You don't understand. Lin's sick. He's dying, Marky."

"What! That can't be true. Maybe it's just an excuse they made up."

She shook her head. "I spoke with him myself. Lin has pancreatic cancer. He tried treatments, but the prognosis wasn't good. He's terminal."

My eyes teared up thinking of such a sad ending for a good man. "What can I do?"

"Come to Traverse City with me. Lin specifically asked for you. I don't have any specifics, but I know he admires you."

I could hardly refuse. Two days later, I made my final pilgrimage to Traverse City, accompanied by Kim and Violet. Hospitals terrify me, and I'm ill-equipped to deal with death. As Violet reminded me, however, it was important to honor the wish of a dying man. My personal comfort was immaterial.

Munson Hospice House surprised me. Instead of being an institution, it was a pleasant eight-bedroom home located in a verdant tree-lined area. Kim explained that each resident had his own room where family was always welcome. We met Lin on the covered porch overlooking a lovely nature area.

The tranquil surroundings were enhanced by comfortable furnishings in pastel fabrics. At Lin's request, Fantasia accompanied us on our sad journey. I found her presence a great comfort as did everyone else.

"Try not to react when you first see Lin," Kim said. "Focus on his sweet smile. That hasn't changed at all."

Violet squeezed my hand as we joined Lin on the porch. Illness had taken a mighty toll on the once vital man, but his spirit hadn't flagged. He greeted us warmly and wrapped his arms around Fantasia.

"Thank you for coming, ladies," Lin said. "I haven't much time left, and I wanted to share something important."

I gulped back tears and gripped my aunt.

"Don't cry for me, Marky. You're wise for one so young and very kind. Those qualities are rare. My sister Linette was like that. Maybe that's why I was drawn to you. I'm ready to leave this life without regrets, but before doing so, there's something I must say."

His voice faltered, and Kim poured Lin some water from a nearby carafe. "As you know, my sister Linette was a beautiful girl. A child, really. Very innocent. She loved music and poetry, so we reluctantly agreed when she went to Paris to study."

He hesitated but, after a few minutes, was able to continue. "She fell under the spell of an evil man. Mario Ricci. He was charming but very cruel. Linette adored him. She never saw him for what he was. When he tired of her, he rejected her in the most callous way imaginable. I brought her home and tried to save her, but her spirit was crushed. My sister, Linette Annabel Baugh, died of anorexia six months later."

Annabel. Something clicked in my mind, and at last, I knew the identity of that lost sonnet. It was Poe's touching tribute to a lost love—the beautiful Annabel Lee. Lin's eyes momentarily brightened. He nodded at me.

"Now you see. I sent those poems to Mario to frighten him. Make him suffer like so many of his victims had." He shrugged. "I realize that he was a Philistine who would never appreciate the connection, but I derived some small satisfaction from those acts."

Kim and Violet looked downward as he spoke as if anticipating Lin's confession.

"I thought I had forgotten him—not forgiven. Never that. I followed his career as the years passed still hating that demon. Then, like a gift from heaven, came the Beauty Expo featuring him, Mario Ricci. I'd already gotten my diagnosis, and this seemed like my chance for redemption. To rid the world of her tormentor and avenge my sweet sister."

Lin's confession continued as we sat transfixed. I'd sought answers and now that they came, I yearned to close my ears to those words.

"I planned his demise, took pleasure in maximizing the humiliation he'd feel. The evening before, I mixed liquid nicotine in his conditioner. Ricci Rich—what a joke. Then, while the audience cheered him, I watched him die."

Lin made no excuses and voiced no regret. I understood his need for retribution, but that left one question unanswered.

"What about Nona? She didn't know your sister."

His face fell. "That was unfortunate. Collateral damage, I think they call it. Nona saw me tamper with the conditioner that night. I don't know how, but she did. Later, she confronted me and threatened to go public unless I repudiated the beauty industry. Foolish, really."

"Would that have been so bad?" Kim asked. "You knew the outcome anyway."

Lin sipped his glass of water. "I didn't mean to hurt her, but Nona was a venal person, much like Mario. She enjoyed inflicting pain. She called Linette a slut! Can you believe it? Said that my sister got what she deserved." He shook his head. "I couldn't bear that. Before I knew it, that wooden poster was in my hands, and I struck her. You know the rest." He chuckled. "I was the one who put that painting in her room after someone returned it to my office. I had the pass key, and it was one final act of disrespect. That and the lipstick."

His voice was fading, and I realized our time with Lin was almost up. Violet rose and took his hand. "Where do we go from here, Lin? How can we help you?"

He reached into a folder at his side and retrieved a sheaf of papers. "I've written everything down. My confession. If you ladies agree to witness this document, I would be grateful."

"What should we do with it?" I asked.

Lin smiled, and for a moment, he had recaptured the vibrancy of old. "When I'm gone—it won't be long—give this to Gideon Hall. He's a good man, and he deserves to know the truth."

Violet nodded, and Kim agreed. "We'll take care of this for you. Peace, my friend."

We left soon afterward for the sad journey back to Harbor Bay. Three weeks later, Kim called with the news that Lin had passed.

Lin Baugh hadn't wanted a service but the four of us joined his friends from Traverse City in a celebration of his life. I saw Gideon Hall in the group, speaking with Aunt Violet. She handed him Lin's document and quickly turned around wiping away tears as they spoke.

"What did Gideon say?" Gemma asked. "I'll bet he was shocked."

Violet shook her head. "Gideon doesn't shock easily. As it turns out, he had already figured things out. Now he can close the records and move on."

Lin passed without expressing any remorse or regrets. He had lived with pain since losing his sister, and death came as a blessing. I understood his reasons, although I couldn't condone his actions.

Life returned to normal or what passed for it in Harbor Bay. Gemma spent an inordinate amount of time planning her wedding to Benny, and I reluctantly agreed to be her maid of honor if she let me choose my dress.

Lin's story went public when Malcolm wrote a chilling expose of Mario's misdeeds. The librarian turned scribe finally made the big time and relocated with his new bride Althea to Chicago.

As for me, I was comfortable with a quiet life, savoring the blessings of friends, a thriving business, and a spot of romance. Aunt Violet says that my time will come, and I believe her. She's never been wrong yet.

Acknowledgements

Thanks to Deb and Jerry Salmestrelli (Chatham Hair Studio) for their invaluable insights.

About the Author

Former Treasury Executive Arlene Kay crafts clever mysteries with dazzling dialogue, clever plots, and snarky characters. In addition to the Cosmetic Crimes Series (*Murder at First Blush*; *The Mascara Murders*, and *Murder Masque*), she is the published author of The Creature Comforts and Boston Uncommon Series (available in audio), three standalone mysteries and the forthcoming novel, *The Acolyte*.

SOCIAL MEDIA HANDLES:
https://x.com/Arlenekay1?prefetchTimestamp=1723127689503
https://www.facebook.com/Arlene.Kay.author

AUTHOR WEBSITE:
arlenekay.com

Also by Arlene Kay

Intrusion

Die Laughing

The Abacus Prize

Swann Dive

Mantrap

Gilt Trip

Swann Songs

Death by Dog Show

Homicide by Horseshow

Murder at the Falls

Murder at First Blush

The Mascara Murders

www.ingramcontent.com/pod-product-compliance
Lightning Source LLC
Chambersburg PA
CBHW020721130726
47899CB00011B/673